Karen Blomain

A Trick of Light

The Toby Press, *London & Connecticut*

First published in Great Britain 2000

The Toby Press *Ltd, London & Connecticut*
www.tobypress.com

ISBN 1 902881 42 7

A CIP catalogue record for this title is available from the British Library

Designed by Fresh Produce, London

Typeset in Garamond by
Rowland Phototypesetting Ltd., Bury St Edmunds

Printed and bound in Great Britain by
St Edmundsbury Press Ltd., Bury St Edmunds

For Michael, guardian of peace and light

Chapter one

Ben Darling died in the season of mock oranges; their tart, sweet, tantalizing scent filled the air of Fenston. The trees were fleshing out behind the houses and even the most reticent among them leapt riotously into view. The cool nights grew shorter and fog from the lake threaded itself through the quiet morning streets as, here and there, a lighted window punctuated the darkness. Three miles away, the Interstate hummed benignly.

Neither Athena Wescott nor Eleanor Rodiri took any notice of the breathtakingly beautiful clear night as they hurried to Hattie Darling's house. Quite sure that her husband was dead, Hattie's first instinct had not been to call the emergency crew or her daughter or Reverend Park, or Clem Tomkins, the police chief, but to call Athena and Eleanor, her two, lifelong best friends.

When the phone rang at Wescott's, Will and Athena had just fallen asleep. The nightstand alarm was set for 5:30, the hour they dug themselves out of heavy sleep to start the daily routine of Wescott's Dry Goods and General Merchandise. They slept on the second floor, in the back, the quiet side of the house, away from the occasional car passing Fenston Corners and the steady pulse of the blinker light. She and Will had put in a hard day. After a twelve-hour stint in the store, they drove over to the Lazy Lanes and bowled a few games in preparation for the couples league tournament they would be part of the following week.

In between work and bowling, they stopped at the Red Bird Diner and had soup and sandwiches where they ran into Tom Miller and his cousin Foxy who were also going bowling. Sherlene, the waitress, had a long involved story about the people who had inherited the Dempsey place, people coming down from Binghamton with no idea at all how the place had fallen apart.

"That's not the half of it," Will said. "I've been delivering to old Mrs. Dempsey for years. She's a pack rat. This last year it got so I couldn't navigate the door. She'd move a few things and then I'd follow the aisle she'd kept clear between the back door and the kitchen. You never saw so much junk—stuff piled to the ceiling, old magazines, radios, clothes, boxes of tools—all heaped up."

Athena smiled, waiting for the punch line. Will

flattened his hands on the Formica counter and looked around at his audience, "She took decorating lessons from Athena, you know."

Everyone laughed, including Athena, who was used to being kidded for her collections of what others might consider junk. Behind the store and the house, she had a shed and barn crammed full of things that she thought she might just need sometime.

They had bowled well. Will was convinced they had a chance in the competition. When they got home it was already nine, but Will insisted they take a short walk across the street and through the woods to the edge of the lake. As usual, they held hands, talking over the day's events. Will was a romantic sort, and Athena appreciated his tenderness, his need to take a little time each evening for them to be quiet together. The tragedy of having lost their son nine years before had made them careful with each other, knowing how vulnerable they were. Most times, when they walked they talked for a few minutes, and then fell into a contented silence that allowed them to appreciate the beautiful hillside and view of the lake.

When she finally got into bed Athena was so tired that she fell quickly into a deep sleep. She had worked the noise of the ringing phone into her dream, and it rang three times before she reached for it.

Before Athena could say hello, Hattie said, "Athena, it's me. Ben . . . Something's happened. Please come!"

"Hattie?" Athena answered groggily, unable to keep up with what was being said. "What did you say?"

"It's me. Just come. Call El too."

Next to Athena, Will stirred and thrust his foot out of the covers. "What's going on?

"Don't know. It's Hattie. She wants me to come. Something about Ben."

"Ben's home?"

"Don't know. You don't have to get up. She wants me to call El. I'll do it downstairs."

"Good," Will answered, twisting his large body into a comfortable position and blocking his eyes from the light as Athena quickly threw on jeans and a polo shirt.

"And I'll call you if it's anything we need you for," she said softly, as she pulled the wild snarl of graying blond hair back into a ponytail and fixed it with a rubber band.

"Yup," he grunted after her, lying still as if to keep himself in touch with sleep.

In contrast to Athena's quiet, dark house the Rodiri household was a noisy hive of activity. Eleanor was on her hands and knees in the dining room of her house, cleared for the occasion of finishing the border of an immense, hooked rug, an Indian design in earth colors with a turquoise medallion in the center. In the next room, *The Johnny Carson Show* blared. Eleanor would peer into the living room each time a new guest was announced, losing her place in the rug.

"Slow business," she muttered as she turned back to her project. The rug seemed to be taking her a very long time as Eleanor could only work it at night; during the day she was busy with the correspondence courses in speed-reading and shorthand that she and Eddie were taking.

Eddie Rodiri was sprawled out on the couch, watching television, and keeping up a steady stream of comments about the show. "That guy has no talent at all," he said about David Soul. "*The Dukes of Hazard*, shit. I don't know why they book these jokers."

"Yes, you do. It's their publicity agents who get them set up for the shows.

"Yeah, but what's in it for Carson?"

"You don't think for a minute he'd be on television at all if it wasn't for the guests. It's the cheapest kind of show to do," Eleanor concluded, her expertise the result of a magazine article she had read at the doctor's office the week before. Joan Rivers appeared on the screen.

"Look at that hair," Eddie whistled under his breath. "That woman's made a career out of having a big mouth. Guess there's a lot of people staying up late at night watching tee vee. People with nothing better to do."

"Must be," Eleanor concluded. She was biting her tongue. She often complained that Eddie was the biggest television viewer of all time. And she was fond of saying he'd watch the test pattern if nothing else was on. Eddie was a voracious reader, but he read only while he was watching television. In the way that people long married complain to themselves about each other, Eleanor thought, "All he does is gripe. If he hates it so much, why does he watch? And why can't he keep his complaints to himself?"

When the phone rang, Eddie was just formulating his

opinion of Olivia Newton-John's skimpy outfit. Robbie, Eleanor's and Eddie's seventeen-year-old son, stretched the telephone cord from the kitchen area around the doorway to the dining room and handed it to Eleanor. "It's Aunt Athena," he said, using the honorary title the Rodiri kids had long ago bestowed on their neighbor.

A short chubby woman, barefoot in plaid Bermuda shorts and a T-shirt, Eleanor scrambled on her hands and knees to reach the phone, motioning to Robbie to turn down the volume so she could hear.

"Are you dressed?" Athena asked.

"What? Why, yes. I've got my hands full finishing this rug. Promised it for the Fire Company's raffle, Friday. And I still have the border to do. What are you doing up?" Athena, it was well-known, was asleep most nights by 9:30.

"Something over at Hattie's. Some trouble. With Ben."

"He's home?"

"Guess so. Just be ready. I'll pick you up in five minutes," Athena concluded, then hung up.

"Robbie, come here. I need to show you how to do this." Eleanor pushed back her salt-and-pepper hair and lifted the edge of the rug, the hook in her other hand. "You'll have to keep at this until you finish it."

"I don't want to. Why do I have to do it?"

"Because I'm needed over at Hattie's, that's why. And because I promised this rug for the weekend. Come on, it won't kill you."

"But Mom . . . Guys don't do that stuff."

"They do if they want to borrow a car from their mothers for the movies."

"But Mom . . ."

"I'll make a deal with you. If you do it, no one will ever know. If you don't, well, I just might let it slip at the Altar and Rosary meeting that you were such a help; so interested in learning how to hook."

She smiled up at him sweetly and Robbie knew he had lost. Picking up the hook, he began jabbing the short pieces of yarn into the eye and punching them into the holes before Eleanor could instruct him. "I've watched you enough times to know how. You just go. If you get back soon, can I stop?"

"Not on your life. Now that I know I have an expert under my roof, I might promise them two rugs for next year."

"Mommmm," Robbie wailed. Eleanor winked at him and kissed the top of Eddie's head as she dashed out the door.

Chapter two

Fenston lay amid cornfields and dairy farms and barren quarries, a little smudge of a place on the map of history. The houses and farms were connected by a thin pencil line of road weaving along with no discernible focus or forward thrust, a road that took the course of least resistance, skirting the mountains and rock formations and unhurriedly connecting Fenston to Crystalle on one side and Winton on the other.

If anything was Fenston, it was the Beste family. Hattie's great-grandfather, Ezra, had made his way north from the lips of the Susquehanna River in Wilkes-Barre. As the story went, he had a thirst for mountains and wanted to be away from the squabbling of the people he knew. Those who knew the local history thought the explanation flawed and self-serving. For if ever there was a squabbler, Ezra Beste was one. County records showed that he was no stranger to the courts, filing seven lawsuits during his life in Fenston, most of them having to do with guarding his acreage from encroachment. He had chosen prime land in the area, outstanding both for its position and richness of the soil.

Alone, he came into the valley before the village had a name, and he built the first part of the homestead in 1840, far enough away from anyone else that he didn't have to be sociable. Hattie had not been told any more of the story. Whether that's as much as anyone knew or had felt was significant enough to pass on, was one of the questions that nagged at the back of her mind, especially when she became owner of the homestead and custodian of her family's lore. That was the way of it, she thought: all families had secrets that fell away after a few generations.

Hattie's old house and the family land were the tangible connection that linked her directly with those early times. It was a beautiful home that hugged the ridge a hundred or so yards from the road and had a view up and down the valley. Ezra's original house had been two rooms and a lean-to. Electricity, plumbing, seven new rooms and many closets, a carriage barn which later became a garage, a summer kitchen (no longer in use), a television antenna, one indoor bathroom, then another, then a powder room on the first floor, a stone courtyard outside the kitchen where, in the previous century, women had toiled on hot days doing the laundry, had been turned into a lovely terrace.

Over the years, a wall of hydrangeas, peonies and Rose of Sharon shielded the house from the driveway, while immense oak trees lined the roadside, making a canopy overhead in three seasons. Air-conditioning was installed in the bedrooms; there was a fancy parlor with overstuffed chairs, tatted doilies and a big piano. The powder room was laid with pink and black tiles. There was a recreation room in the basement with a ping-pong table and a pool table. The yard boasted a trellis for yellow roses, a grape arbor and various bird feeders. Fruit trees dotted one meadow; a sheltering stand of evergreens bordered perennial gardens.

Chapter three

When Ben Darling came to town in 1955, everyone took notice. A month out of the service, he still wore his dark hair cropped, showing off his large, engaging smile and intelligent eyes. When he swaggered in, it was as if he were still wearing a Marine captain's uniform. After his stint in the service there was no reason to go back to Maine—he'd left home deliberately and his years away hadn't improved upon his memories of a childhood spent with an aged, cranky father.

A month before Ben's discharge, he got word that his father had died. That same day, Lennie Rodiri invited Ben to visit Fenston where Lennie's brother Eddie and sister-in-law, Eleanor, a former priest and nun, had settled in, commune-style, with a group of friends, and were all living in a spacious, old farmhouse. Ben, young and not quite at ease with his new freedom, was relieved to be offered some direction, and accepted gladly.

Hattie had finished secretarial school in Binghamton and was helping her father with the farm accounts. She also kept the books for the Wiggam Dairy, a taxing job that involved trying to unravel the serpentine business and bookkeeping practices of the senior Mr. Wiggam, who had insisted on maintaining control of things into his senility. All day she poured over sheaves of paper filled with crimped numbers and painfully tight handwriting, trying to get them into some order as she struggled to come up with a system that would make sense of the enterprise's accounts. Although Hattie loved her father all the more intensely since her mother had died the previous year, she was often bored. She would frequently find herself wondering what, if anything, would make her life interesting.

But it was summer time in rural Pennsylvania, and there was so much pleasure to be had from just living. Almost every day after work, she raced home and changed and went down to the lake. Evenings inside Fenston homes, everyone, like the rest of the country, was glued to *The Lucy Show*. Neighborhood kids thronged the woods wearing raccoon hats and singing about Davy Crockett; but in the balmy evenings, there was a new, throbbing music to be heard everywhere. On weekend evenings, Hattie would go out with her girlfriends to the record hops, learning all the steps to the jitterbug, "Rock Around the Clock."

When Ben Darling showed up on July 20, 1955, it

was as if he and Hattie had plotted and steered a course toward each other. Out of the dark fragrant evening, he stepped into the Chaplin Lake Dance Pavilion and looked around the dance floor that was lit by myriad strings of tiny white lights suspended from the ceiling. It was as if he were searching for one specific thing. His eyes came to rest on Hattie, sitting with a group of girls, her red hair pulled back in a high ponytail to reveal her lovely, winsome face.

As he walked toward her, Hattie had a momentary rush, as if she both craved him and was afraid. Little pin-pricks of nervousness ran up the backs of her legs and settled in her lap. Even as she was aware of him approaching, she tried to hide herself in the conversation with her friends. The country air seemed to hold its breath in the damp night mist. By the time Ben put his hand out to her, The Platters were singing "Only You," and it was all decided.

Chapter four

Ben moved into the homestead which Hattie had been mistress of for a year. Hattie's father, already ailing, was glad to have the newlyweds with him. Since his wife had died, he'd lost interest in things and had let the house go downhill. When Ben and Hattie discovered how costly the upkeep on the place was and how much of it had been neglected, they knew they would have to struggle to hold on. But it was the only home Hattie had ever known and she was tied to it in many strong but subtle ways.

Two years after Reverend Alton Flax, pastor of the Primitive Hill Baptist Church pronounced them man and wife in the most lavish white tent ceremony Fenston had ever seen, Alice was born, and the following year Hattie's father's died. By the modest standards of poor, rural

Fenston, for Hattie and Ben things looked golden. The only unforeseen problem was Ben's work. Or lack thereof. During the first ten years of their marriage, he had a series of short term and unsatisfying jobs. Nothing seemed to stick; or rather Ben didn't seem to stick to anything.

Filling in with bookkeeping work and renting out parcels of their land to local farmers, Hattie managed somehow to keep the bills and taxes paid. Adversity made her realize how something she had taken for granted her whole life—her family's land and home—might be taken from her. There were nights when worry kept her awake, and she'd stand at the door of what had been her own childhood room, and look in at her sleeping daughter. The love she felt for Alice tugged at her, especially when she thought of the future. With all her heart, she wanted Alice to have just the same kind of childhood she had enjoyed: secure in the small, safe place her family had made in the world. Only when that world was threatened did Hattie understand how vital it was to her very being. Just when things seemed bleakest, Ben's luck changed. He received an attractive offer to travel for Harden Tools. The hitch was that he'd be working in New England.

Chapter five

Hattie Darling had looked forward to making love with Ben for weeks while he was gone. She believed his frequent, prolonged absences kept their sex life fresh yet comfortingly familiar. When she heard him singing Goggi Grant's "A Wayward Wind" she knew they would have a good evening of lovemaking. Hattie slipped into a soft pink nightie, sprayed musk in her cleavage, positioned herself seductively on the bed and waited.

A modest man, predictable and fastidious in his ways, Ben had creased his pants and hung them and his suits in the closet. He had emptied his suitcase of dirty laundry into the hamper. Before he left the bathroom, he put a little Canoe on his face, toweled the sink clean of toothpaste and water and donned fresh pajamas, navy with white piping at the collar and cuffs, and began to sing in his clear, sweet voice, "And a wayward wind was born to wander . . ."

Catching a glimpse of himself in the mirror, Ben grew silent staring back at his own reflection. Taking a bottle of Tums from the medicine closet, he quickly cupped a handful of the pills, chewed and swallowed them. Then he returned to studying his features in the mirror, gazing into his own eyes. A look of sorrow and resignation washed over him as he straightened up to full height as if steeling himself.

Hattie knew all of Ben's favorite tunes and when he sang them. A walk in the woods provoked "Edelweiss." The lake made him trill "Indian Love Call." Driving on a sunny afternoon with her would inevitably call up "Daisy, Daisy," the charming Edwardian melody. If he were in a lonely, mellow mood, he would croon "Eleanor Rigby." Ben simply loved to sing. Hattie pictured him driving on the long trips alone in the car singing at the top of his lungs to pass the time, his face a permanent smile around the vowels of a verse. "A Wayward Wind" meant sex. And Hattie was ready.

Outside the bathroom door, Ben composed himself and then swept into the bedroom. Hattie grinned. He went to her side of the bed and lit three candles on the night table. Serious now, he and Hattie smiled at each other before turning off the light, then he started to undress his wife of twenty-five years. Just as slowly they made love. Over the years, their pace of lovemaking and intensity of pleasure had evolved gradually and by mutual consent. After many kisses, Ben began to caress Hattie's feet, then moved, attending to every inch of her body with his hands and mouth. Hattie lay back on the pillows, as her sighs increased. She knew Ben would wait until she was completely satisfied, knowing that she would give him equal moments of ecstasy. Sex had always been good for them, especially on Ben's first night back from the road when they made a special effort to please each other.

In Ben's absence, Hattie had replayed the scene over and over in her mind and longed for it. The candles were lavender, a scent Ben particularly liked. The old house crouched around them like a satisfied, friendly cat, warm and complete with Ben and Hattie together in their room and the slight breeze of early May moving the curtains above the hall table.

After lovemaking, Ben lay in Hattie's arms, listening to the local gossip, catching up on all the changes in Fenston during his absences and filling her in on his work life. They were quiet, waiting for a thought that one of them might like to share. Ben's homecomings were exciting, yet there was sometimes a tinge of unfamiliarity which made them shy with their own thoughts, as if they had to relearn their intimacy.

"Six weeks. That's the longest you've ever been away."

"Nothing I could do about it. They kept piling on the work. And it seems that with the new line it takes longer at every stop," Ben responded, his tone calm and warm.

"When you first got the New England territory, you always wanted me to come along," said Hattie. There was just a trace of resentment in her voice.

Ben's tone changed too, a slight edge to his voice, "That's not how I remember it, Hat. I recall that I wanted us to move up that way."

Each of them could reach inside and touch the sore spot in their relationship around the issue of moving. "You wouldn't hear of it. Couldn't move Alice. Couldn't sell the farm. Couldn't leave Fenston."

Hattie shrugged away from Ben, adjusting her posture in the bed just a little apart from him, though still in his arms. "Ben, this is our home. I just didn't feel right charging all over the country like gypsies. Couldn't imagine selling a place that's been in my family for generations to go God knows where."

Ben answered slowly and wearily, "There's no use going over all that again. What's done's done. Made the best of it all round, I guess."

"I just brought it up because with Alice gone so much, I can't seem to find enough to do, even with the Auxiliary and Meals on Wheels. I thought I'd go with you sometimes. Help with the driving."

Ben did not respond.

"Ben? Some of the shorter trips, I thought."

"Time was I would have loved to hear you say that."

"So, we can do it now."

"Times change, Hattie. Work changes. You'd be bored to death. Sometimes I'm in a place the whole day now."

"I could bring a book. Some needlework." Hattie felt the room draw a breath around them.

After a long pause, Ben finally said softly, "Hattie, there's something I've been meaning to tell you. Needing to tell you."

"Yes," she said, her voice now soft like his. Oddly, she felt a welling up in herself. She didn't know why, but tears were very close to the edge of her eyes.

"Something I should have said a long time ago but just went on without saying it. Now it seems like so long, I don't know how to get started telling you."

When Ben hesitated, Hattie said, "What is it?"

Still Ben didn't answer.

Hattie said, "People married as long as us, Ben, is there anything we can't say?"

Ben made a small throat-clearing noise. Patiently, Hattie gave him some time to think about what he wanted to say. After a few minutes, she began to wonder if he had drifted off, a not uncommon event after a good dinner and sex. But he had made her curious, almost nervous with his talk. She wanted to know what he'd been about to tell her. He was too far into something important for him to stop now. She nudged his arm and said kidding, "Guess it was real important, Ben, for you to fall asleep right in the middle of a sentence."

Still, he did not respond. Nothing. Then she realized that if Ben were asleep he was not making his usual putt putt noises.

Nudging him again, this time more forcefully, Hattie grew afraid. Suddenly, thousands of images of Ben flooded through her as she lay there, afraid to touch him again:

Ben, the year they learned how to ski, Ben walking Alice to school on her first day. Ben hanging from the back of the fire truck in a Fourth of July parade. Ben, the way he looked first thing in the morning and his secret look when they were making love. She grabbed his arm and shook it aggressively. "Ben, Ben." Afraid of what she might and might not see, she lay back for a moment, gathering her courage. The country night hummed outside the open window. Hattie felt paralyzed. The nascent tears were gone. In their place, dread and knowledge edged into her consciousness.

Then suddenly she reached up, turned on the light, and screamed "Ben" at the top of her lungs. Ben was staring back at her, his mouth wide as if he were about to say something very loud and very funny.

Chapter six

When the two women arrived at the Darling house outside Fenston they were in a somber mood. One look at Athena's face had dispelled Eleanor's good humor. Hattie ran into the yard to meet them, barefoot and dressed only in a thin nightgown.

"Oh, my God, Hattie, you'll catch your death of cold," Eleanor said.

"Ben's dead," Hattie shrieked and began wringing her hands frantically.

"Where? How did you find out?"

"In bed . . ."

"He's home?"

"Got home last night. Oh, God," she moaned. "Oh, God, Oh, God."

"Oh, dear," Athena said softly, then put her arms around Hattie and led her quickly back into the warm kitchen and rushed to the hall closet to find a robe and slippers and help Hattie put them on. Eleanor went to the phone and called Clem Tomkins. In less than five minutes, the ambulance screamed up the long drive and the crew leapt out.

Hattie led them all up to the bedroom where Ben still lay, his arms at his sides. Hattie had closed his eyes. The same smile, as if he were enjoying a pleasant dream, played on his features.

After a brief examination, one of the ambulance crew said kindly, "Won't know for sure for a while, but it looks like his heart just gave out, Hattie. Didn't suffer at all."

Hattie nodded gravely; she knew how easily Ben had left her for good.

"What next?" she asked, dry-eyed.

"We'll take him into town and prepare him for the viewing. I guess you'll want Eldon Questor to do the funeral?"

"What? Oh, yes. He's the only undertaker I know, I guess."

"I'll call him and tell him we're on the way. Why don't you go downstairs with Athena and Eleanor? I'll see to things here."

"What will you do?" Hattie asked, her voice now quiet and frightened as a child's.

"We'll take Ben to Eldon's in the ambulance," he explained again more slowly, looking carefully at Hattie, his voice echoing her short, slow syllables. Athena approvingly noticed how his hands moved in small, reassuring gestures, and how that seemed to calm Hattie. He and the ambulance crew approached the bed to remove the body.

"Wait. Wait. Don't just pull him from the bed," Hattie grabbed Clem's arm, although there was no indication that he intended to do that. She sprang away from them and stepped beside the bed with her back to it, as if shielding Ben from the view of the others in the room. Underneath the sheet, Ben was naked. Hattie thought about their lovemaking just hours before. She wanted to preserve the privacy of their last intimate moment. She went to the side of the bed and knelt beside Ben's body almost as if she were preparing to pray. Instead, she loosened the sheets and folded them carefully upward around her husband's body, wrapping him securely in the soft green sheets she had changed only a few hours earlier in preparation for his homecoming, all the while staring at his face.

Her own face showed a rage of emotions as her hands moved across the sheets, smoothing and tucking them in around him. "Ben, Ben," she whispered as she drew the fabric along his arms and legs, which had already begun to cool and stiffen. Hattie's thoughts were no longer in the room, but coursed over the whole long history of their marriage, darting here and there to images of Ben, her Ben, in times of great joy.

"Ben, are you really gone?" she crooned over and over as she patted and molded the material to the contours of his body. She lifted his hands free of the covers. Putting them to her lips, she kissed each finger and then folded his arms.

Ashamed to look but unable to move, Athena and Eleanor and the men silently watched this private ritual, as Hattie Darling made her dead husband comfortable for the first part of his last trip.

When Ben's body had been removed, Clem came back into the kitchen to speak to Hattie. As if they were trying on widowhood along with their friend and judging themselves unequal to the task, the other women watched as Hattie, now clearly having regained her composure, answered the necessary questions and signed official papers in several places. The questions Clem asked seemed cruel and pointless; after all, Ben was dead and nothing could change that. Their minds kept going back to Hattie on her knees at the edge of the bed, covering the body of her husband. How could they comfort her?

By dawn, the officials had left and everything had been taken care of. The traffic of food and condolences wouldn't start for another couple of hours when Betty Tomkins having heard the news of Ben's death from Clem when he returned from work, would appear with the first Jell-O mold salad and her chili jumble, soon to be joined by other dishes from her kindly neighbors. Soon the refrigerator bulged with funereal foodstuff.

Chapter seven

Fenston, like most small towns, had a number of news conduits. Eddie and Robbie had heard the police band radio sputter out, "10–81, 10–81, 10–81 at State Route 1001 off 107," the location of Hattie's and Ben's farm and the code to report a possible death. Will Wescott, unable to sleep after Athena left, had gotten up, taken in the papers and started to open the store for the day. On his way back, Clem saw the light on in Wescott's General Store and Dry Goods and stopped in to tell Will what happened. Paul Wilson walking to his garage and shoe repair shop at Fenston Corners and Tom Miller, Fenston's postmaster, saw the police car at Wescott's and came in out of curiosity.

All four men were Ben's contemporaries and had

known him since he first arrived in Fenston fresh out of the Marine Corps. Though none of them could say they knew Ben well, their quiet talk that morning centered on what a good neighbor he had been.

"Hattie and Alice . . . strange how I always think of Alice as a kid, even now when she's off on her own. She and Hattie, they'll miss him sorely," Will Wescott said, his bloodshot early morning eyes misting over behind his glasses. "And so sudden . . ."

"Yes," Clem added. And he looked over at Will, recalling Will and Athena's own sudden loss, their son Gordie, who had been killed in Vietnam.

Paul flipped a quarter expertly into a can on the counter, breaking the silence. Then another and another.

"My treat today," he said as he poured coffee into Styrofoam cups.

"Ben didn't have a chance," said Clem. "Heart attack. Mighta felt a few tickles during the week. More than likely, he didn't even know what hit him."

"Seems funny," Paul remarked, "Hattie's been alone a good bit of the time up there on the hill anyway. But somehow now it will be different."

"It's strange, you know. You're neighborly and all. And Hattie and Athena being as close as they are. But I don't think I knew him all that well," Will said.

"Singing. That's how I think of him. Singing. That voice of his booming out behind us in church. You could always tell he was in church of a Sunday by the way Eleanor started pumping up the organ," Tom observed.

"He was more like a visitor than a husband. That Hattie's some woman. Taking care of that big place by herself all these years," Paul turned toward the others and lifted his cup.

Immediately, Will bristled, "No good letting your own feelings for Hattie show just now. Doesn't seem right, talking bad of the dead." Will looked Paul over quietly. He and Athena had always thought Paul was more than neighborly fond of Hattie. Though a number of men were taken by Hattie's good looks and friendly ways, Paul's interest was singularly obvious and intense.

After a moment, Clem said, "It's one thing when she expects him home from a trip from time to time. This is something altogether different. It'll take Hattie some getting used to." Then he shook his head as if to acknowledge how foolish his own words sounded once he'd said them.

"I guess Athena's over there?" Tom asked inclining his head in the direction of Hattie's farm.

"Yes. I expect she'll be there a good bit until all this is over," Will answered. They all understood he was talking not just about the funeral and the next few days, but also about the time it would take Hattie to adjust to Ben's death. Even for a town where everyone knew everyone else's business, and where it was commonplace for families to depend on each other, the special bond that Hattie and Athena shared was considered deep.

"Wouldn't have it otherwise," Will said softly. "I know all too well how much you need your friends in time of grief. Don't know how we would have gotten through

Gordie's . . ." he broke off and turned from the other men who looked elsewhere as he wiped his eyes.

"Gotta get across and open up," Paul said, draining his coffee cup. "They'll be lining up at the pumps. Coming, Tom?" He nodded to Will and Clem and left. The tinkle of the store bell hung in the air.

Chapter eight

Hattie's large, tidy kitchen had the feel of a place where someone lived. A large picture window looked out onto a garden filled with spring blossoms and bird feeders. A cushioned wicker sofa and rocker sat by the Swedish enamel stove in the corner. Next to the chair, a large wicker basket brimmed over with books, papers, and magazines, and binoculars and a bird book were in easy reach. But the table, a thick, round oak claw-foot table, held the center spot in the room. In a large, beautiful home, Hattie spent most of her waking hours in her kitchen.

Perhaps because the three women were so frequently together in that room, it was hard for them to focus on what had happened. Knowing where every item was kept, Athena set about making a pot of tea. Eleanor sat across from Hattie, studying her face. Both women knew the best thing they could do for her now was to simply let her talk. The arrangements, the busy work of death, would claim her attentions soon enough. But for now, they waited for the words to come.

Slowly and deliberately Hattie said, "One minute we were lying there talking. The next he was gone." She did not begin to cry, but her face, a crumple of confusion and fear, was all the more painful for her friends to see. Although Athena and Eleanor were awed by this sight and the revelation of this new possibility—the uncharted territory of widowhood into which Hattie had been thrust—neither could offer any suggestion or help beyond common sense. Athena set a cup of tea in front of each of them. Sensing her struggle with the flood of ideas and images that came to her, they waited for Hattie to compose herself enough to speak.

Finally Eleanor said, "Hattie, just let it out. You'll feel better if you do."

"Yes," Athena added, "Just say what you're thinking. What you're feeling. It'll help you."

They waited. Her two friends looked at Hattie as she began tentatively, "I feel . . . I feel . . . I feel." She fell quiet, sobbed for a moment, then paused as if to concentrate on naming the emotion that engulfed her.

Hattie closed her eyes and began again. "I feel . . . betrayed. It's not bad enough that Ben was gone half the time anyhow. But now with Alice moved away to Pittsburgh, I was thinking I'd be able to go with him, maybe have some real time together . . . but now he leaves me completely. I . . . without any explanation."

She stopped. The corners of her mouth worked as she gestured confusion with her palms upraised. Then she wailed, "I can't believe I'm saying that. Ben's dead and I'm . . . angry."

She broke off, as she recalled Ben's last words and wondered what he had wanted to tell her. Abruptly, she stopped crying and looked up at Athena and Eleanor. "Oh, God, I almost forgot. Ben had just started to tell me something important. Now I'll never know what it was."

"Maybe you can figure it out. What were you talking about?"

"His job. We were just lying there and talking about his job. I said I thought I'd like to travel a little with him. But I have no idea what it was he wanted to tell me . . ." Suddenly Hattie let out a short laugh that startled her friends and seemed to brush the corners of the kitchen. "Isn't that just like Ben? To leave me. And leave me guessing . . ."

Eleanor had been praying under her breath on the way over in the car as soon as she realized how serious it was. Now she dipped her hand into her sweater pocket where her rosary lay. Athena stood up, moving around the table to stand behind Hattie and put her arms around her shoulders. A chill came into the room as both women watched Hattie live out their secret fear. In her own mind, each tried it on: What if it had been Eddie, sick for most of the last five years? Or what if it had been Will? Athena's thoughts went back to Gordie's death; the horrible loss that had just begun to scab over in her heart would burst open again. Having lost a child, she couldn't imagine a fate cruel enough to take Will from her too. Each woman, in her own way, alone, tried to finish the statement that Hattie had begun—"I . . . I . . . I . . . feel"—each woman attempting to name the face her own grief would take.

"Oh, Hat," said Athena, "Let me call Alice. If I get her before she leaves for the hospital, she'll come right away, probably be here by evening. You know you'll feel better when she's here." Maybe the best thing Athena could do for Hattie would be to save her having to tell Alice that her father, perfectly healthy and only fifty-three years old, had died quite suddenly in his bed.

Hattie nodded her assent, relieved that she wouldn't have to tell Alice herself, but not at all sure that she'd feel better when her daughter arrived. Just as Athena went to pick up the phone, it rang. She spoke softly for a few minutes.

"Eldon wants you to come over to decide on a few things. I'll drive you, as soon as you can get dressed," she reported the conversation to Hattie.

"I'm not going," Hattie replied, her face set at a combative angle.

"Now, Hattie, I know this isn't easy. But you have to do it."

"I'll go along if you want," Eleanor added.

"I mean it. I'm not going. Tell Eldon to come here." Athena and Eleanor were familiar with Hattie's imperiousness, chalked up to her having been spoiled as a child.

"But, Hat. Ben's already over there. You have to go to pick out the casket," Athena's voice dropped as she spoke. "And you have to decide what Ben will wear for the viewing."

"Of course I'll pick out the clothes. But I'm not going over there."

"You're just overwrought. We don't have to rush right over. Why don't you rest for a while first."

"I'm not going there. Tell Eldon to pick out the casket himself, I don't care. Ben's dead, he won't care either. I want Ben's wake to be here, at home. Eldon can get him ready . . ."

"Why don't you go upstairs and try to take a nap. This will all seem easier when you're not so tired."

"Nap or no nap, I'm not going to Eldon's. He can come here for the arrangements. I'll get Ben's clothes ready and he can take them back with him. I'm not leaving, and that's final." Athena and Eleanor exchanged looks that said they couldn't change her mind, so why bother to upset her further.

Instead, Athena got up again to make the call that had been delayed by the discussion of the funeral arrangements with the undertaker. She didn't want to postpone telling Alice.

Chapter nine

Hattie went alone up the stairs to the bedroom, the room that Ben had died in. It was only that morning, but it felt to her like eons ago. She pulled back the quilt that Clem had placed over the bed when they had taken Ben and the sheets she had wound around him. Then she took off her robe and nightgown and lay down naked on the unmade bed that was still scented with their lovemaking and thought of Ben, her husband of twenty-five years. Her husband no more.

She replayed every minute of Ben's homecoming, from the way he surprised her at the door, to the dinner she had cooked—his favorite pot roast with potatoes and carrots and sprigs of fresh mint she had snipped that morning. Ben had walked through the house slowly looking at each room. "Odd how cool and dark the rooms are. Last time I was home the trees weren't in leaf yet. The light changes everything," he said as he picked up an old photo of Alice from the desk. "How old was she here?" he asked and nodded as if verifying something when she told him the picture was taken at the church picnic when Alice was ten.

They had eaten slowly, talking about Alice and her job in Pittsburgh. In a routine that was second nature to both of them—like a well-rehearsed and silent ballet—Ben and Hattie washed the dishes and then he shut out the lights and followed her up the stairs. All evening she had had the sense of something waiting between them. Just the sense of it. Something far off at the edge of her consciousness that she could not have brought into words.

Later when she thought of what Ben had said, how he had something to tell her, she shivered a little and tried to go back through the evening looking for clues to what it might have been.

Often when Ben was away, if she felt lonely, she'd close her eyes and visualize his face, always smiling. But this night, when she tried to summon him for comfort, she could not. She had cried, but not as much as she would have liked. She wanted to cry and shriek and sob and deplete the tears, but that didn't seem possible. The pillows still had the indentation where she and Ben had nestled next to each other, and she tried to recall that feeling of safety and fullness after their lovemaking. She pulled the pillow over her face and breathed into it slowly, waiting for some kind of clarity about what had happened, something to explain her loss. The idea that Ben was dead wouldn't stay with her.

Finally, she arose and went into the bathroom and showered, meticulously scrubbing each inch of her body. The water felt good against her skin, but her eyelids stung from the pressure of tears. She dressed carefully in a dark skirt and sweater and went back into the bedroom where she removed and rolled the mattress pad into a ball and stuck it into a plastic bag. Next, she took fresh linens from the hall chest and slowly and carefully dressed the bed of her widowhood.

Chapter ten

From the closet Hattie took the suits Ben had hung there just the day before when he returned from his trip. Her next task would be to decide whether the world would get its last glimpse of Ben Darling in a light gray jacket flecked with charcoal, the one he had worn just the day before when he returned to Fenston, or dressed in a trim navy. Hattie lay the jackets side by side on the bed and went to the tie rack where she found his favorite, his lucky tie, the red and gold stripe on a cream background that he had donned for all important and happy occasions since the day he had first worn it eight years before and won a Dodge Dart at the Knights of Columbus raffle.

Lifting a freshly laundered white shirt from the closet shelf, she laid it and the tie on the bed between the suits.

The tie looked best with the navy. That decided, Hattie took shoes and socks and clean underwear and put them in a bag, carefully wrapping the shoes in squares of old flannel as Ben had always done.

Glad that she had something to do, she focused on the task. Even on such an extraordinary day, she could keep her emotions in check by concentrating on the details of her work, investing each small decision with her full attention. Not just any socks, but new ones without any worn spots, though for a moment she wondered if they actually put socks and shoes and underwear on the body. Literal-minded, Hattie responded fully when asked to prepare her husband's clothing. Occasionally, Ben's face would come up before her eyes, and she'd think of the great pleasure he'd always taken in selecting and caring for his clothing, his pleasure in a good shirt and tie.

Easily the best dressed man in Fenston, Ben never left the house without looking himself over in the hall mirror and giving that squinty smile that engaged his whole handsome face. Hattie stood in front of her dresser looking at the photo of them taken at her forty-fifth birthday party. She and Ben made an attractive couple. Half a head taller than Hattie, Ben looked more like forty than his fifty-three years.

Hattie examined her own image in the picture frame: a voluptuous figure, large breasts and round hips and a small waist that she always took care to emphasize with belts and fitted clothing. She had looked especially appealing in the gray silk dress she had worn for the party. Her long hair, freshly done for the event, a glossy auburn; with only a few strands of gray showing through its Loving Care rinse. Ben's hand lay on her shoulder and her hand reached up to it, her fingertips touching his. She was smiling guilelessly into the camera, but Ben's expression was a mixture of candor and mystery. She had not studied his expression before, though she had looked at the photo hundreds of times. Now she wondered if Ben had known he was so close to the end of his time with her.

Determined to finish her task, Hattie turned from the photograph and crossed the room. As she passed the mirror she caught sight of herself there. Was she still the woman in the photograph, the happy wife? She paused, examining her face feature by feature—her high cheekbones, deep gray eyes, aquiline nose. Yes, they were *her* features. But who *was* this woman?

Hattie again glanced at the extensive and orderly closet, his doing entirely, where every article of clothing was neatly in place. She took the clothes brush from a hook inside the door, lifted and replaced the gray suit and took the blue one up from the bed and began to brush it methodically, as she had seen Ben do a thousand times. There was comfort in this faithfulness to his routine, as if somehow she was taking over where he had left off, somehow holding his place. She carried Ben's funeral ensemble downstairs.

Chapter eleven

In the office of his funeral parlor on Cain Street in Carbondale, Eldon Questor tapped the fingers of his left hand along his cheek waiting for Athena to finish speaking at the other end of the phone. He betrayed his agitation in his fidgety manner but not by his voice as he answered. "I know they used to do it in the old days. I know that. Lots of people held wakes for their loved ones at home. But this is 1982. Why would Hattie want Ben laid out in the parlor?"

Again he waited and fiddled with his hair and various objects on his desk. "Yes. I know it's her call. It's her husband. No one would disagree with that, Athena; I just wanted to talk to you about it. Maybe she'll regret it later."

At the other end of the phone, Athena was trying to explain how Hattie felt.

Eldon interrupted, "You saw her. She's out of control. I've seen lots of people in her position and I know what I'm talking about."

Athena began speaking again, but Eldon interrupted, "Of course there's no set way for people to react. All I mean is I think Hattie needs some help. She's taking this far worse than it appears. And her not wanting to leave the house even for Ben's viewing is part of it."

He waited again.

"Okay. I just wanted to see what you thought. If that's what she really wants, we'll give it to her."

He waited.

"I know it's hard for her. Yes . . . yes . . . yes, we . . . okay, Athena. Whatever you say." As he hung up, he opened his desk drawer and took out a notebook and a bottle of Scotch.

In the cluttered kitchen of her half made-over farmhouse, Eleanor Rodiri was mixing eggs in a huge bowl, enough eggs to make seven or eight cakes, one of which she'd take to Hattie's house and the others would go into the freezer for future use. One-handed, she broke each egg with a practiced crack against the side of the bowl and dripped in the contents. Dolly Parton was playing back up to Eleanor's voice. When the phone rang and Eleanor answered, Parton was crooning the phrase, "I will always love you."

After the initial hello, her face darkened and she was

quiet for a long while. Then she shrugged and said, "What can she be thinking of, Athena? Can't you talk her out of it?"

Pause, listening.

"I guess we've all become so used to the way Hattie is we scarcely take notice. But not leaving the house for weeks on end is, excuse me for saying so, not normal. And this, holding Ben's wake at home so that she doesn't have to go into Carbondale, well, I don't know that it's the best thing for her either."

Pause, listening.

"Well, yes, I know they used to do it all the time."

Pause.

"Well, not that I can think of. Yes. Of course. Seems like it should be up to her."

Inside the Fenston Borough Building in his office, Chief of Police, Clem Tomkins answered the phone and listened until he could restrain himself no longer, "Eldon, it's not up to me to tell folks how to bury their dead. This sounds plain foolish. But you know Hattie as well as I do. Gets a thing in her mind and there's no telling her. Absolutely no telling."

"Wilson's Gas Station and Shoe Repair," Paul Wilson said absently into the phone as he peered through the front window wondering if the car that just pulled in wanted gas or was just making a U-turn. When the caller gave him a chance to speak, he said, "A wake in the living room. No, I know it's not illegal. But it does seem strange."

Pause.

"Not strange as in bad but strange-weird . . . Kind of ironic, too, don't you think? Ben was almost never home when he was alive. I don't know what's in her mind, but I've thought about Hattie quite a bit, her not liking to leave the house or Fenston. Maybe she's reacting to Ben's always having been away. Now she wants him right there in the living room. But whatever Hattie wants, I'd say. A funeral is not about the person who died. It's to comfort those left behind."

When he hung up the phone he walked out of his building and into the post office next door. He stood for a moment as if trying to work something out, then said, "Wait till you hear this, Tom."

Chapter twelve

Athena showed Eldon Questor into the kitchen where Hattie sat. Folded neatly over a chair next to her were Ben's clothes.

"It's a sad time, Hattie. I know that. I hope I can make it a little easier for you."

"Thanks, Eldon. I appreciate your coming out here. Somehow I just don't feel like going anywhere right now."

"I understand completely. We just have a few details, a few things you need to decide on and I'll take care of the rest." His mouth moved smoothly over the unctuous syllables of explanation: What would happen next, what his services would entail. The home viewing was no problem at all; Eldon made it seem like a good idea that he should have thought of himself. Finally, he explained that it would cost no more or no less than if she had chosen the more traditional wake in his funeral home. Athena was at Hattie's side throughout, patting her hand and making suggestions. She behaved as if picking out a casket was as ordinary an occurrence as choosing a dress for a concert . . . What color? What finish? What kind of satin?

Confused by all the possibilities, Hattie chose what seemed the simplest thing. As he fawned and counseled, Eldon's lugubrious tones emitted from a mouth freshened by numerous wintergreen breath mints. Hattie stood back a pace or two to avoid the cool blast. Athena, who had first spoken to Eldon, gave Eleanor a glance, lifted an eyebrow and fanned her nose surreptitiously to indicate how unsuccessfully the mints provided coverage for Eldon's whiskey breath. Everyone knew he would be the first to take out the hard stuff at the evening viewing, and that the other men would follow him onto the back porch periodically for a sly drink to sustain themselves through the dry rite of mourning.

By late afternoon, the preparations were well underway. Will and Athena's son, Al, arrived to move the furniture around the living room to allow space for the casket by the long wall. Chairs and tables were repositioned for groups of mourners to sit and talk, and additional folding chairs dotted the dining room, ready to handle the anticipated crowd.

By six, Ben's body arrived in the gleaming gray casket Hattie had picked out from the photos in Eldon's catalogue. Dressed in the outfit Hattie had chosen, he lay in the alcove of the living room as friends, food and flowers began to appear.

Chapter thirteen

The viewing had already been planned when Alice arrived. She went up to her room before she greeted her mother. Athena, sensing trouble, followed her and tapped lightly on the closed door.

"It's open," Alice said, quickly turning to face Athena. The young woman's lovely face was clouded with anxiety. She buttoned the jacket of a dark suit and straightened the collar, adjusting her long blond hair around her face.

"Oh, Aunt Athena," she said, and her composure faltered. Athena had to reach up to put her arms around Alice's shoulders. The young woman stiffened for a minute and then relaxed into the loving embrace of an old friend. After a few minutes of quiet tears, she stood apart and looked around the room, which held all her childhood and girlhood memories. Alice's glance took in the books and photos that lined the walls.

"Oh, God," she echoed her mother's words earlier that day. "I can't believe he's gone. How? What happened?"

"Turns out it wasn't his heart. An embolism."

"I keep thinking—that if I had been here . . . But, of course, that's foolish. Even if I'd been sitting next to him, I couldn't have done anything, if that's the case. Kind of strange, you know, to be a nurse. And not to be able to . . ."

"You can do something. Try to be gentle with your mother. She's taking it very hard."

Athena looked steadily at Alice.

"I'll try. But you know how it's been these last few years. Somehow things flare up and neither of us seems to be able to back down."

"Well, try. That's all I'm asking. I know you love her. Just try."

A few minutes before the stream of mourners began, Alice stood beside her mother and faced her father's body. Dry-eyed, Hattie turned to her and the two embraced, a clearly emotional yet somehow clumsy and distant hug. Then both turned to face Ben and stood quietly.

"Doesn't he look fine?" Hattie asked.

"Yeah, Mom. He looks just great, Alice answered, a slight edge to her voice. "Dead but great."

Hattie drew in her breath sharply. "I mean . . ."

"I know what you mean. I'm sorry."

"I mean I want everyone to see him looking his best for the last time."

"I know what you mean. Looking good, yes, that's important."

The two stood silently looking down at Ben.

Suddenly Alice let out a huge sigh and said in a whispery hissing voice, as if she were trying to prevent herself from speaking or avoid letting Hattie hear, "I can't believe you've done this."

"Done what," Hattie asked, surprise and confusion in her voice. "Don't you think he looks all right?"

"You know what I mean."

Hattie sighed, "You've blamed me for so many things, I'm really not sure I know what I've done this time."

"Here—in the house. How could you? What were you thinking to have this here? Who ever heard of such a thing?"

Hattie recoiled in hurt, "I don't know. I just wanted it."

"God, Mom, I don't know what you're about sometimes."

"I guess I just wanted him home."

"Well, that's a switch," Alice's voice now had a hostile edge to it.

Hattie's voice, too, got sharper, "What do you mean?"

"I mean you never seemed to care whether he was home or not. Why now?"

"That's not true. I always wanted your father here."

"But not enough to . . ."

"To drag you all over the countryside after him."

"Maybe I would have liked it. Maybe I wanted to go. Did you ever think of asking me?"

"Don't be ridiculous. You were a child."

"It wasn't about me, a child who wanted to have a father more than once a month. It was about the crazy fear or whatever it is that won't let you leave this place," Alice interrupted.

Athena who had been closely observing them from the doorway, suddenly moved between mother and daughter, "Alice, Emily Simpson just came in." She pointed to the door where a young woman and about five other people, the first visitors, were waiting, unwilling to intrude upon the conversation between Hattie and Alice.

When Alice walked off to greet her friends, Athena put her arm around Hattie, "Don't worry about it. She's just sad and can't take care of it except by striking out. You know Alice's always been that way. She'll get over it and be back to herself right away. Don't take it to heart." But Hattie had heard. Alice's words would stay with her for a very long time.

Soon the large house bulged with more people than it had contained in years. Almost everyone in Fenston would show up that evening or the next day, even though some had never actually spoken a word to Ben Darling. What mattered was that the Darlings were neighbors. All of Alice's classmates who still lived in the valley, some she hadn't seen since high school graduation, arrived. Even Eddie Rodiri, crippled with gout, hobbled in, leaning heavily on Robbie's arm.

Hattie stood by the coffin, not to one side as custom would have it, but right in front. Most of the time, she didn't look at the people who came through, but at Ben, forcing the visitors to turn their back on the body and squeeze in between Hattie and the coffin in order to offer their condolences. Hattie seemed almost detached from those who wanted to console her; she was so absorbed in looking at Ben. Her mind played over and over, "How could this be?" as she gazed at him in the casket. She couldn't get beyond that one startling thought.

By the time the six o'clock fire whistle sounded, the room was full. Plates of food were consumed and replenished, and the evening went by. Every so often, one group or another would forget why they had gathered and a spate of laughter, the pleasure of friends in company with each other, would break out and then be quickly and self-consciously stifled. Hattie was aware of the time passing in massive blocks. She watched the sun dive over the edge of Crystalle Hill and sometime later Eleanor tried to get her to sit down and eat a sandwich, saying it was almost nine. Finally, the last of the callers left. Eleanor, Athena and Betty finished cleaning up the dishes then joined Hattie in the parlor.

"Time for bed, I think, Hat," Athena said. "You're about done in for the day."

Alice added, taking her arm, "Yes, Mom, let's go upstairs."

Hattie opened her mouth to protest, but no words came. After Alice's sharp words earlier, Hattie knew the girl was ashamed. They had avoided each other's eyes all evening. Now Hattie was glad for her daughter's solicitousness, though she knew some chasm had widened between them. Tears, the first all evening, began to leak from Hattie's eyes as she hugged her daughter silently. She hoped they would be able to talk to each other again, but not just yet. Hattie felt unable to tolerate any more upset. She suspected that Alice felt guilty and disloyal. Hattie knew her daughter must have been harboring some strong feelings that neither of them could deal with right now.

"That's right, now. Up, up you go. We'll see to the last of things down here," Eleanor said.

From her room, Hattie listened to the women downstairs—her old friends and her daughter. In the intonation of their familiar voices she could make out Athena's crisp voice and Eleanor's wheezy speech, then Alice's high, quick accent. She felt like a child listening, made safe by the sound of voices somewhere in the house, words unintelligible and uninteresting but comforting. Hattie undressed and fell into a deep, dreamless sleep.

Chapter fourteen

When Hattie awoke for the first time, it was still early, around midnight. The house was quiet. Although she had been asleep less than an hour, she felt jittery and restless. She walked into the bathroom and drank a glass of water and started back to the bed. Abruptly, she turned and went down the stairs. Instead of switching on the hall light, she steadied and guided herself down each step by pressing her fingertips against the wall as she had done a thousand times before. Fear was the only thing different in Hattie's life: her fear of the casket and of the knowledge that Ben had been about to tell her something important.

At first, when she entered the room which only hours before had been filled with mourners, she was so afraid that she couldn't focus her eyes. Hattie approached the casket and forced herself to look at him. Ben lay with his hands folded on his stomach; his left hand on top. He had never worn a wedding ring, and now Hattie wished he had. She thought back over the events of the past two days—from her anxious anticipation of Ben's homecoming to their lovemaking, his horribly sudden death, the crush of people around her . . . Hattie needed to think. Something nagged at her, preventing her from crying. She felt it like a pressure in her abdomen, her back in the grip of a crushing pain.

A bank of candles in large glass cylinders at either side of the casket threw shadows about the silent room. A car labored up the highway in the distance. Hattie recalled how she had listened those nights she expected Ben home late, thinking she could tell his car's sound from all the others as he left the Interstate and wound through the valley road, starting up the drive back to her.

For a very long time, she stood there waiting; she wasn't sure for what. Ben would never come home again. And she couldn't seem to cry about it. Her body felt icy and separate from her mind.

"What was it, Ben?" she whispered. "What did you want to tell me? Why did you leave me? I don't think I can forgive you for this."

Lying in the casket with the play of candlelight on his face, Ben's expression seemed to change from the benign confusion his features had held earlier in the evening to a look of sinister amusement.

Hattie looked up past the casket to the glistening banner on the floral arrangement Alice had insisted on,

"DADDY, I LOVE YOU." Hattie's eyes blurred with the pain of her grief for her daughter. When she looked back at Ben, his features had rearranged themselves again, this time into indifference.

Suddenly Hattie touched the ring on her own finger. She reached out to Ben. His skin felt cold, rubbery and stiff, completely different than it had before. She startled at the sound of the refrigerator motor unexpectedly kicking on in the next room, shivered, drew back, but then touched him again; resolutely this time. She still didn't know what she intended to do, but her fingers took over. Fearing that someone might come into the room and stop her, she moved quickly as she spun the ring from her finger. Working hard to separate Ben's hands, she thrust her ring between them and out of sight. Absently, she tugged his sleeve into place over his wrist and touched his hand again, the small bristles of hair on his fingers and the turgid skin, which felt nothing at all like her Ben Darling.

Hattie moved back from the casket and stood for a long time staring intently at Ben's face, just as she had throughout the viewing, almost as if she expected him to respond to her actions. Still no tears coursed down her face as she expected and hoped they would. Everything about the house she had spent her whole life in, had changed and shifted as it accommodated itself to this death. She thought of those other deaths—her parents, Gordie dead in Vietnam, the five Beste generations who had lived and died in the house—summoned to witness how she would grieve. She could not fix her mind on any particular emotion. But she did feel something—a chill coursed through her body so intense that her teeth chattered. Again, she moved closer to the casket and bent over as if to listen to Ben whispering. She pressed her cheek against his chest.

The man she had loved and had spent her life with was dead. All the ways she had ever thought she might feel in this situation eluded her. Hattie continued to study Ben's features, which seemed to change again and again in the shifting light. She suddenly knew one important thing about her life with Ben. She had lived alongside him through both the glorious and the mundane days of a long marriage, and yet they had borne their individual loneliness. Hattie's body trembled again at the daunting knowledge that she had never really known Ben at all.

When she turned to climb the stairs to her bedroom again, Hattie felt a weariness so intense that she could hardly lift her feet to clear the treads. At least, she thought, she would be able to rest. But during the night, her first night of widowhood, sleep moved away from her like an elusive lover. Each time she felt herself near to it, she'd be pulled back to wakefulness, imagining she heard a thick, phlegmy breathing on the pillow next to her. As she tossed and jerked the covers this way and that, trying to find a cool space to rest, she struggled to make sense of her own emotions. What she was experiencing didn't feel like the grief she felt entitled to. Had she been forced to put a name to her state, it would have been confusion.

It was as though too much was happening at once, too many images crowded about her, too much for her to process, especially with the house full of people all afternoon and evening. She simply couldn't think. Occasionally, she'd relive her recent action, placing the ring, touching Ben's dead flesh. How strange he looked and felt; then the thought would frighten her and quickly disappear, only to surface in images of Ben holding baby Alice on his lap.

Since Alice had moved to Pittsburgh two years before and with Ben on the road, Hattie's life had been solitary and private, shared only with her good friends and neighbors. The day had been too much for her and the viewing and funeral the next day would be even more taxing. She knew she needed sleep, yet how was she to turn off her mind enough to rest? How was she to endure it? When she thought of the numbers of women she knew who had been widowed, she was astonished that they had been able to survive the rituals of bereavement.

And Ben. How could she even make herself begin to realize that the central person in her life was gone? Ben. How could she cope with everyone talking to her, trying to comfort her, but saying things she didn't want to hear, forcing her thoughts back to this or to that good time they had spent with her and with Ben? What about the other times just the two of them had shared, the not-so-perfect times? Did anyone else remember them? She felt her mind refuse those images.

Still another thought pulled at the edge of her consciousness, one that she couldn't quite bring into focus. She dozed fitfully until two, then fell into a deep sleep for another hour. She woke up with a start, now knowing with certainty the elusive thing which had been bothering her: She still didn't know what Ben had started to tell her. What had he been thinking of in the moments before he died?

She must have slept again for when she woke next, the room was stuffy, much too warm for early May and gray with predawn light. She lay there, willing herself to get up; even imagining herself seated on the edge of the bed ready to stand. The house was completely still; Alice was asleep down the hall, in her childhood bedroom. There had been no traffic on the road since the milk truck's four a.m. delivery. When she heard the hall floorboards creak a small kernel of happiness bloomed in Hattie's heart.

It was night. Long, long ago. Long before Ben had begun to travel, before Alice and she had begun to misunderstand each other. The covers moved and she felt her daughter's small, sleep-warmed body slide in next to her. For a moment, milky-sweet baby breath feathered Hattie's cheek, then the child turned and nestled close, her back curled into her mother's chest. Greedily, Hattie inhaled Alice's scent and drew a few strands of her daughter's downy blond hair into her mouth. Only partially awake, Hattie adjusted her body around her daughter and Ben moved slightly, to make room in the cave of his arms for his wife and child.

Chapter fifteen

Alice stood beside Hattie's bed. "Mom, it's time to get ready . . ." she said, her voice full of concern.

Moving seemed a superhuman effort that Hattie was not capable of. But she stretched out her hand to Alice, and with her daughter's help sat up.

"I guess you didn't get much sleep last night," Alice shifted to her nursing voice.

"I'm okay. Just slow. I'll be right along," Hattie insisted.

It was clear from the set table, the waiting coffee and juice that Alice had been up for some time. As Hattie lowered herself into her chair, Alice poured some coffee and shook a little white pill into Hattie's hand.

"Take this, Mom, it will make things easier today." And that's just what happened.

The funeral was a blur. Alice had insisted that she take a little pill every few hours. Since her angry words in front of the casket, Alice had been a model daughter, plying her mother with endless cups of tea and as many of the white pills as she could force Hattie to take. She fussed and hovered, suggesting walks and late night movies and popcorn.

Hattie kept trying to remind herself that Alice had lost Ben too. But Alice seemed to function best focusing on Hattie. Finally, a week after the funeral, Alice said, "Mom, I can't stay here much longer. Why don't you come out to Pittsburgh with me for a few weeks? It'd be fun. We can do some things together, spend some time. You could use a change."

"I don't think so. Not right now. I feel like I want to stay close to home."

"Mom, I've seen what you've been doing here. I've had to drag you out of the house even for a walk over to the lake. You're not answering your calls. You can't let yourself turn into even more of a hermit."

"I'm not ready yet. Give me some time. Maybe I'll come out later, during the summer."

"I wasn't going to tell you this, but . . . Well, I've taken a new job. Starting July 15. I'm going to head up a critical care unit."

"Oh, how wonderful. Oh, Alice, your father would . . ."

"I know. Dad would be proud. But, there's something else."

"What?" Hattie asked, warned by some tone in Alice's voice.

"The job. It's in California. In Santa Barbara. I'll be moving the first week in July."

"The first week in July? And you didn't tell us?"

"Mom, I remember how you carried on when I moved to Pittsburgh. I wasn't eager to tell you that I was leaving for California. Besides, I was waiting till Daddy got . . ."

Alice's words trailed off as the reality of her father's death startled her again like a splash of cold water. She held her hand out to her mother as if to steady them both.

"This is hard on both of us. Do you really have to go back to work so soon?"

"Yes, Mom, I do. I'm training my replacement and can't be away much longer. But the offer still stands. Won't you come with me?"

"I'd like to but I just can't. I have some things I need to take care of here. I can't go to Pittsburgh just now."

"Mom," Alice said, her voice rising again, almost angrily, "what I said the other day. I'm sorry I said it because I shouldn't have upset you, but not because I was wrong. You've let yourself get so tied to the past, to this place, this town; you'd sacrifice anything for it. You couldn't go with Dad. And now you won't go with me."

"Now, I don't think that's called for. If I choose to do my grieving here where my whole life has been, I don't think you should fault me for it."

"If that's what it was, it'd be okay. But you just seem so . . . so stuck."

"Maybe I'm happy right here."

"I just hate the way you mope around this place, preserving the past, not noticing the present."

"Oh?" Hattie felt anger quicken inside her.

"This shouldn't be news to you."

"What do you mean I don't notice the present?"

"For instance. Well, just for instance," Alice hissed, "Dad left a long, long time ago. Did you notice that?"

"What in hell do you mean by that crack? You act like you're the only person whose father traveled for a living. Lots of families had to get used to having their father be away. He worked hard for us. Everything was for us. He didn't like being on the road any more than we liked his being gone."

"Is that so? How often did he come home?"

"Well . . ."

"Or weren't you paying attention to that either?"

"Of course I was. I missed your father every day he was away."

Mother and daughter looked at each other silently. Both were afraid to say anything that might do more damage, but neither could back away from it.

"Mom, you have everything in the world to look forward to. You're still young. You're a beautiful woman. You know you won't have money worries. You can make a good life. But you're going to sit here moping around just the way you always did when Dad left. Sad, but not sad enough to get up and go with him."

"As a matter of fact, I'd just about made up my mind to start going with him," Hattie protested.

Alice snorted, then looked at her mother. Her heart expanded. Her arms followed, and Hattie tearfully folded into them.

"Oh, Mom. I'm so sorry. I'm just sad. And so worried about you. You can't go on like this, living only in the past. My room is kept as if I'll waltz back in the door in my seventh grade tutu and settle at the kitchen table for cookies and milk."

Hattie smoothed her daughter's hair as the young woman continued.

"You're not old. There's a world out there. Frightening, yes, but interesting and absorbing and wonderful too. I just want you to live. Dad did. You can too."

"You make everything sound so easy," said Hattie, looking at Alice and once again seeing the hurt little girl whose Daddy had gone and was not coming back.

"I think we've covered this, Honey. I don't want to go. But you can stay here as long as you like. I'd love to have you."

Alice dried her eyes and looked up, "God, I don't know what gets into me. I can't believe I said that stuff to you. I'm so sorry."

Hattie now held out her arms and Alice hugged her back. This was not the first time they had exchanged such harsh words. Despite Hattie's deep love for Alice, she was constantly mystified by her daughter's ability to work things around to being Hattie's fault. Usually she was able to ignore it, but today it stung with the painful poisoned arrow of truth.

Chapter sixteen

After Alice left, Athena and Eleanor checked in on Hattie regularly and were alarmed that she seemed not to be getting over her grief at all. If anything, she seemed quieter and sadder. It was as if she were becalmed on the sofa for days on end, her eyes closed, barely answering any of their questions or acknowledging their presence. One afternoon, Athena drew a chair close to the sofa, "Hattie," she said softly, "I picked up your mail for you. Lots of cards and bills. Some things you should see to."

"Maybe tomorrow. I just don't feel like it now."

"I know. But maybe you should get up and get moving. How about a cup of tea?"

"Not just yet."

The two fell into silence. Hattie's eyes were closed,

but she could picture Athena's wild graying strawberry blond hair in a long braid, wispy strands escaping around her face in a blurry halo of color. Athena's slight figure would be clad in the usual old jeans worn soft and a white cotton shirt. After a while, Hattie began to feel something, some kind of comfort in Athena's presence beside her. Their friendship stretched back years and years through all the stages of their lives . . . they had once been young brides learning to cook and can and clean, they had been through endless plantings and tree decorating and sick children's bedsides, they had been through middle age, with its new-found leisure and lovely days which widened before them with time to enjoy as they chose. Once, with the pressures of family duties, their free time had been so scarce; then suddenly, Hattie had almost too much of it. And finally, there was this new stage.

"Athena," she said, her voice somewhat creaky with disuse and emotion.

"Yes."

"Just checking to see if you're still there."

"I'm still here. Do you want me to leave?"

"No."

"I don't know what good I am, Hat, but I'm here."

"Yes."

"I'm supposed to be cheering you up, you know. At least that's what everyone is hoping."

"I know."

"But I don't think I can. All I keep thinking about is that I've never felt what you must be feeling now."

"I hope you never have to," Hattie answered.

The two women were silent again. Then Hattie said, "Remember old Mrs. Degar who used to live over on the ridge by 108?"

"Sure," Athena answered. "We used to pass her place on our way to Towson's to pick tomatoes." She waited to see why Hattie had brought up the old woman. After a minute, Athena continued, "Haven't thought about that old lady in years. Her crazy old house with its outbuildings and lean-to falling down around her, the yard overrun with asparagus and rhubarb and her face at the door, peering out as you passed. Never speaking, just watching till you moved up the lane and out of sight.

"Remember how we used to invent a past for her? What would have made her want to go to live on a hilltop all by herself? An old woman lugging water from the well and carrying the buckets up hill alone, refusing power, the gas line, the phone."

"Yes. And how she wouldn't have a mailbox, and when they put one up across the road for her, she refused to look inside."

"Up there by herself, cut off from everything. How I wanted to understand it. Now I do. I think I know what might have happened to her."

"Oh, Hattie," Athena cried picking up her friend's hand. "I know it must hurt terribly. And even to say that . . . of course, I don't know. But I hate to think of you feeling this way."

"It's not just that Ben died. But I keep having these

odd feelings, like he was somehow not with me for a time and I only realized it when he died."

"I'm not sure, but I think those feelings are probably natural."

"Maybe. To some extent. I think that. But then I keep feeling like there's something more underneath. Something I can't quite get a grip on."

"Fine, so let's try to talk this out."

Hattie waited. Then a deep shudder escaped her.

"There was something Alice said. She said he left us a long . . . Oh, I don't know. The whole thing confuses me. I look around and he's everywhere. No matter how hard I try to block it out. Then I think he's just away on a trip, this is how it's always been. Then I have to force myself to understand, and just for a moment I do, that he'll never come back. Then I think about it and realize he'd been away more than he was here. But this time, it's different."

"I'm sure being surrounded by all his stuff makes that seems even worse." Then tentatively, "It's been two months. Maybe you should think about getting rid of some of Ben's things."

It was so long before Hattie answered that Athena thought she hadn't heard. Finally, Hattie whispered, "Maybe."

Hattie seemed to brighten slightly. "You know, something like that would make me feel better. At least I'd be accomplishing something."

When Eleanor dropped by, the conversation changed to Eddie's newest craze. Every morning he would spend two hours listening to audiotapes, trying to teach himself Hebrew. "Says he wants to be able to read the Old Testament in Hebrew," Eleanor grimaced. "But it's not a language you want to do your ironing too."

"Tell him to use the earphones. You won't have to hear it."

"He does. That's not the problem. What he's listening to isn't the problem. It's how he sounds when he tries to repeat the words." They collapsed into laughter as she imitated Eddie's Hebrew pronunciation. At the sound of Hattie's welcome laughter, Eleanor and Athena glanced at each other in relief.

Chapter seventeen

The next day, Hattie gave up the couch. After weeks of nightgowns and robes and slippers, she went into her closet and selected a pair of tweed slacks and a beige silk blouse, pleased to see that she had lost weight and that the small roll at her waist had disappeared. Her clothes now fit in a way that pleased her.

Many women envied Hattie's figure and men still looked at her approvingly. A feeling of ironic bitterness passed over her as she thought of Ben, so secure in her love that he left her alone in Fenston half the time. She toweled her auburn hair, noticing that she badly needed a root job.

Hattie set about the chores she had planned out for herself: she began by getting rid of his clothes. Ben had prided himself on never gaining an ounce. Every year around his birthday, he would come down wearing his Marine Corps uniform. He'd strut around the house proud as could be. She would keep the uniform, Hattie thought. The only man in town built like Ben, the postmaster, Tom Miller, seemed thrilled when she asked him if he'd like to have Ben's clothing. He showed up promptly at noon, his lunch hour from the post office.

As Hattie led Tom upstairs and opened Ben's closet, she felt curiously detached. He stood there uncomfortably, seeming not to know what to do until Hattie began hamming it up, acting as if she were a sales clerk in a pricey man's clothing store.

"And this elegant jacket, pure wool, woven by hand, was designed by Joe Schmoe, especially for the House of J.C. Penney."

"Elegant," Tom answered.

"And here we have the classic gray, suitable for any occasion," she said slipping a gray jacket from the hanger. Then she realized it was the one Ben had worn when he came home for the last time. Quickly she undid the button and shook it wide for Tom to try it on.

Taking his cue from Hattie's mood, Tom narrowed his eyes, looked himself over in the mirror, slouched and thrust his hands into the pockets, striking a pose. When he withdrew his hand, he said, "You might want this," and placed a piece of paper in Hattie's hand.

Both became instantly ill at ease once more, recalling why they were there. Soberly and quickly they finished the transfer of Ben's wardrobe with few words. After Tom left,

Hattie went back upstairs and sat on the bed looking into Ben's empty closet. "Am I supposed to feel better now?" she asked aloud, then absently picked up and looked at the tiny piece of paper Tom had retrieved from Ben's pocket, an ordinary appointment card for Drs. Downs, Field and Rook, Hartford cardiologists. Filled in on the patient name line was one word: Darling.

Alice had notified Harden a few days after Ben's death. A company representative, Mr. Holmes, a kind-faced man in his late fifties, came to Fenston the following week. He offered condolences and gave Hattie information about the benefits and life insurance she would receive. As Alice had predicted, Hattie would be well cared for. She had her farm, the rented land, Ben's social security and half a million dollars in life insurance.

When Mr. Holmes shook Hattie's hand, she felt he meant it. "Didn't know Ben all that well. Didn't socialize much. Seemed eager to get his work done and head home. They were standing on the porch and he took in the view of the valley. "This is some place you have here. No wonder Ben wanted to be here as much as he could."

"Didn't seem that way to me. He was always rushing off to do something with Harden," was all Hattie could squeak out in answer. Finally Mr. Holmes sighed and looked at her again. Hattie had the unnerving feeling that she was somehow different from what he'd envisaged. But what had he expected? And why did she have the impression that he didn't approve of Ben? Before he left, Mr. Holmes made arrangements for someone from the leasing agency to come for Ben's company car. As Mr. Holmes said good-bye, he drew in his breath as if he were about to say something else, then thought better of it. She watched him walk to the car.

After disposing of Ben's clothes, Hattie moved on to the fishing gear and tools, feeling a compulsion to finish what she'd started. She called Will Wescott to come and take the tools and gear away, to keep what he wanted and to get rid of the rest.

When they opened the door to Ben's workshop at the back of the barn, dust swirled up at them and it took a few minutes to accustom their eyes to the dim room. On the workbench lay a small stool, which Ben had evidently been making. Its size reminded Hattie of the table and chair set he had once made for Alice and her friends when she was a child, for tea parties.

Will drew air in through his teeth in a soft whistle of appreciation when he looked over the tools in Ben's shop. Some had never been used, but all were oiled and hanging perfectly on the wall of the pegboard, each tool outlined in black marker so they could easily be replaced in the correct spot. The saws gleamed; the vise jaws were open and waiting.

"Are you sure, Hattie? Maybe it's too soon to be doing this. Maybe you'll regret it later."

"I want to get rid of all these things. I'll feel better."

"You could get a pretty penny for this stuff. Mint condition, I'd say."

"Just don't feel right selling Ben's things. Alice has no use for tools. And I think Ben . . ." she paused, realizing she was about to choke on the emotion of what she was about to say next.

Will put his arms out and Hattie walked into them, lifting her own arms up to Will's meaty, comfortable, flannelled shoulders.

"I want," she said into his shirt, "I want you to have them for all the times when Ben was away and I needed to call on you. You and Athena were always there for me. I want you to have them, Will." She stood back and looked at him steadily.

"Well, if you're sure . . ." Will answered quickly, almost embarrassed by the emotion in his own voice. He hefted a tool. "I've always wanted one of these Yankee screwdrivers. You know I'll put them to good use. If you need anything fixed, just call me. Anyhow, tools or no tools, we'll always be there for you."

Chapter eighteen

Hattie wasn't sure whether she was sadder because Ben was dead or because she thought he was capable of keeping a secret from her. What she should do next came to her as she slowly realized that she would not find comfort from the running discussion she had been having with Ben in her head, nor be eased by the fact that she had given away all his possessions. Alice's words haunted her throughout the day and night.

Yes, Hattie thought, if she actually measured the time Ben was gone, well, it added up. Why hadn't she understood that Ben was spending half his life away from her? Had she become so little a part of him that he didn't share important information with her? What was wrong with him that he was consulting a cardiologist? Why hadn't he told her?

Without allowing herself time to change her mind, Hattie picked up the phone, the appointment card in her other hand. The receptionist answered immediately, and put Hattie on hold for five minutes during which Hattie ordered her thoughts and decided what questions she would ask.

Then, after the wait, the woman abruptly came back onto the line and responded curtly to Hattie's request for information about Ben's condition, "Our policy is not to give out information about our patients over the phone."

"But he was my husband. And he's dead. I just want to find out what was wrong with him."

"I'm sorry. But . . ."

"Please," Hattie pleaded. "Please. I really need to know."

"I'm sorry."

For a minute, Hattie thought the woman was going to hang up on her. "Isn't there someone else I can talk to? Is the doctor in?"

"Just a moment, I'll see." The moment stretched to another five minutes. Hattie waited, almost ready to hang up each second.

Finally, the woman said, "I talked to the doctor who is on today. He has an office full of patients to see. He told me the same thing I told you. No exceptions. We can't give out information over the phone."

Hattie sighed heavily and said, "Okay."

Something in her voice must have softened the receptionist, "I'm sorry. I really am. We can't say anything over the phone. Surely you can understand that. But if you come in to the office and have some identification we can release the patient's information to the next of kin."

"But I'm in Pennsylvania."

"That's our policy. You'll need a death certificate and your own ID." The woman returned to her initial briskness. "Now I really have to attend to the other phones. Have a nice day." And she hung up.

All night Hattie thought the conversation over, and by morning it was clear to her: She would have to go to Hartford. She just had to find out what Ben had been keeping from her. If she waited she might lose the momentum of her decision. After three months in which brewing tea had been a major effort, she packed the car in less than an hour, infused by the strange rush of energy that comes with new purpose.

Just as Hattie was closing the trunk on two suitcases, which contained more clothes than she thought she'd need for the time she'd be away, Athena arrived in their beat-up old Buick. Tears welled in Hattie's eyes. Could she really leave? She knew she'd miss Fenston so much, and she'd miss everyone, especially Athena with her wild hair and blue jeans, her loud laugh and spicy talk. She'd miss Athena's determination—a strength of mind you could crack nuts on—and she'd miss her friend's built-in second sense for when something was going on that she should know about. From the expression on her friend's face, Hattie knew she'd have some explaining to do.

"Okay, what's this about?" Athena dove in before even saying hello.

"I'm going to Connecticut. I found a card, some cardiologist that Ben had an appointment with. I'm going there to see what it was about." The words came tumbling from Hattie.

"What?"

"I'm leaving for Connecticut. Today."

"You really amaze me. For years you won't go anywhere, no matter how you're begged. Now you take off by yourself, with not so much as a goodbye to anyone."

"That's not so. I was going to call you and let you know I was going."

With her usual intensity, Athena had been watching Hattie's expression change. She paused. "So, there is something else?'

Hattie hesitated.

"What?" Athena asked.

"I can't stop thinking about what Alice said. That Ben didn't stop living. Somehow I just keep thinking that I didn't know anything about him."

"What are you talking about—that you didn't know enough about him? You were married to him all these years. What more is there?"

"I want to see how he lived on the road. What his life was like away from us. I'll go to Hartford first. That's where he spent a lot of time. I'll stay in the Idyll Away, where Ben always stopped. See some of the things Ben was always talking about. Try to get a feel for what that part of his life was like."

Athena looked skeptically at her friend, "If this is about that appointment card, you could just call the doctor. Ask him some questions?"

"I did." Hattie quietly looked away. "They won't tell me anything over the phone."

"But what do you want to know? A cardiologist. Ben didn't die from a heart attack. You know what they said. An embolism. Something he never even knew was there."

"That's not the point. If he had something wrong and didn't tell me, it only shows how separate he was from me, from our life."

"I wish you'd just forget about this. Obsessing about Ben's health after he's dead. I just don't understand you sometimes, Hattie. It's just another face on the same thing Alice said, living in the past. I think you should just forget about it and get on with your life. I have an idea: Why don't you call Alice and talk to her about it? Her being a nurse and all, I bet she'll know what to do, how you can find out without going all the way to Connecticut."

"For the time being, I don't think Alice and I have very much to say to each other. She made it clear to me before she left that she blamed me for Ben's being away, for our not going with him. I didn't tell you this, but she's moving. She planned it all along, the past six months or so. Just didn't get around to telling us. Next week, she's off for California. Got a great job offer with the nursing shortage out there. Said she wants a new start and I don't think it includes thinking about me or visiting the homestead."

Athena put her hand on Hattie's. "Kids can be so cruel sometimes. But Alice will come around. She's grieving for Ben and doesn't know what to do with the emotion. I'm sure she didn't mean to hurt you."

"I know. I also can't stay angry at her long. But that's not the point. I want to be in charge of this. It's about my husband, things I should have known about."

"I'm against you doing this; that goes without saying. But since you're so determined, what can I do to help? And you must promise to call me and let me know what's going on. I want to hear from you as soon as you get there. How long do you figure it'll take you to drive to Connecticut?"

"Ben always said it was six hours. We'll see."

Walking through the silent rooms of her house for the last time before leaving, Hattie thought about the four generations of accumulated stuff—heirlooms and possessions and junk—that the house contained. Since her father died, she had been responsible, turning into the caretaker of it all, for that is how she thought of it. She had culled and selected, discarded, repaired and replaced until the old farmhouse had the composure of history and the elegance of money.

Hattie had loved the work of making her home beautiful. It had seemed her life's work and a valuable, interesting focus. She had meticulously researched various pieces of furniture, types of molding and even door handles and hinges, working toward a consistency and grace she had a clear picture of in her mind. As she looked around the living room and through the arch to the dining room, she took in the wide plank floors gleaming buttery and smooth in the morning sun, the beautiful old tables, the needlepoint and crewel pillows worked by her mother and grandmother, she felt curiously unmoved.

What had it all mattered in the end—all these things she had devoted her life to preserving? Those women had died anyway, and Ben had died and she would die. Even in between all that, there was no certainty. And what did any of her effort, her large beautiful house crammed with four generations of lovely and carefully executed things, have to offer as a solace for the pain she felt like a sharp stone next to her heart?

Chapter nineteen

Once she was behind the wheel, Hattie didn't want to stop, but as she passed Paul's gas station she realized she was running low on gas. She hit the brakes and backed up awkwardly nearly clipping one of the pumps.

Paul looked on with amusement. "What'll it be, lady? One pump or two?"

"Oh, Lord, Paul! I nearly put you out of business, didn't I? My mind's just not where it should be."

He leaned into the window as the tank filled and noticing the map on the seat, asked if she was going on a trip. Hattie was reluctant to tell him that she was heading for Connecticut and glad when he accepted her explanation that she was going to visit friends. "I just need a change of scene."

"Good for you. Best thing to get out and about in the world and involved in something else when grief comes our way. Nothing else we can do about it."

When she handed him her credit card for the gas, he held her hand just a second longer than was needed and Hattie felt the pleasure of knowing that she was important to him, that he had long admired her.

"Don't stay away too long, Hattie. We'd be lost without you around here," he said as he handed back her slip and card.

Hattie drove out of Fenston. Before she turned onto the Interstate she passed the gas station on the highway where Ben had stopped on his way home for the last time. This was the gas station with the telephone where he had placed his last call. Even though she didn't know what he had done, she began to retrace his steps to a place she'd never been before. Instead of feeling afraid or nervous or any of the emotions Hattie would have thought of for herself in this predicament, she felt eager. The air felt good and she switched on the radio to an unfamiliar station and heard John Cougar singing about some Jack and Diane.

As the car moved farther and farther from the center of her known universe, Hattie felt her mood change. She was filled with a light, expectant buoyancy that she imagined all explorers must experience. For a time she wasn't sad, and she ceased to think of herself as a woman whose husband had just died. Hattie felt her identity slip away from her like a silk scarf in the wind and she welcomed the cool, fresh air around her neck and cheeks. She felt herself expanding to meet it. For once, she thought, I'm really acting on something I want to do. I'll find out what was going on with Ben. Then I'll be peaceful. The phrase, *have to know, have to know, have to know*—which had formed the background of all her thoughts since Ben died and since she found the appointment card—had to be quieted.

Through the rear view mirror, Fenston got smaller and smaller until it disappeared. When she turned onto Interstate 84 and the long yellow, markered highway on her map, she didn't even notice it was gone.

Chapter twenty

"Can I help you?"

Florene, according to the name on the tag and the voice, which Hattie recalled from the brief phone conversation, looked up at Hattie with firm purpose through large, square glasses adorned with a gold rosebud in one corner. Her uniform and the large waiting room were very white.

"I'm Hattie Darling. I called you last week. My husband was a patient here. I wanted some information. About his condition."

Florene looked past Hattie into the waiting room. "Where is he?"

"I told you on the phone. He died. I just wanted to find out about his condition."

The woman frowned in sympathy. "I can't give out the

information. Maybe the doctor will talk to you. I'm sorry. You'll have to wait until he's finished with his appointments."

Two patients waited and were in turn called in by Florene. Hattie sat on a chrome and vinyl sofa and studied the decor. The waiting room was a veritable jungle. Plants hung from the ceiling and trailed from every surface. The only reading matter in evidence was a stack of old *Woman's Day* magazines and two pamphlet holders on the corner table. During the hour the receptionist kept her waiting, Hattie had read about diabetes, anemia and the perils of smoking. Finally, the room had emptied, and Florene went in the back office to confer with the doctor.

She emerged to tell Hattie that Ben was not and never had been a patient in that practice. Tears of frustration stung Hattie's eyes. "But you must be mistaken."

"I checked the files. No Ben Darling. And the doctor doesn't recall anyone by that name."

"Can I at least talk to the doctor?"

"He left for the day."

"How can that be? I've been sitting here all the time."

Florene was becoming frustrated with Hattie. "He left by his own entrance."

Hattie gripped the edge of the desk, "I'm sorry to be such a bother. But I have to know what was wrong with my husband. I know he was here. I have the card. I should have shown it to you before." Hattie rummaged in her purse and put the small slip on the woman's desk.

"And I'm his wife. Here's my identification. You told me to bring it. And his death certificate."

"I know I said that. I remember talking to you on the phone. But, well, that was when I thought he was our patient. It's hard for us to keep track of everyone. With such a big staff—three doctors, well you can imagine. The practice saw seven hundred patients last year."

"But what about the card," Hattie said insistently, looking at it again herself as if she might notice something more, some evidence that would force them to produce whatever they knew about Ben's condition.

Florene shifted back to her kind demeanor. "While I was in the back, I even called the billing company. If anyone would know for sure whether we had him as a patient, they would. But he's nowhere in our files."

Then Hattie did see something on the card that might help, the date. "May 15. Can you look up May 15? His last appointment was for that date. He died that night."

"Maybe," Florene said, more softly now. "Could be he made an appointment and didn't keep it. In that case, he wouldn't be in our files. If he wasn't actually a patient, that is." She rifled officiously through the pages of the appointment book with the air of someone who was good at solving problems, shuffling back through the months until she came to May. Hattie tried to look as well, reading the months and days upside down as best she could. In response, Florene moved her arm to shield the book from Hattie's view.

"All files are confidential, even appointments."

"I'm sorry," said Hattie, somewhat insincerely. "Well?" she asked, when Florene had stopped shuffling.

For a moment, Florene said nothing though she looked confused or surprised.

"Please. Oh, please," Hattie said. "You can't know how I feel. I didn't come here to make trouble for anyone. But I need to know what was happening to Ben." Emotion flooded her and spilled out into the room. Somehow the whole of Ben was represented in this information. Had his health been failing and he didn't want her to know? Didn't want her to worry? Had she come all this way to be denied?

Florene looked behind herself as if to make sure that she was not being overheard. She looked again at Hattie, concern evident in her warm eyes, "I'm not sure what I can tell you. There is no appointment in the name of Ben Darling on May 15th at 10 AM. Another person, a regular patient, had that time and kept the appointment."

"No appointment for Ben," Hattie repeated, her voice cracked as if trying to let the information sink in.

Florene very carefully opened the book wide, laid it on the counter, and turned it toward Hattie. "I think I have to check on something in the examining room. Sorry I couldn't be of more help," she said, glancing first at Hattie then down at the book in front of her.

Seeing the name, Darling, on the 3 PM slot on May 15, Hattie impulsively reached over and pulled the book toward her. Florene was heading slowly away from the desk, as if wanting to avoid seeing Hattie who had abandoned all subterfuge. Hattie peered at the waiting page. The 10 AM appointment slot was filled in with the name Darling, Anya.

Chapter twenty-one

Even after all of Ben's descriptions of tie-up's and bumper-to-bumper traffic, Hattie was not prepared for the difficulty of driving in the city. The good part was that it kept her mind occupied and away from the dangerous territory of her encounter with Florene. She just couldn't allow herself to think about it—whatever the confusion was regarding Ben's appointment. Hattie resolved to think that they had made a mistake and transposed names and now wouldn't own up to having been so careless with medical records.

The Idyll Away bleeped out *vacancy* as she rode by on the Interstate. Ben had always stayed at this motel when he was in Hartford. It was a good sign that she was on the right track in her search for Ben's time away from home. How lucky to have come upon it so easily. She'd stay there.

Getting to the Idyll Away was another matter. After three wrong roads, all of which were in plain sight of the hotel without giving access to it, Hattie concluded that her trip so far had been pitted with cross purposes. For a fleeting minute, she considered going home. Then the hotel sign came into view again, beckoning with second-hand familiarity. The right access road was at last in front of her, and she soon pulled into the lot. Relieved, she climbed from the car, her clothing sticking to her in the early summer heat.

It was just where she imagined Ben would stay. Not new and modern, but a solid kind of place with a facade straight out of the 1950s, a one-story red brick version of Ben's favorite songs. Well-tended shrubs hugged the small patio in front of each room. Comforted by the solidity of the place, she could just imagine Ben pulling in at the end of the day, carrying his sample case to the room and then emerging again in shirt-sleeves to walk across the parking lot to the small flower garden which she knew he'd enjoy. She recalled him talking about how often he looked forward to eating in the Meadow Room, how the chicken and biscuits were served with a tiny carafe of honey to drizzle over them. Hattie thought about food for the first time that day. Once she'd checked in and freshened up, she'd treat herself to a really nice lunch, probably the chicken.

As she handed her credit card to the young woman at the desk, she said, as if in answer to an unspoken question, "It's my first time here."

"We hope you enjoy your stay," the woman's voice

was robotic and somehow off, as if miscued, issuing a dismissive statement too soon in the transaction.

"My husband, though, he stayed here all the time."

"Unh-huh," the girl responded, shifting a book and handing it to Hattie to sign.

"Ben Darling. You probably know him. Do you?"

"Sorry."

"The last time he was here was May, early May," Hattie added, trying to prod some kind of a response.

"Wouldn't then. Know him, I mean. I'm only here for the summer."

"Oh," said Hattie. "He died. My husband. He died. I thought maybe you knew him."

The young woman looked up briefly at Hattie. "Gee, I'm sorry. Maybe Hal, he's the boss, part owner. He's been here for years and years. He probably knew your husband. Prides himself on remembering everyone who stays here more than once. How long did you say you'd be staying?"

"I didn't say. Probably a day or two. When will Hal be around?"

"He's gone into town right now. Should be back at lunchtime. He's usually in the dining room through lunch and then at the desk for the afternoons when we have most of our check-ins. You can't miss him. He'll be the tall guy with the string tie."

The girl giggled at some private joke about Hal and handed Hattie the key to her room. "We hope you enjoy your stay," she said, finally getting to use her canned phrase at the right time.

As Hattie opened the heavy drapes in Room 44, dust motes swirled in the stream of sunlight. Otherwise, the unit was spotlessly furnished with the traveler's comfort in mind: a large easy chair, a neat pinewood table and chairs and good lighting. Yes, it was obvious why Ben had liked the place so much.

Suddenly exhausted, she drew the drapes, adjusted the air-conditioning, took off her shoes and fully-clothed climbed into the bed and fell asleep. She awoke ravenous and hoped they were still serving lunch.

The chicken and biscuits were excellent. Hattie, who had never eaten in a restaurant alone before, fought off her self-consciousness long enough to be able to enjoy her meal. Although attached to the motel, the restaurant appeared to be a local spot, as the few late lunch or early dinner patrons greeted each other. Just like home, Hattie thought, as the Red Bird Diner on Route 7 came into her mind. She pictured the booths against the window, the countless days she and Athena and Eleanor had gone for breakfast or lunch on their way to go shopping. It was her first thought of Fenston all day. Suddenly, she missed her life. She recalled her promise and decided she'd call Athena right away.

Absently, she registered Hal's presence in the room as he moved from table to table greeting people. There was the string tie, the kind worn by cowboys and certain other types who affected a good old-boy swagger and colloquial style. A gregarious sort of guy, just the type to have a place like this, she thought, munching her way through the second piece of chicken. Dipping a biscuit in the small honey pot, Hattie realized that she was no longer in pain.

Despite that morning's setback at the doctor's office and the mystery of why Ben had had some other person's appointment card in his pocket the day he died, she felt good about her trip so far. She felt Ben close by. Yes, this was what she had come for. Hattie was very proud of herself—the way she had driven so far from home alone, the way she had handled things as she checked in. All the years in Fenston she would never have thought herself capable of just making up her mind and driving away alone. Over the years, it had occurred to her a few times to just get in the car and drive up to Hartford and surprise Ben, but she had never been able to summon the courage to do it. Now here she was. And there was nothing to it. How she wished she had known how easy it was. Ben would have been so surprised to see her.

As Hal passed her table, Hattie flagged him down with a small wave. "The young woman at the desk said you might be able to help me."

He nodded to the chair and then sat across from Hattie. "Hal Duggan. Anything wrong?" He put out his hand and Hattie took it.

"Hattie Darling," she responded, expecting some kind of a reaction as she stressed the last name.

"What can we do for you? Except feed you the best lunch in town." His jovial manner set Hattie on edge. She had no time for corny flirtation.

"Information, I guess," she said. "My husband used to stay here all the time. He's the one who told me about the Idyll Away. And the chicken dinner. I'm just traveling around to places where he used to work. He died." Hattie surprised herself with the catch in her voice. "In May."

"I'm sorry to hear that. What did you say his name was?"

"Ben. Benjamin. Ben Darling."

"Yes. I do recall him now. Trim. Young-looking guy. He died?"

Not trusting her voice, Hattie nodded.

"Long time ago he used to stay here pretty regular. Traveled for some tool company or something."

"Harden Tool. But it wasn't a long time ago. At least not that long. He was here in May. Came home May 15."

"I don't recall him being here that recent." The man had begun to infuriate Hattie. "No, I'm sure of it. I pride myself on knowing who the regulars are. Seems to me he was here ten or more years ago. Maybe came in for dinner once in a while after that, but didn't stay here."

"That can't be," Hattie interrupted. "He was here in May. Talked about it the night he died."

"I wouldn't want to argue. But . . ."

"Can't you check your books or something? This is important."

Hal looked at her for a long moment, his eyes squinting with concern.

"Sure I can do that. But why don't you relax for a few moments. You've got yourself all worked up. Here," he handed her a napkin. When Hattie reached out her hand to take it she realized her eyes were filled with tears.

"Oh," said Hattie. "It's been a frustrating morning. I'm fine. Really, I am. But I'd appreciate it if you'd check for me."

"Sure," Hal said firmly.

The chicken, which had moments before been succulent and flavorful, seemed to turn to sawdust as Hattie attempted to finish her lunch while Hal checked.

Hattie knew that he was going to affirm that Ben had not stayed at the Idyll Away in May. Her heart had begun to pound in her ears. What was going on? First the doctor's office putting her off, trying to mislead her. Now this. It was obvious that some ridiculous twist of fate was at work, trying to prevent her from claiming Ben's life.

Later as Hattie sat on the edge of the bed trying to sort out what had happened, she remembered the call she had promised to make to Athena. The motel phone system had a complicated dialing procedure for long distance, and she had to refer to the sheet on the front of the phone book to figure out how to place her call. The Hartford directory was ten times the size of the Susquenock County phone book, which contained not only Fenston, Winston and Crystalle, but also six or seven other small towns in the outlying areas of rural Pennsylvania. She hefted it onto her lap and absent-mindedly thumbed back and forth through the dense block of pages, thinking of how she was going to explain to Athena about Florene and Hal and her dead ends for the day.

Her fingers, knowing on their own what they were looking for, stopped at the D's and idly leafed page by page until they reached what she must have been looking for all along: Anya Darling, 751–2820. She lived at 321 Gordon Street, Hartford.

Suddenly Hattie saw herself back in the barn at home in Fenston carrying an old chair to the driveway for the dump when something totally unexpected, something she had never felt before, a whispering pressure atop her right foot and across the sandal she was wearing, made her put aside the chair. A large copperhead, whose nap she must have disturbed, slipped between the rock foundation of the barn and scurried out of sight. And now, as Hattie focused on the name before her, she felt threading pinpricks at the back of her head and along the calves of her legs, pinpricks of terror racing toward her heart, the way the venom would have if the copperhead had chosen to bite.

For the very first time since Ben packed the car and headed out on the road all those years ago, Hattie let herself have the worst thought she could imagine, the one thought she had refused every day he was gone, the one thought she connected vaguely with her inability to leave the house for days on end, to drive the car alone, to shop in the new big mall in Binghamton, to set out herself to surprise her husband. What if Ben had been unfaithful?

Chapter twenty-two

Perched on the edge of a steep hill, the string of row houses from a distance had the uniform look of shabby poverty. As Hattie drew closer, she saw that each house on Gordon Street, each window, each front door, was poor in its own way. The first porch she passed, shaded by many awnings, overflowed with scabby, old-fashioned metal furniture. On the next, a faded, overstuffed sofa squatted near to a bicycle. Farther down the block, there was the gentility of wicker and chintz next door to a jungle of houseplants with scarcely room for the single web chair. And next to that, the small space contained a play pen, a baby swing, and a pram, presided over by a fat, bald, happy boy of about a year, who stared back at Hattie as she pulled the car up to the curb and with much difficulty parked in the lone free spot on the street.

Two things struck her as she walked up Gordon Street. First, that the front porches were like tiny, condensed farms, lives turned inside out, with so much of the necessary machinery left visible. She thought about the naked, public way city people live. She also thought that considering it was a sweltering summer afternoon, there were very few people out on their porches. Just as well, she concluded, as she neared the address. She had no idea what she intended to do next and hoped she'd have a few minutes to look around and decide after she found the house. She hoped that this was a wild goose chase, a huge mistake; best of all, it might turn out to be something she could laugh about when she called Athena to recount tracking down some unknown person who just happened to have the same surname.

The unsettling idea that Ben was somehow connected to this address, this name, nudged into her consciousness and quickly retreated.

What she had first sighted on Gordon Street encouraged her. In her wildest imagination, she wouldn't have connected Ben with these surroundings—Ben who liked space and luxury. Everything about this place seemed wrong in connection with him. And the more incongruous it seemed, the more Hattie felt reassured that there was no possible connection between Ben and this person, this Anya Darling. Somehow, she would solve the mystery of the appointment card and go back to Fenston and her life, to mourn Ben as she should.

She located 321 and walked up and down the opposite

side of the street a few times trying to figure out what to do next. She didn't want to call attention to herself by continuing to walk back and forth, but she wasn't sure how to proceed.

The front door of 321 opened and a little, blond girl who must have been seven or eight years old, came out to the porch devouring a cherry Popsicle. She was dressed in shorts and a jersey. Giving herself a little extra time, Hattie walked up to the corner and slowly crossed the quiet street. Noticing the heavy traffic on the perpendicular avenue, she walked back down and stood in front of the porch and asked, "Is this 321 Gordon?" Though the number over the door was clearly visible.

"Uh huh," the girl replied, distractedly trying to catch the last sweet drop of her treat on her tongue.

"That Pop looks good. Just the thing for a hot day. I'll have to get myself one."

"Stop & Shop," said the child. The inside of her mouth all red from the frozen colored water. Something about her, the way she talked and held her head touched Hattie. And she recalled summers of those red and green and orange mouths from so many Popsicles. Alice's face had been stained with them for weeks at a time. The child's voice was sweet and musical with a hint of something familiar.

"What?" Hattie asked, wanting the child to speak again. The porch was a tidy oasis with a green metal glider and armchair, covered in a faded green and white old-fashioned leaf print. In the corner sat a table with a few small but thriving plants.

"Stop & Shop. Over on Sisson Ave . . . But I think you have to buy the whole box."

Hattie was still enjoying the voice, an echo of something forgotten, when the door opened and a small, tidy woman with strawberry blond hair and bright blue eyes came out onto the porch and looked at Hattie.

"I thought I heard someone talking." Her speech was clipped with a strong European accent, and she had a breathy, strained voice, which was not without music. German, Polish, Austrian? Hattie thought. The woman stared at Hattie as if asking for an explanation. Of course, Hattie thought, this is the city; people are suspicious if you speak to their children.

"I was looking for 321 Gordon Street."

"This is 321," the woman said, pronouncing it scree two one.

"Oh," said Hattie. Her mind raced to its far corners trying to think of what to say next. She stared at the woman wondering how and if she was connected to Ben.

"Are you selling something?" the woman asked; her gaze, an odd mixture of hopefulness and suspicion, moved to Hattie's large handbag. The woman seemed breathless and moved slightly as if to rest herself against the back of the door.

"No," Hattie answered. Then thinking quickly she recalled a sign she saw in the window of a house she had passed on her way to Gordon Street, she added, "I've come to see about the room for rent."

"Room for rent?" the woman seemed startled, "No, not here."

"Oh, don't tell me. I can't believe that I . . . I might have gotten the numbers jumbled when I took them down. I do that sometimes when I'm in a hurry, mess up the order of numbers."

Hattie felt herself flush as she hurtled headlong into this makeshift explanation. Her slacks and blouse clung to her in the heat and her large pocketbook that had been light and unobtrusive as she walked up and down the street now swung, a dull heavy weight against her legs.

Standing in the bright sun looking into the shade of the porch, Hattie could hardly make out the woman's features, but she read her tone and expression as kind and quietly waiting for Hattie to explain herself.

"I'm new in town," Hattie said.

The woman continued to smile politely. She drew in a long breath, and then paused as if to breathe again, "And someone told you there was here a room to rent?"

"Yes."

"How strange. I can't imagine . . ." the woman continued.

"I'm in Hartford to do research for my company, and I'll have to consult the county archives, look up some properties and deeds and other documents. For the company business. Looking into population, things like that." Hattie scarcely knew what was going to pop out of her own mouth next. Even with her, minimal knowledge of the business world, she felt that the implausibility of what she was saying must be painfully obvious. She could only hope that she could get herself out of there fast enough that she wouldn't make a complete fool of herself. Maybe this woman knew as little as she did. She certainly didn't seem to act as if she doubted Hattie. But where did the story come from? Documentation was not a word she could ever recall using before. The tiny woman gazed at Hattie.

"When I travel I don't like to stay in hotels, too impersonal. If I'm going to be anywhere for any length of time, I prefer to rent a room in a private home. I'd been told that at 321 Gordon Street, a quiet single businesswoman could rent a room by the week." Hattie stood, the afternoon sun slanting down, her clothes sticking to her skin, her hair a sweaty swirl of auburn ringlets matted to her face. As she talked, Hattie took a tissue from her pocketbook and wiped her brow, then backed closer to the edge of the sidewalk. Neither the woman nor the girl said anything, but both looked at her closely. "Oh, well. Maybe I can find the place . . ."

"Your face is very red. You look exhausted. The sun is really very strong." Again, the strong, charming accent.

Yes, Polish, Hattie thought, as she said, "Just can't believe I wasn't more careful writing down the numbers," looking again at the slip of paper she'd also taken from her pocketbook. She felt tears welling up behind her eyes, the result of recognizing the impossibility of the task she'd set herself.

"Things like that happen." The woman seemed to interpret Hattie's agitation as a sign of frustration at being so careless.

"Why don't you come up on the porch for a minute,

rest a bit? I'll get you a glass of water," the woman's voice had genuine concern in it.

"I'll do it, Mama, let me do it," said the child, who had been silently watching, and vanished inside the house. Hattie climbed the three steps to the welcome coolness of the shady little porch.

"I'm Anya Darling," the woman said. "And that's my daughter Kasia. Hattie drew in her breath sharply. Oh, God, Anya Darling, her mind shrieked. But she heard herself say in a calm tone. "Nice to meet you." The woman appeared to be in her late thirties. Her face was drawn but very pretty, dominated by lively blue eyes. There was a sense of composure about her, but also a feeling of vulnerability, perhaps due to her size, which Hattie judged to be little more than five feet. The woman wore a pair of yellow shorts and a green striped shirt with the tails hanging out, all neatly pressed; on her feet were a pair of black rubber thongs. Hattie was aware of her own clothing, almost all of it ordered through expensive mail-order catalogs.

"Where did you say you were from?" The lovely accent again gave Anya's words a particular weight.

"Pennsylvania," Hattie answered, watching for a reaction and finding none. My name is Hattie Beste, and I'm from Pennsylvania. The northeast, almost up by the New York border. Much cooler there, I'll tell you that."

Later, Hattie would go over the conversation in her mind. Anya simply didn't look anything like the kind of person who might be the other woman. That woman Hattie could easily picture, a strumpet with coffee dribbles down the front of her frowzy robe, eyes racooned with leftover makeup and a cigarette in hand. This woman was so kind, so concerned about the well-being of a total stranger. Surely there was some explanation beyond the frighteningly obvious. And how could she have jumped to such conclusions about Ben? Didn't he deserve better than that?

Chapter twenty-three

Too fast. That's the only thing Hattie could think about what had happened. Just moments before she had been getting out of the car, looking up the street with a keen curiosity and a feeling that maybe somehow she'd come across a clue about Ben. In her imagination, she was always talking with Ben. How could he have done this to her—how could he have put her in such a position?

Hattie hadn't known what she'd do when she arrived at 321 Gordon Street, or really what she'd been looking for, except that she was prepared to follow even the faintest thread of Ben's story. Now that she was standing there, she lost her nerve. Could what had seemed so straightforward just a few hours ago, now be the cause of such terror?

It was like her first glimpse of this street from a

distance—when all she had seen were poor people. Poor people, that's what she had thought at first; poor people eking out a living; trying to keep themselves alive with variations on the same tedious story. But up close, it was anything but uniform. Every life had a remarkable individuality. The old woman on the next porch who had just emerged from her cool dark house without looking over busied herself hanging a birdcage at the edge of the porch amid pots of asparagus and Boston fern. One only had to slow down and really look to see the particularity of a life expressed in the flutter of hands, a life expressed in choices, in the selection of color, the decision as to quantity; a life expressed in the order of priorities.

The child returned with a large, sweaty glass of cold water and handed it to Hattie, then went over to the table and began working on a connect-the-numbers book. Hattie drank greedily—almost half the glass—before she put it down on the table in front of her. Anya sat watching, looking friendly but a little preoccupied, as if trying to figure something out.

"It's cool here. Relax. You look so red, as if you're going to get heatstroke. Just sit and rest."

Surprisingly, Hattie did. Although her thoughts were racing, she felt comfortable sitting there in the shade. She picked up the glass and drank the rest of the water, relishing its coolness. She felt almost drowsy. Drowsy and surreal. Kasia's pencil squeaked across the alchemy of numbers, as she worked to reveal a picture of some ordinary object in the lines she connected. Hattie began to feel more connected, shaking herself out of whatever daydream had compelled her to find Gordon Street. Ben could not possibly have had any part in all of this. Hattie felt sure of it, whatever the confusion about the appointment card.

"Mama, look," the child said, holding up her work. "It turned out to be a butterfly."

"Very nice," the mother replied absently.

Hattie realized then that it was time to go, that Anya had been kind and there was nothing else she could gain by staying any longer. The puzzle of her elusive grief and Ben's life would take her away from this place. *Except.* "You've been so kind. I really hate to trouble you any more. But I think I have to use the bathroom . . ."

"Oh, of course. By all means. Up at the top of the stairs. There is a guest towel on the shelf." Anya responded warmly. Suddenly, a worry shot through Hattie. Does the woman always invite strangers to roam around her house? What could she be thinking?

Chapter twenty-four

Inside the house, Hattie looked around at the dark woodwork and heavy furniture covered in maroon and deep green. The house had the shuttered feeling of nineteenth-century parlors. The furniture looked at least that old. The walls of the tiny vestibule, the living room and the dining room beyond were all covered with gold brown, swirled paper. The floors were plain wood, clean and polished to gleaming. The house was poor and shabby. Hattie felt sorry for anyone who had to live in such a place. Her mind drifted back to her own large, lovely house, the deep porch and the windows giving onto the meadow and her feeders. She imagined Ben walking through the rooms satisfied with their light and beauty. She almost laughed to think that she had imagined she'd find something of him here.

As she walked toward the stairway, Hattie noticed a framed photo on a table and felt herself drawn to it. Involuntarily, she moved toward it, across the wooden floors, past the worn couch and the odd lamp with the faded fringe, past a window with lace curtains, past the smell of something sweet from the kitchen door. Almost as a whooshing of sound in her ears, she felt something coming toward her that she could not or would not have imagined. Both knowing and not-knowing that it would shift her world, she walked slowly toward it.

The wooden frame of the picture was carved and warm in her hands. She lifted it. At first, her mind refused to register what she was seeing. Smiling up at her were Anya and Kasia. And Ben. A recent photograph judging by Kasia's size. Ben's smile was that carefree, loving smile she had always believed was solely for her. Her body shook with the effort of directing her hands to replace the picture in the center of the dresser. Her hands leapt away from it as if they had been singed, and she felt her stomach lurch.

Flying up the stairs, Hattie held her hand over her mouth as she gagged. Once the door was closed behind her, she leaned on the sink and felt her stomach churning. Trying to avoid vomiting, she closed her eyes, but the picture of Ben with the other woman and the child was with her. After a moment, she opened her eyes and slumped down weakly onto the toilet, disoriented and horrified by what she had seen. Had she really seen it? She wondered if her eyes could have played a trick on her. Could that be it? Her Ben had been keeping another woman and her child.

But could she have been projecting Ben's face onto someone else? After all, her eyes were unaccustomed to such a rapid shift in light, coming in as she had from the shady porch to the dark room.

But that was all sophistry: She just knew it was Ben. Maybe she had always known. She wondered how long it had been going on. Not very, she thought. Maybe the deceit of it was what brought on Ben's embolism. Oh, God, Ben, why did you do this? How could you let this woman use your name? Wasn't there enough in our life together to hold you?

Deliberately she pushed these thoughts away by trying to concentrate on the room, which, in contrast to the downstairs part of the house, was light and lovely. Someone had evidently painted over the old wallpaper. The walls were creamy white, immaculately clean; stenciled around the room were pale pink flowers connected by green vines. A small pot of geraniums sat on the windowsill and fresh pink hand towels echoed their color. Involuntarily, she picked up the flowerpot and stood poised to drop and smash it. Then she put it carefully back onto the sill. Sobs wracked her body.

Fearing that she had been in the house too long, she washed her face and hands and went back downstairs. Passing the photo, she examined it once again; her eyes welled up as she noticed the lucky tie Ben wore, the one he had been buried in.

"Find everything you needed?" Anya asked, when Hattie returned to the porch. She almost recoiled at the question's awful resonance.

Feeling tormented by what she had discovered, Hattie could not imagine where her surface composure or her words were coming from, but she heard herself answer: "Yes, and thank you so much. You've been more than kind. As I said, I must have just transposed the numbers. I'm like that sometimes, especially when I'm in a hurry."

A huge sob escaped her, and she mumbled, "Well, goodbye."

"Good luck finding the right place," Anya said, obviously mistaking Hattie's state for concern over finding a place to stay.

Kasia looked up quickly from her coloring, her blue eyes quietly questioning. "Goodbye," she echoed after Hattie and Anya.

Hattie's face stung as she walked away from 321 Gordon Street. "Well, there it is," she said to herself. "I just had to find out. Couldn't leave it alone. And instead of feeling better, I feel even worse than before. I guess Athena was right—nothing to be gained by knowing what we can't change."

How she wished she could have remained so philosophical, but she knew this revelation would torment her for a long time. Now that she knew there had been another woman, did she feel what she thought she would? Now that she knew that there was an Anya and even where she was living—well, would that help her deal with Ben's death? Hattie was waiting at the corner to cross to her car when she realized her hands were empty and that she had left her purse behind. Turning, she saw Anya running down the street behind her, with Hattie's large satchel pocketbook bobbing awkwardly against the small woman's legs. She had not heard her name called again and again as Anya tried to catch up with her.

Red in the face and out of breath, Anya paused and coughed vigorously and seemed to shiver all over for a minute, waving her hand up and down in dismissal of Hattie's thanks. Anya put her hand up to her chest and signaled for Hattie to wait until she caught her breath. It occurred to Hattie that if Anya had only looked inside the purse and found her wallet, she would have known who Hattie was. Maybe that would be best—to get it all out. In that very moment Hattie knew how it would all have to happen; she wouldn't be able to make herself say the words.

Trucks rumbled by on the avenue and Hattie noticed a small grocery store on the corner where a cluster of teenagers congregated. She was suddenly weary and missed Athena very much and wanted to be home, far away from the noise and confusion of this unfamiliar city. If she could go back just one day, she'd never leave Fenston again. She wanted to be home, living the life of a widow and not here trying to make sense of someone else's life.

But when Anya caught her breath and said, "We do have an extra room. It's not much. But it's clean. Do you want to take a look at it?" Hattie found herself nodding her assent.

Chapter twenty-five

The plate of soup in front of her cooled to room temperature slowly in the hot kitchen. Anya bustled at the stove. As soon as she sat down at the table, Anya and Kasia bowed their heads and together said a short prayer in Polish, a grace before meals. Hattie sat staring wordlessly into the fresh, straight part of the child's blond hair, knowing that she should be feeling something.

Hattie found that part of her mind was shrieking in anguish at Anya about Ben's infidelity and what harm it had caused. The muscles in her arms were as tense as if she were engaged in a physical struggle to prevent herself from reaching across the table and grabbing the woman's neck in her hands and pressing down as hard as she could to choke her.

The other half of Hattie Darling's mind was carrying

on as if the pretense she had come up with to gain entry to this house were the actual truth. She was the nice lady who simply wanted to rent a room. With this split-off part of her, she was able to notice and record what was going on, then react and answer and smile and respond.

Anya's accent seemed to be in everything, from the prayer to the child's hairdo, to the savory steam from the vegetable soup. Anya had ladled soup into each bowl directly from the stove; then she placed a basket of bread and some butter on the table. Hattie didn't realize she had eaten, but when she looked at her bowl, it was nearly empty. She examined the tidy kitchen. A small gas stove and an ancient refrigerator were its lone appliances. But on the shelves over the sink sat an array of interesting pieces of crockery, no two matching, but the whole arranged in a tasteful, thoughtful way. Hattie placed the table as a 50s set. Chrome legs and padded chairs in red vinyl, ornately and conspicuously studded. The dishes were chipped and mismatched, but somehow there was harmony in their combination on the table. There was something about the way things were put together, deliberateness, a kind of charm.

Again with the practical second half of her mind, she attended to the odd details that are never filled in when she read about such goings-on in books. She wondered how much money Ben had given the woman for his visits? And the vexing problem of Anya using his name surfaced in her mind again. But how could she find out the things she wanted to know? Perplexing, too, was her almost insatiable curiosity about Anya and Ben. Questions increasingly complex and relentless popped into her mind until she thought she'd go mad. At one point, she had tuned out the conversation between Anya and Kasia and looked up to see Anya's frowning expression as they waited for a response to whether she wanted more soup. But mostly she found herself astonished at her own ability to go in and out of this shifting reality.

Neither mother nor daughter spoke during the meal. It was not an uncomfortable silence but one that acknowledged the importance of the meal. Hattie watched Kasia eat, and thought that the simple meal was not nourishing enough for a growing child. Both Kasia and Anya were thin. The girl ate intently, spreading butter carefully onto several slices of bread. Kasia had finished long before Anya and Hattie and waited politely. Hattie was glad she had declined a second helping when she saw Kasia eagerly eat the remaining serving. Remembering Alice's voracious appetite when she was small—often she had eaten as much as Ben himself—Hattie thought a plate of soup and some bread wouldn't have satisfied her. Anya's daughter was tall, like Alice had been, but smaller boned and thinner; her shoulder blades moved loosely and the square plates of her knees showed beneath her skin.

The small wooden door of a cuckoo clock over the sink swung open and a bird peeked out to celebrate the magic spell of six p.m. "Time to wash up, Kasia." And the little girl got up and collected the plates. Anya poured two cups of coffee and placed one in front of Hattie, as if she had been doing it every day for years.

Disoriented again, Hattie had to force her thoughts back to where she was. She thought there was something oddly comforting about the place, a sense she could not explain, the way it sometimes feels when dreaming, as if you know that all that's happening defies credulity, even while you're inside the dream, but it still feels perfectly logical at the same time.

Perverse as it seemed, now that she had found Anya, Hattie realized she was in no hurry to tell her about Ben. Hattie's marriage to Ben, his sudden death, his life with her in Fenston, all of it, everything that she eventually would confront Anya with—could wait. For she knew that as soon as she told her side of the story, the odd chemistry of having this secret would dissipate. A kind of voyeurism had surfaced; she would force herself to maintain the pretense she had set out, however painful, in order to solve the puzzle of Ben's other life. It was her secret mission to find out who her husband had been when he was away from her. A mission. She said the word over and over in her mind to prevent herself from screaming in rage and anger. She told herself she was on a mission that made her being there somehow special.

Eventually, of course, she would tell. For that would truly destroy the woman. Not only had the wife been in her house, but she had known all along that her lover had died. Hattie could wait for just the right moment when what she knew would hurt Anya most.

The small room was hot from the cooking and the bodies of its three inhabitants. Kasia pirouetted around the table, moving back and forth from the sink. She started to hum, and a look of great sadness passed over Anya's face. Suddenly a terrible awareness overtook Hattie. She looked around the room and realized she had been sitting in the last remaining chair, the chair Ben sat in when he was there with them. It had been his place at the table. Anya hummed notes so familiar to Hattie that she herself sat smiling and waiting. The room drew even closer about her. She smiled hard into the faces of the two other people in the room. The first words were so familiar they might have been bubbling from her own throat. Sweet voices, soft female voices without Ben's powerful baritonc to balance them. A song familiar to Hattie. The song Ben always sang when he helped her with the dishes, "Edelweiss" was piercingly beautiful.

The blond child and the woman who sat opposite at the table with her eyes closed—who were they again? Hattie thought she heard herself groan "Oh, God." The kitchen grew dark at the edges and the voices, though still powerfully sweet, came to her from afar. It was all so lovely but dark somehow. And darkness continued to seep inward toward the center of the room, toward Hattie. Anya still wore sadness in her face and voice like an animal born to the yoke. Somewhere there was the sound of glass breaking, and Hattie slipped from Ben's chair, dropping the cup of hot coffee into her lap and hitting her head on the table.

Chapter twenty-six

Hattie and Anya were sitting on the front porch again. After Hattie's fainting spell, Anya had sent Kasia out to play. Then she retrieved a first-aid kit from under the kitchen sink and gently and carefully washed and dressed the gash on Hattie's head where she had struck the chair in her fall. The yards of all the row houses terraced onto an alley, a favorite haunt of the neighborhood children. The house was dark and quiet though the children's voices could be heard in the distance. Hattie was feeling much better.

"Have you fainted like that before?" Anya asked, concern evident in her voice.

"I don't think I actually fainted. I just got very woozy and lightheaded. I've had a long day. The drive, the heat, and then the mix-up about the room. Maybe I was hungry, too. When I finally sat down . . . I guess it caught up with me."

"I'd be glad to call a cab. Take you to the hospital. You've got a good cut there. Maybe you need stitches."

"No. You know how head wounds bleed. I'm sure it's nothing."

"If you're sure. I'd take you . . ."

"No, really. I'm okay. I think I'll be fine. Just needed some air."

"Let's see if you're feeling better tomorrow."

The warmth and concern in Anya's voice pricked Hattie's conscience. Odd that just hours ago she had been thinking about guilt, not hers, of course. Now she herself was feeling guilty for her deceit.

"Do you know how much you'll charge for the room?" Hattie asked, shifting the conversation away from herself.

"I have no idea. What do you usually pay?"

"Depends," Hattie answered. "On the location mostly. Maybe we can . . ." and she indicated *The Hartford Courant* on the porch table. "Let's see what the going rate is."

Sitting on the darkened porch, Hattie felt herself on the brink of something. She knew that at any moment she might open her mouth to tell Anya who she was and to demand to know what the woman's connection was to her dead husband. No words came. Instead, her mind traveled back to a bad time, before Ben traveled, before the Harden Tool Company came into their life.

*

There was the hot evening that Ben had been sitting out on the back stoop of the house in Fenston, years before they had added the Florida room and patio. Alice was asleep and Hattie thought it would be a good time to talk. She slipped out behind him and watched her standing shadow looming large over him. Ben must have seen it too but said nothing. She sat next to him and he didn't move or speak; yet she knew he was aware of her there beside him. She put her hand on his shoulder, felt the warm muscles under his blue shirt. He didn't shrug her hand away, didn't do anything, didn't, in fact, seem to notice.

Hattie remembered exactly what she had wanted to talk about. For a long time, she had wanted another child. Every time she brought it up, Ben said not now. She had confided in Athena and Eleanor about wanting another baby. Athena said she should get Ben in a good mood and seduce him. Eleanor advised her to accidentally on purpose misuse her diaphragm. Each month as she put off the decision, Hattie felt more and more fiercely the desire to give Alice a childhood with siblings. The kind of childhood she herself had not had. But Ben had seemed miles away from her. Obviously that was not the time to try to talk him into anything.

After what seemed like several minutes, Hattie began to feel foolish sitting there, focusing on her husband when he so clearly was far away from her. She withdrew her hand, got up and went back inside the house, leaving Ben to his own thoughts on the porch.

It was odd how memories came unbidden, secret

emissaries from the inaccessible regions of the mind, reminding one of things submerged, prompting memories of distant times . . .

Had her life with Ben always been good? Where was he that night when she tried to enter his thoughts? What had sent him so frequently into the yard or the basement those years he was always at home? So many nights he'd stay in his shop, she'd hear the power tools whirring away for a time and then there would be a long silence. To remember only the happy times was the widow's way; memory's trick of light. It couldn't be trusted.

Chapter twenty-seven

The next morning, Hattie left the house, ostensibly headed for "the courthouse and the necessary research." She walked to the car, got in and started the motor, not at all sure where she'd go. For an hour, she just drove around looking at the city, an activity exciting and unfamiliar in itself. So many people crammed together in a small space. She couldn't recall the last time she had been anywhere outside of rural Pennsylvania except for a short trip to Philadelphia for Alice's graduation from college.

The pretext of a job would require some effort. During the hours when she should be at work, she'd just have to figure out a way to pass the time. She had no idea how to be a tourist. Because Ben traveled for his work, he always wanted to spend his vacations at home. Hattie had no desire to travel alone and no real wish to go anywhere. Sometimes, especially after Alice went away to school, she'd thought about visiting an exotic place. She had always wanted to see California or Paris. But the prospect of making the arrangements, packing her bags and leaving, made her realize travel would be just too much trouble. So many years she had watched Ben lift his suitcases up the last step on the front porch and sit heavily in a kitchen chair and sigh. Travel seemed eternal weariness.

Everything she knew about cities, about the differences of city life from the slow-moving rural pace she'd known at Fenston, she knew from flat, inanimate things—movies she'd seen or novels she'd read. Long before she'd read *The Catcher in the Rye*, but she still vividly recalled the descriptions of the train station, the sluice of people moving around one person. Loneliness so discrete and incommunicable that a young girl would be driven to muteness. Cities full of flash and danger, brimming with sound and swirls of light. All her imaginings had stopped there; now was her chance to find out what city life was really like.

She drove around for another hour, trying to get the feel of the place, trying to figure out how people lived their lives. She spotted a telephone and circled the block three times before she got a parking space she could navigate her way into. Then she called Athena. The phone rang three times before she heard her friend's voice, "Wescott's."

Chapter twenty-eight

"It's me," she interrupted before Athena could finish.

"Oh. Am I ever glad to hear your voice: I've been sick with worry since you left, imagining all kinds of things—that you'd got in an accident or got lost and ended up in Miami. Where are you?"

"Believe it or not, I'm where I set out to be. Hartford. And I drove right here with no problem."

"I didn't mean anything by that. I just meant. Well, you know. You haven't exactly been a world traveler. Most times you'd as soon stay home even from a trip to Binghamton."

"Could be I've changed. Anyway, I haven't forgotten how to drive a car and read a map."

"Obviously you haven't," Athena responded in her

own calming fashion, realizing that she was close to hurting Hattie's feelings.

"So?" The rest of the unstated question was clear to both of them.

"So. It's hard to explain."

"Did you find what you were looking for? Did the doctor tell you what was wrong with Ben?"

Hattie sighed with the weight of all that had happened since she left Fenston. Then as coherently and briefly as possible, keeping the emotion out of her voice as best she could, she gave Athena a full account. When she got to the phone book in the Idyll Away motel, Athena broke in, "So you went there?"

"How did you know?"

"I've watched you since the beginning of this thing. Once you went that far, I assume you'd have to see it through."

"Yes. And yes, I found it right away. Or rather I found Anya. Right there, right where the phone book told me she'd be—321 Gordon Street."

"And?" Athena's voice was calm and noncommittal, but Hattie knew she was disguising her feelings.

"And what? There is a woman named Anya Darling. I met her. Evidently she and Ben had been seeing each other. She's poor, an immigrant. She has a child."

"But the name. How is it she was using his name?"

"I don't know. Maybe because she's an immigrant. Maybe she's not legal or something."

"What did she say when you told her?"

"So far, I haven't told her anything."

"What do you mean, so far. You went there to confront her. And now you're telling me you didn't."

"I know this is going to sound a little crazy. But I realized that just knowing she existed and where she was, was far worse than knowing nothing at all. All at once, I knew I'd have to find out other things, like what she was like, why she got involved with a married man in the first place, where she thinks he is now, what she knows about me."

"That's all very well and good, Hattie. But it's a tall order. Of course, you'd like to have those answers. I mean, how do you expect to get all that information? She's certainly not going to come looking for you to tell you the story of her life, is she?"

"I thought if I could just spend some time with her, I'd be able to understand better."

"Maybe, but how do you propose to do that?"

Hattie spoke quietly, as if she did but didn't want Athena to hear, "I've rented a room in her house."

On the other end of the line, Athena sucked in a deep breath. "Now, I think you've gone completely crazy. You're going to be living in the house of your dead husband's mistress hoping that you will become her confidant. Hattie, have you lost your mind? How much heartache do you want out of all this anyway? What good will come of knowing any more than you already do? If you're thinking that knowing these things will heal your pain, you're going to find out just how mistaken you are."

"I knew you wouldn't understand. I don't know why I even called. This is hard enough . . ."

"You called because you promised you would. And because you knew I'd tell you what I really thought. I'm thinking of you. But I know you'll do what you need to anyway. Just promise you'll keep calling. I'd be crazy with worry thinking about you there, especially now, in her house. Just promise."

"Okay, okay. I promise."

"Okay."

"Well. How are things in Fenston?"

"God knows how Eleanor goes on with those terrible kids of hers. Sharon seems to have run away with some guy who was working on the paving crew over in Winton. And Shirley, everybody knows she's pregnant, shipped down to Eleanor's sisters for a few months."

"Oh, poor El. I feel terrible that I'm not there to help." In her mind's eye, Hattie could see Eleanor's dilapidated, old farmhouse and her children, the Rodiri kids, in all their smart, beautiful, troublesome particularity. Eleanor and Eddie, the true eccentrics of Fenston—they had seven languages between them and not one thread of common sense or purpose or a nickel. Hattie and Ben or Athena and Will, whoever had a few extra dollars at the time, had bailed Eddie out of two bad investments, loaned various sums, which were always repaid and fronted the money for braces and parochial school tuition. Hattie enjoyed being able to help the people she loved and wished she could be in Fenston to comfort Eleanor and see what she could do.

"For once it seems you have more to worry about than Eleanor. Just you take care of yourself."

"But she always needs us so much in these emergencies."

"Don't worry. With the Rodiris there's plenty more where that came from. If you miss this month's crisis, you'll catch up when the next one hits. And it might be something even juicier, like them getting kidnapped by gypsies or taking off on a flying saucer."

Hattie hooted with laughter, and a woman standing nearby glanced at her sharply, as if she disapproved of someone having such a good, hearty laugh on a city street. Hattie said, "Athena, you're something. That's the first laugh I've had since the day Ben came home and died on me."

"Really, now, you exaggerate. Did he die *on* you?"

"You're the most irreverent person I've ever met. And I miss you very much. I'll call you again soon. Promise."

Chapter twenty-nine

Already missing Athena, Hattie hung up the phone and suddenly realized that she was standing on a street corner in downtown Hartford, with traffic swirling around her and a hot dog vendor ten feet away. A young black woman with a baby carriage and a fellow dressed entirely in leather paced the edge of the sidewalk, obviously waiting to use the phone she had tied up for the last fifteen minutes. She was just formulating the word, sorry, when she realized they didn't expect it. They were used to waiting for the phone; next time it might be her turn to wait.

The anonymity of the city fascinated her. She thought about how different it was from Fenston where everyone knew your problems. She had never really considered whether she liked or resented the lack of privacy; she had just accepted it. Now, face to face with another way of life, she found herself adapting very well, glad for once that every pair of eyes didn't glance curiously at her.

Was the anonymity part of the draw of the road to Ben, too? At times he had chafed at the curiosity of the small town about them. Hattie was used to it—to being the family on the hill, the family with all the land and what must have always looked like a fortune to many. When she and Ben got married, every person in town could recite the details of the decorations in the tent by the pond, the picture frame hats and the enormous Alice Long petticoats of the bridesmaids, the local country club Tommie Watkins band, the seven tiers of their wedding cake. Having lived in Fenston her entire life, Hattie took such interest in her stride. For her it was a matter of course, but Ben had resented it even then.

Later, when his work life didn't seem to be working out, he resented it even more. "That snoop," he had called Eleanor when she casually and innocently asked how he was doing over at the new Agway where he had been hired to sell feed to large farms, a job Ben detested from the start.

In her mind's eye, Hattie saw Ben walking the streets of Hartford not having to nod to people or to wonder what they thought of him. He could go about his business and return at the end of the day to Gordon Street, nod to his neighbors and enjoy his privacy.

Hattie couldn't fault him; there was certainly liberation in anonymity. With that new freedom in mind on this summer's morning, she looked around her at the swell of people on Third Avenue and felt herself merging, blending in, one story among many. Yet there was also a curious pride; who else among them had achieved what she had in the last few days? Who would have had the courage and imagination to see it through? She felt happily unnoticed, and pleased with herself that she was able to hold this vast secret inside herself.

But back in her room that night, Hattie felt quite different, as her self-congratulatory bravado gave way to pain and longing. The odd sensation of hearing Ben breathe on the pillow next to her the night after he died returned to her whenever she began to slip into sleep. She'd turn toward the sound of his breath and then startle herself awake again. Finally, she got out of bed and went into the bathroom and looked out the window into the alley where someone was pacing and smoking. She felt a kinship with this other, late night, tormented soul. The night air was cool when she opened the window. Taking a few deep breaths, she tried to calm herself. It worked for a few minutes, but as soon as she drew back inside, she again felt Ben's presence in the house.

Fifty times during the night she felt the strongest impulse to walk to the end of the hall to look into the big room where Anya was sleeping, where Ben had slept beside her. The following day she thought of an excuse in case Anya came up and found her there: she'd say she had wanted to look out onto the street to check the weather. Fortified with her alibi, she headed for the room. The hall was papered in dull green, old paper that was graying to brown, like in the living room and dining room. The light leapt too easily from square glass panes of the ceiling fixtures. During the day, Anya propped the hall window open and the immaculate, white lace-edged curtains, a contrast to the evil, dingy wallpaper, billowed against the frame of the window.

Hattie did actually peer out the window looking at the weather, steadying herself, telling herself all she wanted was a quick glimpse into the bedroom. Six steps from the hall to the door and then she was inside. Incredibly old-fashioned, heavy wood furniture held down the corners of the room. The bed seemed mammoth, high off the floor and piled with many articles of bedding. It was European in style and arrangement, with bolsters behind loose pillows and a soft knitted shawl covering the foot of the bed. There was the same billow of curtains as the hall window; all soft white and cream tied back with pale ribbons. Like the rest of the house, the room was impeccably clean, its bare wooden floors polished and glistening in contrast to the pale, soft bedding.

Despite the heavy furniture and ugly wallpaper, an inviting room, Hattie thought with a stab of jealousy, but no more so than her own beautiful room in Fenston. She noticed an ornately framed picture on the dresser and longed to pick it up and examine it. A moment later it was in her hands. Ben and Anya smiled back at her. Anya's blond head was garlanded with baby roses. Kasia was not in the picture. Ben looked like himself, though he seemed to need a haircut and she didn't recognize the suit. She hadn't heard the footsteps in the hall, but turned just as Anya entered the room, a look of agitation on her face.

She walked toward Hattie, her expression moving from surprise to anger and took the picture firmly from her. She held it for a moment, studying the figures.

"Our wedding photo," she said. "I look very different, don't I?" The firmness of her voice startled Hattie. Small prickles moved up the back of her scalp. Trying to recall one of the excuses she had prepared to cover for her snooping, she looked at Anya who was regarding her squarely. Her mouth was so dry; she wouldn't have been able to speak, even if words came to her. The two women held each other's gaze.

"Kasia and I are walking over to the park. Do you want to come?" Anya still studied her face.

Hattie knew she should say something, but her lies, for once, failed her. "Yes," she squeaked and sheepishly followed Anya from the room. Halfway down the stairs, Anya's words started to sink in like iron claws dragging her below the surface of her consciousness, "Wedding photo." God in heaven, Hattie thought: Wedding photo!

Had Ben really married someone else while he was married to her?

The wedding photo continued to torment her. She kept wondering if Ben had been sleeping in that room with the curtains all those nights she thought he was somewhere else, all the nights he called from the road, alone in some motel? All those years, what did she really know of Ben's life? Her picture of him had been driving the car, singing, shaking hands and unpacking his cases, holding up one tool after the other, explaining their uses. And then he'd eat at a diner and sleep somewhere, the same sleep as at home. That's the image Ben had carefully cultivated for her. He had even supplied the label: his life on the road.

Chapter thirty

Each day Hattie awoke sure that this would be the day she'd finally tell Anya everything and drive home to Fenston. She could imagine every part of it except the actual telling. How would she start? And each day Hattie left the house, unsure of what she'd do to fill up the hours until she could return to the house on Gordon Street. For the first two weeks, she drove around the city and its suburbs, idly watching people and continuing her mental conversation with Ben. At a luncheonette one day she picked up a tourist book and systematically worked her way through its recommendations: the Mark Twain House, the Travelers Tower and the Charter Oak. She spent the better part of a week in the Wadsworth Athenaeum, discovering art she never knew existed.

After exhausting the official sights, Hattie thought about how much she liked to read. Cuddled up in the kitchen or in her bed, she'd often go through two books a week when Ben was on the road. She found the public library and spent much of each day happily leafing through newspapers and magazines and reading the fiction books displayed. One morning on the bulletin board, she saw a notice asking for volunteers to read for the blind. Immediately, she saw herself sitting in a chair surrounded by blind people and guide dogs as she read aloud in a clear, impressive voice.

She copied down the address and drove to the office of the Recording for the Blind. Mr. Miles, the pudgy-faced, cheerful middle-aged man who presided over the organization's schedule, handed her an application, telling Hattie that she could work at her own pace and timeframe, but that she would be reading into a tape recorder and not directly to people. She thought he looked at her a little too long, pausing to smile a little too often, "You can do bestsellers, but most of the good ones are taken already. But we always have a call for the classics. Right now, we're looking for someone to take on *Great Expectations.*"

"I'll do it," Hattie said quickly as she followed Mr. Miles into the booth to be instructed on how to use the equipment.

"New in town?" he asked, looking directly into Hattie's eyes as soon as he had shut the door. The first person since she left Fenston to pay her any attention, Mr. Miles was clearly interested in more than her speaking voice.

Unbidden, a flush of pleasure came into Hattie's face as she realized he was attracted to her.

"Yes. But how did you know?"

"Your accent. Not that there's anything wrong with it. But I knew you weren't from around here. And lots of people find their way in a strange place by helping others."

"Really?" Hattie was giving herself time to see how she felt about the conversation. All the weeks she'd been in Hartford she'd begun to think that the anonymity of city life agreed with her. Now here was someone wanting to know more about her. He was short, perhaps not much more than three or four inches taller than Hattie herself, trim with wiry gray hair and metal-framed glasses behind which his magnified eyes were a watery blue. Deep lines underscored the corners of his mouth, but as he smiled they folded into themselves. Laughter lines, Hattie thought. And she smiled back.

"Yeah, people volunteer for all kinds of reasons. But mostly out of their own needs. Works out well all the way around."

"I guess so," Hattie answered.

Even though she had already measured Mr. Miles against Ben and found him lacking and had given off her best version of body language that said *not interested*, he continued, "So where are you from?"

"Pennsylvania. Northern part." And then she added "Here with my husband's work." That did the trick. Mr. Miles remembered what he was about and resumed the training session.

Pleased with herself on both counts, Hattie settled into the booth to begin the test read of ten pages. When she emerged and handed the tape to Mr. Miles, who had taken his place behind the desk, she smiled.

"Didn't mean to be forward back there," he said, jerking his head toward the booth. "I didn't notice you wearing a wedding ring. What I said about the volunteers goes for me too. Wife died two years ago."

He looked at Hattie as if he wanted to say more, but couldn't figure out what. "Anyway, we're glad to have you with us. And the work we do is important." Then he looked down at the schedule Hattie had filled out and his face brightened, the lines again disappearing into a wide smile, "See you Monday morning."

The recordings became Hattie's work. She liked reviewing the material ahead of time, thinking about how she'd read a long passage, where to break it up, how to use her voice to emphasize something or to create suspense. In the break room she met a number of seasoned volunteers who gave her some good advice.

After their initial encounter, Mr. Miles, now satisfied that Hattie was a happily married woman, began visiting her in the booth and telling her his woes. He just couldn't adjust to single life. He missed having someone of his own to talk to at the end of the day. But of course, he sighed, Hattie wouldn't know about that. Mr. Miles only hoped she'd never have to.

"When you came in, I thought it was too good to be true. All the nice ones are already taken." While he talked,

Hattie thought about the reading session. Mr. Miles didn't require any kind of response other than Hattie's sympathetic gaze.

One afternoon he appeared at her booth with a particularly forlorn expression and a newspaper in hand. "Can you believe this?" he said, jabbing his index finger at a front-page photo. Hattie stifled a laugh as he put the paper in front of her. The Reverend Sun Yung Moon had married 4,150 people in one ceremony. The front page blazed with accounts and photos. "All those people willing to get married in a pack like that. Most of them had never even met each other before the wedding."

Hattie waited for what was sure to come next. "All I'm looking for is one really nice woman. And what kind of luck do I have? What do I have to do, join a mind control cult or something to get a date?"

Murmuring sympathetically that she was sure he'd eventually find the right person, Hattie ushered him out of the booth and started to work. But the image of those couples crept into her mind throughout the day. She wondered if they knew all the things that could go wrong and whether their religion would help them cope with life when things did.

Every day, the heat settled on the city like a warm, wet cloth, thick and suffocating. When she left the house in the morning, it was cool. But by noon, the tiny dark rooms were stifling. Hattie, Anya and Kasia settled into a routine. Hattie was out early in the morning and back by mid-afternoon. She often went to her room and changed out of her work clothes, a skirt, blouse and light blazer, into shorts and a sleeveless shirt. At Anya's suggestion, Hattie often joined her on the porch for a few hours before dinner. Sometimes she and Anya sat together; sometimes she sat alone.

Hattie had the sense that Anya had a good deal on her mind. Though polite, Anya seemed listless and preoccupied, so it did not surprise Hattie when she never questioned her further about her work or her life, thought she seemed glad enough to have her there. It was a relief for Hattie that Anya seemed to exhibit neither great curiosity nor much energy for remaining questions about the propitious appearance of her boarder.

Often, throughout the day, Ben would enter Hattie's thoughts; flashes of memories from different periods of their marriage visited her. One moment they were dancing at their twenty-fifth wedding anniversary party and the next, leaning over Alice's crib looking into her huge blue eyes. There was no telling what would appear next on the screen of her memory.

Hattie also knew Anya's silences had to do with Ben, with his unspoken absence. The two women sat together, each wrapped in her loss and isolation, both grieving, but unable to share their grief. Oddly, it comforted Hattie to know that someone else was thinking about Ben too.

Chapter thirty-one

It was the rottenest love story ever told Hattie decided that evening, at the beginning of an unusually hot September, when Anya poured out her memories and emotions. After tucking Kasia in Anya returned to the darkened porch where Hattie sat drowsing in the sweltering heat and puzzling out her feelings for this other woman. A long moment of quiet stretched between them. Then Anya caught her breath and said, "Kasia mentioned you in her prayers tonight."

Hattie was surprised by the flush of pleasure that came over her, "She did?"

"Yes. That's progress."

"How so?" It wasn't just Anya's accent; sometimes she'd phrase things in a stilted, old-fashioned English that only lent what she was saying more charm.

"I'm glad she's thinking about other things. Up to now, she's only been praying for her father to come home."

"Ouch."

"She's even been bargaining with God." Then Anya lapsed into a small voice, imitating Kasia, "If Papa comes home I'll never misbehave again. I'll do all my chores and be so good."

"That's awful. She shouldn't feel like everything's in her control," said Hattie, "especially bad things."

"There hasn't been much else lately."

"Oh?"

"I'd just come home from the hospital, and that in itself terrified her. When I'm sick she really gets upset. Ben's away most of the time and she depends on me."

"Oh." Hattie tried to keep her voice noncommittal.

"And now Ben seems to have disappeared," Anya spoke in a brisk, almost detached tone, belied by the stricken look on her face Hattie could discern even by the faint light from the street. Her comment implied that Ben's disappearance affected Kasia and not herself.

Hattie's face stung in the dark. This was her moment. She could end the charade right here and let Anya know just why she had come. Before she could say anything Anya continued, again imitating Kasia, "And thank you for letting Hattie come to us. She helps us so much and makes us laugh sometimes. Even though Papa is still gone away."

"She calls him Papa. She must really have taken to him?"

"What do you mean?"

"Well, just that most step-parents . . . well, they aren't so easily accepted. That's all. But Kasia . . ."

"Stepparent. What gave you the idea of a stepparent? Ben is Kasia's father."

"Oh, oh, oh, I guess, I guess . . . I mean, I'm sorry. I thought you meant. When you said she was your daughter."

"Oh, I see." Anya inclined her face toward Hattie as if looking her over very closely.

The air was heavy between them; a misunderstanding that hummed like insects in the summer air for a moment. Hattie was afraid to let herself think about anything, afraid to feel. Could it be that the child was really Ben's child? But Kasia was eight years old. Oh, God. She couldn't even let herself process the words. She'd have to contend with that information later, alone in her room. Now she had to go forward and find out as much as she possibly could. For the time being, she forgot about telling Anya the truth about Ben. She wanted to know how it was that her husband had commenced this hidden life. How? And when?

She drew in a deep breath as if she could hardly get enough air in the summer night, "Tell me about Ben. About when you first met." A car made its way slowly up the street.

Hattie watched Anya tense and realized that even now, almost five months after Ben had died, Anya was expecting him to return. A young woman in white shorts bounded from a porch on the opposite side of the street and slid into the passenger side. The car sped away in a blast of rock music.

After a moment in which Hattie imagined that Anya was trying to decide whether she should tell, her words were slow and the accent that Hattie had found charming since she had first encountered it was never more so. The words seemed to drift of their own accord around the porch and flesh out into complete scenes and images for both women somewhere between Anya's telling and Hattie's listening. Anya began, "Twelve years ago . . ."

Unable to breathe, Hattie sorted through her own life and found the place that was twelve years ago. Alice was just finishing junior high school and Ben had been working the prized New England territory for two years. Finally there seemed to be enough money to do some of the desperately needed repairs on the farm. She recalled it as a happy time. The picture that moved to the forefront of Hattie's mind was not one in which suspicion was even a part. Their life was seamless, punctuated by Ben's comings and goings and the delight of watching Alice mature. Where inside that time, Hattie wondered, had Ben found a part of himself that wanted to deceive her? How had she not known that he was about to act so desperately and out of character?

Chapter thirty-two

"I was twenty-four years old and had just come to this country. My parents had died, my father shortly after the war. I don't remember him at all. And my mother when I was fifteen. It was only my brother Piotr and me. He was much older—fifteen years older. By then he had his own life. I stayed with him, finished school and was working in a bakery. There was a house and a little money, so we got along. But then Piotr had a friend here, Stan, who sent for me, asking me to come over to marry him. He said he would pay my way. When I saw how determined Piotr was that I should go, I realized he had been waiting to get rid of me. So I went. At least, I thought, Stan wants me.

"When I got here, I found Stan cruel and repulsive. He didn't want a wife, but a slave. Someone who was afraid and would have to take his terrible tempers and long silences."

"Did you marry him?"

"I had no money. Nowhere to turn. I convinced him to wait awhile, telling him I wanted to make just the right, beautiful dress for the wedding. I had brought a lot of fabric from Poland, things that were in my mother's chest when she died, almost the only things I have of hers. Every day he would ask me how close I was to finishing the dress.

"At the grocery store, I used to see this woman. Her clothes were strange and her looks frightened and fascinated me—somehow familiar. When I heard her talk to people, I realized she was Polish too. I listened to her talk at the store. You know how that happens—suddenly every time you're in a place, this other person is there too. I was frantic and couldn't think of anything. I just wandered around every day thinking what I could do to escape Stan.

"One day, she came up to me and began saying I was following her. Maybe I was. I couldn't recall. But I meant no harm. I just wanted to hear her speak. "Why are you watching me?" she asked. Up to then, I had only nodded. When I said I thought I knew her, I lied. But then her face lit up. "Polish. Why didn't you tell me you are Polish? How long have you been here?" she asked, searching my face closely as if looking for clues. Then as if she had made a decision, she took my arm, 'Let's go for coffee.'

"We met again and again. She was from Warszawa near where I lived, and she had left long ago, before the war, before I was born. She asked me this and that about

Poland, wanting to know every small thing . . . Of course, this made me more homesick. And she too, after all those years, got homesick. She'd never gone back even once. 'How are the gardens along the Vistula?' she'd ask me as if I'd been there the day before. And then I'd have to describe again each small flower and curved path and fountain."

Chapter thirty-three

When Hattie thought about her own life, the way she herself had clung to the security of the familiar; the idea of leaving all that she knew and loved—her surroundings, possessions, her entire life—and going far away, alone, as Anya had done—it was all something she couldn't imagine. Maybe it was what attracted Ben.

"Somehow, I don't know how, I began with telling her a little lie. Clara, her name was Clara, she just listened to everything without comment, like you're doing now, I suppose, but that doesn't mean that there are no thoughts behind that listening. I told her that Stan was a nice man who wanted to marry me. But the truth must have been written all over my face.

"She said, 'Then why does it look like a gallon of

tears wait behind your eyes for you to cry them out at night.' It happened, I couldn't hold back. She waited until I stopped crying, then gently asked the question that would let me tell her everything.

"While Stan was at work the next day, I met her and we went by cab and got my things and took them to her house. The house was over on Phelps Street. It's no longer there. They tore it down to make a market. But it was lovely—big rooms with windows and a backyard that Clara had transformed, like the gardens she missed in Poland.

"Overnight, Clara had made up a room for me, filled with flowers from the garden and a nice bed and table. A room filled with sunshine. There were pillows made of some of the clothing she had brought with her from Poland and others that she had embroidered. I'd never seen such a beautiful room. I cried and hugged her and then we both cried. Now, looking back, I'm grateful to her still, but I realize she had made the room up as much for herself as for me, because I was the one person she had met who would understand what she had done. As for me, it was the first time since my mother died that I felt safe."

The description was so clear that Hattie found herself inside the story. She too walked into the room and felt the peace and comfort of such warmth and safety as Clara had offered.

"And that's how Clara acted, wanting to take care of me like a mother. I was so glad to be away from my brother's domination and that terrible Stan, I didn't notice at the time, or think about what that might mean. If she wanted to act like a mother, let her, I thought. Clara helped me find work at the Idyll Away, a hotel she knew about." At the mention of the Idyll Away, Hattie drew in her breath. Anya looked over at her. "I think I know where that is," Hattie said.

Anya continued, "I was cleaning and changing sheets. A job that I could do, even though my English was not good. It was hard work, but I was very strong then. At night, I'd return to her house and we'd eat and talk and sometimes take the bus out into the countryside by the river and walk there for hours. It reminded both of us of the springtime riverbanks in bloom in Poland. Like here, winter in Poland seemed so long that we thought we'd never see the flowers again.

"Sometimes we'd work together in her garden, and she'd teach me to plant and what the different flowers wanted. I began to remember other things my mother had shown me years ago. She was so kind, I could have lived like that forever. But always, like a mother, Clara would warn me that men in America were not to be trusted."

"That's where Ben came in, I guess," Hattie said.

"Yes. When I met Ben I was surprised by her anger. She told me to have nothing to do with him. She was so furious she didn't talk to me for a day. All I had said was there was a nice man who talked to me sometimes and liked my singing. Like a mother, she forbade me to even speak to him, which was foolish and impossible. She wanted me only to come straight home, to stay near her. But the next day he was gone anyway. So I didn't think about it anymore."

When Anya mentioned the singing, Hattie summoned a picture of a hotel room with Ben getting ready for his day's work and Anya's voice coming from somewhere down the hall, getting closer.

"In a month, he returned. I saw him at the end of the day as I left. I couldn't believe how glad I was to see this stranger. I didn't even know his name then. So many people coming and going, coming in and out of the hotel, and somehow, this one was special. I don't know how to explain it even now. But there was something inside me that knew. He was there the next day and the next. I'd never done anything like this before, but that afternoon, I went into the office and looked at the reservation book and found out that he would be there for almost two weeks. I was so glad. And why, I didn't know. He had only said a word or two to me occasionally.

"One day after work, I walked with Ben, I don't even recall now how it happened that we did it, how he suggested it or maybe I did, though I doubt that I would have been brave enough to do that. We set off through the park and along the river. We stopped to eat a little and listened to some music. We were in no hurry, just enjoying the early evening. I remember that I felt embarrassed that I was still in my uniform, still sweaty from working, though I had washed up and tried to fix my hair at the hotel. Ben walked me back to the corner of Clara's block. She didn't speak to me for two days. Then she said that if I stayed out late again with a man, I'd be sorry."

From the first mention of Ben's name, Hattie was

straining to visualize the scene more clearly. Finally. This was the conversation she had longed for; this was the reason for which she had come. Hattie felt her body at first stiffen then pass through relaxation, then beyond into a place where her limbs felt strangely liquid, and her body a pulsating mass of matter held loosely in place by her skin, that sensitive, easily damaged sheath, the only defense she now had.

Her mind was keen, able to register these physical changes, able to try to follow Anya's comments well enough to summon up the appropriate facial responses and murmurs to keep the confidences coming; while all the time she was ceaselessly sorting through the index of her own emotional repertoire to see what was happening to her.

As far as Hattie herself could judge, she had moved from curiosity to envy to fear. The curiosity—natural enough; the envy—certainly to be expected; but what was under all the fear she felt? Imagining Ben in the hotel room did not summon the usual comforting picture of his life away from home. Instead of seeing him on the road, briskly involved with his business and then, in the evenings, going over his papers, having a quiet dinner alone, and then watching *Mission Impossible* for a while before going to sleep, she now pictured him in his room, hunched over his papers at the desk, his back in a tired, lonely curve, as he left the door to the room open to catch the song of a young woman working in the hallway.

What had Ben been feeling when he first met Anya? Did he respond to the same vulnerability in her that had so far kept Hattie from telling her about Ben, about herself? There was no end to the questions that plagued her about Ben's other life. Anya had fallen silent, looking out into the street, as if she herself were seeing the whole thing again, Hattie prodded, "And then you fell in love?"

"Ben had a way of making problems disappear," Anya continued. "When Clara threw me out, Ben didn't have to feel responsible for me. After all, that's not what he had bargained for. He only invited me to hear a little music. After he heard me singing, he knew I was European. We got to talking about waltz music. We both liked it very much. I was surprised at all he knew about different kinds of music. It was just that we both loved music and he was doing a good deed, taking me out to hear something nice that he had spotted in the paper.

"Then suddenly he's stuck with me. It was a wonderful evening and we had talked a lot after the concert. I knew it was late; somehow I couldn't make myself care. Ben insisted on driving me the whole way home. As we got to the street, I could see boxes on the porch. Clara had packed all my things and put them on the porch. No matter how long we rang the bell and called out to her, she wouldn't answer the door. Wouldn't let me back in. It had begun to rain, I was terrified. What could I do now? How foolish I had been to go against Clara! Now I had lost the comfort and happiness I knew in her house, the first since my mother died."

Imagining herself in that situation, Hattie shivered with Anya's fear. In a strange place, the only person who had befriended her suddenly was turning her back on her.

"Then Ben said: 'Let's just go back to the hotel.' He said we could call Clara from there, talk to her, explain. We carried my things to the car, there wasn't that much, not even enough to fill the trunk: some clothes and toiletries and my box of fabric, the half-made wedding dress. And one other thing. When I opened the box of cloth, I saw that she had added the lovely old pillowcase, that thick, cream linen embroidered with white silk, faded and softened by time, like her memories of Poland. I think she wanted to remind of me what I had thrown away by not following her advice. I remember the windshield wipers clacking as we drove back to the hotel, neither of us speaking. I couldn't tell how hard it was raining through my own tears. I had felt so good there with Clara, but I knew that she had turned on me now and would never let me come back. I had done the one thing she had warned me about. For even though Ben and I had only talked and listened to music together, I already knew in my heart that I was in love with him.

"When Ben saw that I was crying, he misinterpreted it. 'I won't hurt you,' he said.

"And I cried all the harder.

"That night, I cried myself to sleep on the other bed in Ben's room. All I could think about was how I had ruined the only good thing that had come to me in America. Yet I knew that I wouldn't have given up that evening with Ben, even if I had been given another chance to do it all over again. I could hear Ben in the other bed. He wasn't sleeping either. What he was thinking, I don't know. Even then I wanted him to come over to me. Maybe I was crying a little because he wouldn't.

"The next day, he left for work but came back in a short while. 'I have a surprise,' he said."

Chapter thirty-four

The last week of summer passed quickly. August dove toward September in a swelter of days, while Hattie felt becalmed, unsure that there was any further justification to her being there, but unwilling, unable to leave. After she finished reading aloud *Great Expectations*, Mr. Miles commented on her speed and accuracy, her ability to give tone and inflection to even Dickens' more difficult passages.

He was sitting at his desk, reading, when she handed him the last tape. Looking up, his eyes were unfocused and vulnerable. Hattie thought about what he had told her and what she guessed from reading between the lines. He was the kind of man no one pays much attention to—a good person who tries to get decently through life. Regret that she had lied to him troubled her and she was angry with herself. Yes, Ben's work had brought her to Hartford. But the essence of what she said was a lie and she knew it. Had deceit become second nature to her, too?

"Hattie. I'm glad to see you. I've been saving a newer book for you." *The Hidden Persuaders* was a book she herself would never have picked. Nonetheless, she found herself reading it with relish. She learned that things could work on your mind without your even knowing it. As she read, she thought about the web of deceit she had enmeshed herself in. In a moment of luminous clarity she realized she was assuming Ben's life in order to understand it.

Kasia was about to enter second grade and she talked about it constantly. Often Hattie had to catch herself as she sat with mother and daughter on the porch or in the yard in the evenings. She was transported back into the girlhood days of her own daughter. Her hands twitched at the familiar gesture, as she watched Anya carefully undo Kasia's blond braids and comb her hair long and straight across her back, the golden ripples gathering up and holding memory's strange light.

Throughout these weeks, drenching waves of feeling came and went for Hattie. At times, she felt such grief and rage that she thought that only running in front of a truck would give her the oblivion she needed. At other times, she felt a terrific tenderness for Ben, for the life that was no more. Then she'd think she was over with the angry part, only to have it surface again in her dreams or waking thoughts.

Oddly enough, from the first, Anya and Kasia were

never the focus of Hattie's anger. It felt to her that they were casualties, just as she had been. When she first arrived they would bring Ben's name up as if they expected him to return, but mention of him became increasingly infrequent. Anya's distracted look and Kasia's deepening silence told her they knew that his return was unlikely.

Some nights she would linger on the porch and hear Anya's odd, dry cough, her struggle to breathe in the tight summer air. Kasia had told Hattie about how much her parents loved to sing duets. "Their voices were so sweet together, you could almost not tell them apart." Hattie couldn't help wondering when things had changed for Anya and what had happened to replace her sweet voice with the shortness of breath. Anya had brushed off her questions with, "Allergies. Always at this time of year. Allergies."

Kasia was singing quietly on the glider and playing with her Etch-A-Sketch. The ice-cream truck tinkled its greeting down the block. Kasia looked up plaintively; she seldom asked outright for anything she wanted. The money Hattie contributed to the household seemed to be what they got along on. She glanced at the child, "Just what I felt like. The Good Humor Man must have read my mind." Then she tickled Kasia on the bottom of her bare foot, a gesture she considered, and then allowed herself, "Can I talk you into walking down the block with me? My treat."

Kasia bounded to her feet, slipped on her rubber sandals and smiled at Hattie, "Sure." A pair of beat-up sneakers and these sandals were what Kasia had worn all summer.

As they walked along, Hattie said, "School starts Monday, doesn't it? I thought I could help you and Mom, maybe we could go and get a few things to get ready."

"Mama says we need to wait until Papa gets back. Then he'll take me shopping." In Kasia's voice there was not the slightest shred of enthusiasm or belief that such a thing would happen; her face was averted and Hattie could only guess its expression.

"Maybe I could talk to your mom. You and I could go, if she didn't feel up to it. Then when your dad got back, you could go again." For a minute, Hattie thought Kasia had not heard her. She was ready to repeat herself when the child finally drew in a deep breath and said, "Maybe. Oh, yes, Hattie, that would be very good, very nice." She turned her head slightly and Hattie could see that she was thinking and smiling.

"Three Nutty Butties," she said, handing the money to the man behind the small opening. She could feel herself smiling too. As they walked home in the summer night, Hattie felt unaccountably happy. Not for the first time since she had arrived at 321 Gordon Street, Hattie felt as if she'd been given a chance to relive one of the lost, ordinary moments of Alice's childhood.

Chapter thirty-five

Anya's voice had become weaker and fainter as she spoke, until finally Hattie, sitting only a few feet away, could hardly hear her. "I know it's good for me to talk about this, about the sadness, and about Ben's disappearance. But I'm so tired, I can hardly think of it anymore."

"Yes," Hattie answered, regretting that she still hadn't sated her own curiosity, as each fragment of the story made her greedy for more. Still, she regretted that she had not heard the terrible fatigue growing in Anya's words. "Maybe we can talk again tomorrow night or some other time." Then she added, straight from her own unedited thought, "I do want to hear the rest."

Anya looked at her wearily but gratefully, "And I need to tell it. Maybe somehow then I'll be able to understand what happened." She drew in her breath and paused. "Life is so confusing sometimes. And so surprising. Like you sitting here. I don't know how, but it was lucky that there was that mistake, that you came here."

Chapter thirty-six

By the time she heard the rest of Anya's story, Hattie had lost count of the nights she'd spent in Hartford. Often after Anya and Kasia settled in their room, Hattie lay on her bed ready for sleep, imagining herself some kind of animal led to the barn at day's end, at the whim of some force beyond her own power, not knowing what to expect next. She'd get up and look out onto the many windows across the alley, a lighted table in someone's kitchen, a woman washing out her lingerie, another making a sandwich, filling a thermos, a glint of night light from a child's room. It was not that Hattie particularly wanted to know who the people were, and yet she couldn't help putting her own longings inside them, wondering what simmered in the pot on that stove, what loss or sorrow drove the woman to open the cage at a late hour to let out a bird that would fondly nuzzle her neck.

Hattie recalled seeing people down from the Interstate drive slowly through Fenston, stop and look, finger the cards in Athena's store or pull up to watch Eddie plow a meadow. What can they be seeing, she'd wonder? So close to the fold of dirt and stalk, the colored slice of earth, the smell of loam after spring rain—she wasn't seeing the same thing. And yet it was all there, perfectly preserved in her memory, little pieces of experience coming to her, lit and called forward by some scent, or thought or association. The fragments of her life, its exquisite wholeness in each little part.

A few days after Hattie arrived, Anya showed her the garden, telling her to help herself to any of the vegetables or flowers for her room. The small 15 x 15 plot took up a good portion of the backyard, but produced as if it were acres. Tomato plants and basil bloomed; beans ran uphill and over strings, squash blossoms and lettuce and every manner of herb flourished—the garden was prodigious.

Anya named each plant she passed, pausing here to tidy a row, there to deadhead faded blossoms. At the back of the garden, roses tumbled against a trellis. "Cottage Rose, Scarlet Star, Amber Star, Carolina Lady," she smiled at the sound of each name. She and Ben had made the garden the first year she lived on Gordon Street. One evening he had appeared with trays of plants and seeds and the implements they'd need to get underway.

"You really have a knack . . ." Hattie commented.

"I like to grow things. And it makes me recall the gardens we had in Poland. Little plots outside the city, but everyone spent lots of time working."

Hattie touched a small bush full of bright berries and looked questioningly at Anya.

"Currants," Anya explained. "At first it seemed silly to put so much work into the garden of a rented house. Then we thought: Why not? At least as long as I lived here I could enjoy it. Ben helped me."

"But so much work."

"Yes. Especially now."

"Now?" For a moment Hattie thought Anya was about to say something important.

"This time of year. So much thinning and weeding and hoeing. And with Ben gone . . ." her voice trailed off.

To temper the sadness in Anya's voice and face, Hattie said, "Oh, it's lovely though. Even if it is a lot of work."

"Please enjoy it any time you wish."

And Hattie did. Often she sat on the front porch to escape the heat of the house in early evening; but often, too, she went out into the backyard late at night and walked and savored the small plot and its bounty.

Those nights on the postage stamp of Anya's yard, Hattie realized how the smells from a hundred kitchens could become as real as colored ribbons circling her shoulders, as the stew of voices from the houses around the strip of yard; she came to understand how vital, how fecund somehow, it could be to have someone birthing in the room next to the clink of glasses, and, chiming in, the sounds of celebration of some unknown feat, or someone arguing, someone running a vacuum.

Then she thought of her own hill, which spoke in a single voice, and how the scent of lilac bushes outside her window prepared her for the flurry of spring birds at the feeder—each moment entire and distinct yet linked to the others. Snow falls, and a plow lumbers up the road, its light circling overhead. Hattie had come to believe in that kind of connection, the way she could follow each moment backward to comprehend its path and locus. If such thinking worked, Hattie reasoned, there would have to be some sense to what Ben had done, a way she should be able to follow him through the strange odyssey he had set out before both of them.

Over the weeks of late summer and early fall, Hattie moved beyond incredulity and accepted that her husband had developed and sustained a completely separate hidden life for twelve years. Without notice or volition, her quest shifted from finding out what he had done and wanting some justice for her suffering, to needing to explain to herself how it could have happened. Otherwise, she felt, nothing in the world would ever make sense to her again; she would never be able to believe in love or goodness or compassion or to hope that she could understand anything about life.

Hattie's thoughts jumped like crickets, each landing in a different bath of longing as she considered what her own responsibilities were, what her actions should be. Now that her deceit had brought her to Ben's other family and she had remained silent for so long, she felt herself more conspirator than injured party.

Walking in the garden late one evening, she realized that although she deeply resented what Ben had done, she no longer hated him. The last of Anya's roses were straggling atop tough thorny stalks. Hattie bent to the scent of the Amber Star.

Hattie wrapped her hand carefully around the rose's stem then pulled it across her palm. Pain shot through her, together with waves of unexpected, unexpressed sorrow. And then something she did not understand, a strange inchoate joy; the joy of release born of a deeper knowledge.

Chapter thirty-seven

When the dance was over, their faces were pasted together by a thin glaze of sweat. Embarrassed, Hattie peeled her cheek away from Ben's and realized that her body was trembling. Her thighs and pelvis, which had pressed insistently back as Ben held her close, were charged with a kind of current, a wild electric feeling she had never experienced before. Without speaking, Ben took her hand and led her from the pavilion and out into the night.

"I'm Ben. Ben Darling."

"I know," Hattie said, her voice softer than his. He was still holding her hand.

"I'm staying at the Rodiris."

"I know that too," Hattie smiled at his lack of understanding about how things worked in Fenston. A handsome young man just out of the military, a hero in Korea, according to Eddie, that hardly would have happened without everyone knowing within twenty-four hours. Suddenly Hattie thought of those black silk jackets some of the older girls had been wearing a few years earlier, black with exotic designs of flowers, dragons and butterflies stitched in brightly colored threads. "You were in the Army or something."

"Marines," Ben answered. "There's a difference."

"What is it?"

"What's what?"

"The difference?"

"There's no comparison. Marines—Army?"

"No, I'm serious. What is the difference?" And Hattie was. Everything about this man was a source of interest to her suddenly. The tumult of new physical feelings he stirred in her was taking her by storm.

"Semper Fidelis. That's what we are. Always faithful."

"That's a little bit of information I'll file away for future reference." Hattie surprised herself by the flirtatiousness in her voice.

"You can count on it."

"What's it like over there?" Hattie asked, motioning her head in the direction of the Rodiri farm, a source of endless curiosity to the natives of Fenston.

"Where?"

"The farm."

"Not boring. You can say that. Some pair, those two. We're painting the house and Eddie just sits down and starts reading poems. His favorite poet just died. He just kept reading his poems."

"Who died?"

"Guy by the name of Stevens, he said. From Hartford. Funny thing, I really kind of liked it. On the way over here he said one about the boys bringing the girls flowers wrapped in newspapers."

"Oh, wasn't that sweet of them."

"I'm sorry I didn't bring you some."

From the Pavilion they heard strains of "Sincerely" and Ben took the hand he had held since they danced and placed it on his shoulder.

"I'd do anything for you. Please say you'll be mine." Ben's voice was like some kind of warm liquid breath along her bare shoulder. Hattie would recall that dance in the darkness outside the Chaplin Lake Dance Pavilion, the scent of cedar trees and the words Ben sang softly in her ear as the place where she decided something important. She would have Ben Darling as her own.

Later that night, Hattie saw firsthand the chaos of the Rodiri farmhouse as she and Ben crept past and around piles of books and furniture and baskets of laundry on their way to and from his bedroom. As a sheltered only child, Hattie had never seen a naked man before, nor was she altogether sure of the mechanics of lovemaking. But Ben was both confident and careful, easing Hattie slowly out of her clothing and onto the bed. To Hattie's amazement, he was able to open her bra with a practiced flick of his fingers. She had already decided, anticipating the pain of intercourse, which she had read about in countless *Modern Romance* magazines, that she would not cry out or flinch.

Hattie's fears of the pain she would endure were groundless. When Ben entered her, she felt a passionate surge and automatically moved her hips toward him. Glad that he obviously knew what to do, Hattie surrendered herself to her passion. But not before she watched him take from the nightstand a condom and roll it expertly onto his penis. Of course, she thought, this is the first time for me but not for him.

The black silk jackets and the hard faces of the older girls who had worn them came into her mind as Ben's practiced hand opened the condom. Danger flashed through her mind. Then she lost herself again in the rush of her passion. After their lovemaking Hattie wondered if she was just where she wanted to be or whether she should get up and run.

When Ben pulled up to the Beste farm, he stood outside the car and looked around appraisingly. Knowing that his daughter had been giddy and busy all day getting ready for the big date, Hattie's father stood beside the barn and watched the young man's muscled frame unfold from behind the wheel and approach the house in the company of his daughter.

"Dad," called Hattie, and he entered the house by the kitchen door, taking his time washing his hands before going into the parlor where Hattie and Ben waited. She was smiling up at Ben in a way that he hadn't seen before, as the young man looked around the rooms then at him, "Nice to meet you, sir."

Though he saw how taken Hattie was with Ben, her father had his own ideas about men out of the service and new in town.

"Just take your time, Hattie. You don't know much about the world. That's just as well. But you have to know enough to be careful," he said.

Usually in bed by ten, her father had stayed up until she returned at twelve-thirty. When she saw the light on in the kitchen, Hattie grew afraid and then angry. "Don't you like Ben, Dad?"

"Nothing to like or dislike," he answered gruffly. "Just that he's not from here. Doesn't understand what we're like."

"No, but he wants to. Ben says he likes Fenston, really wants to stay. He's going for an interview tomorrow at the battery plant. Supervisor job."

"What does he know about making batteries?"

"I didn't ask him that. You're getting yourself all worked up about nothing, Dad. Ben's a nice guy. We like each other. That's it."

"So far." Her father spoke with a kind of ironic finality.

Chapter thirty-eight

The house was very quiet in the afternoon. Most days, Anya was in her room resting. Something was very wrong with her. Something more than Ben's disappearance. How much could Hattie pry to find out what it was? Did she even want to know?

When Hattie returned to the house in late afternoon, she often found the child sitting on the porch quietly, moving the glider back and forth rhythmically, a distracted look on her face. She seemed listless, leaving the house less and less often to play in the back alley with the other children. Hattie had fallen in love with the little girl long ago, even before she made the connection and realized that Kasia was Alice's half sister, accounting for the great resemblance between them, she was captivated by the child's sweet, inquiring gaze. But their personalities were very different. Alice had been a noisy, impetuous little person, lording it over the neighborhood kids, both girls and boys, and always thinking up some new project or game. In contrast, Kasia, even when she did go out back to play, was watchful and reserved, always hanging at the edge of the activity, shuffling her feet and pushing back her bangs with the back of her hand. Her meekness invited rejection by the other, more confident children. Hattie had observed Kasia from the kitchen window, her heart going out to the child.

One afternoon, Hattie noticed that the theater over on the avenue was showing *E.T.* Preoccupied with her internal odyssey as she had been in the past few months, she still hadn't escaped the tremendous promotion the movie had been given that summer. At dinner the next evening, when she proposed they all go out to the movies as her treat, she realized she was seeing Kasia's face light up for the first time in weeks. "Can we? Really? Mom?" Kasia stared from Hattie to Anya and back.

"Well. I don't . . . I mean I don't want you to . . . Hattie, we can go, but pay too. How much do you think it would cost?"

"I insist," Hattie said, wondering how much of Anya's worry was a result of her finances. Hattie had become used to the meager meals, most of which came from the wonderful but dwindling garden, and the avoidance of anything that was not absolutely necessary.

"I insist. It was my idea. I so want to see that movie. The billboards are everywhere. It sounds really exciting, and

I hate to go to the movies alone. Just could never get used to that."

Kasia threw a beseeching look at her mother.

"Okay, okay. I guess just this once. We could all do with a little outing."

All three cried as the little traveler was befriended by a child and introduced to the ways of a different life. Sitting in the theater, looking up at the motes of illusion rending the darkness, Hattie said a prayer that the grief and hurt had left her for good. Befriending Anya and Kasia had not only helped them, but she had found a respite for herself as well.

That night after Kasia went to bed with her E.T. doll, a last minute purchase as they exited the theater, clutched in her hand, Anya and Hattie settled in the living room rather than on the porch, as there had been a cool snap that day. Gradually it had begun to darken earlier, the year moving imperceptibly away from its midpoint.

As the intimacy between the two women grew, it was very clear to Hattie it was one-sided. But Anya didn't seem to notice that she was the one telling and Hattie was always listening. Hattie felt herself drawn into Anya's story, which was fascinating enough for its own sake, and so much more so for Hattie because of her life with Ben. She was particularly fascinated by the similarities and the differences.

Hattie realized that she had begun to think of Ben-when-he-was-with-Anya as 'the other Ben,' as if he were really two different people. Sometimes Anya's Ben seemed more likable than the Ben she thought of as hers. It was terribly confusing because he both was and was not the same man with each woman. Occasionally, she had to remind herself why she was there. Shaking her head as if to clear away the mesh that obscured intention and volition, she would try to recall Ben as he was twelve years ago.

The two women sat across from each other in the overstuffed chairs in Anya's dingy and cramped living room. From the first moment she had set eyes on the place, Hattie had been taken aback by Anya's choice of furnishings. Hattie's practiced eye told her that even when they had been new, they had not been costly pieces; but that must have been many years before Anya's arrival. Time had not improved them. Though immaculately clean, the place had the shabby, worn quality of an old hotel lobby.

"What an interesting lamp," she began, nodding at the least ugly object in the room, and thinking that she wanted to find out how Anya had come to select these furnishings.

"Oh," Anya replied. "Yes. It's my favorite object in the whole house. Reminds me of home. It's the kind of thing my mother would have chosen. The kind of thing I grew up with."

It was a moment of understanding for Hattie, who continued headlong, "So that's why you chose it. Chose these furnishings. Because they reminded you of home?"

Anya laughed, genuinely amused. "How completely foolish you must think me. And tasteless. To pick out any of this. Yuck!" She made a funny face and laughed again at Hattie's embarrassment and confusion. "No, I didn't pick out any of it. Not one single thing. When Ben found the place, well, you know it was a big rush because we were there in his hotel room. I had nowhere to go. If Hal, my boss, had found out I was there with Ben, I surely would have lost my job. They feared that the hotel would get a bad reputation. As it was, I worried that Clara would call them and tell them something bad about me and I would lose the job that she had found for me. But she didn't. I guess she had enough revenge just knowing that I was missing the cozy place she had made for me."

"Did you keep trying to talk to her?"

"I did, though I knew it was useless. Ben even went over there to try to explain to her just how it had happened so innocently. But she shut the door.

"It was a few days before he had to go on the road again. I didn't let on that I knew when he was leaving, but I was frantic, thinking he would just go and then where would I be and how would I live?

"Ben had found this place. Furnished. In a little newspaper for retired people. I don't know how he came by it. But the woman had gone to a nursing home. She was very old, but hoped she'd mend her broken hip and be able to come back to her house and all her things. She thought it was to be a short term furnished rental. Completely furnished. Just what we, I mean I, for I was going to be by myself, just what I needed. I only had to move my clothing in and begin living. We put all her personal things in the back bedroom. The one you're in. All her personal things. Everything else I had the use of.

"Everyone—us—Mr. Morris, her nephew and her

only relative, thought it a good solution. When a few months passed, it was obvious she wouldn't be coming home, but no one had the heart to tell her. Whether she knew herself wasn't clear. She didn't talk about it."

"What do you mean, talk about it?"

"I visited her many times. I was living here in her house, using her things. It made me feel as if I knew her. I'd come across something, a recipe for corn soup in a drawer or phone numbers penciled on a sheet inside a cupboard, and I'd be reminded of her, of the other life that had taken place here in this house.

"For a long time I was alone in the house. It wasn't too bad. After all, I had my own place and I didn't have to submit to either Clara or Stan. I had my job. But once in a while after work, I'd take the bus out to the south side where Mrs. Morris was in the nursing home. I'd go to visit her, occasionally because I was lonely too. Sometimes I brought her something special I had cooked or food from the garden. She loved that; she particularly loved the currants, saying they reminded her of her childhood. But whatever I brought her, she would make it seem like it was a treasure.

"She was a small, round lady with wonderful eyes, eyes so dark you felt they could take in anything. When she saw me, she'd get really excited. 'You made my day,' she'd say each time I visited. She felt that someone really cared if I came around. I'd be in for an afternoon of stories: What it had been like moving to the house when she was a new bride. The street had just been built, mostly for the workers in the typewriter factory. Her husband was many years older than she was, and he bought the house as a surprise for her, and I couldn't help thinking of Ben and me. You know how people's lives cross each other. Like that." Anya gestured two index fingers crossed in front of her.

"Yes," answered Hattie, though she was not thinking of Mrs. Morris and Anya, but of Anya and herself. "I think of it more as lives seeping into each other. I've felt it myself at times. Especially when you're using their belongings. Like I'm here with you and Kasia and suddenly we're not strangers and I'm not the outsider."

"It's odd, but you never were. Even that first day. There was something . . ."

Feeling herself on the verge of some revelation that might torment them both, Hattie drew the conversation back to safer territory, "And you felt that way about Mrs. Morris?"

"Oh, yes. How happy she was to know I was living here in her house. She was happy to know that there was a garden. She said there had been one many years ago when she was young. She had lived here alone for thirty years after he died. Now I was living here alone. Would it be for thirty years? I didn't think I could stand that."

Thirty years alone played like a chill up and down Hattie's spine.

"Ben had paid the first three months rent on the house before he left. I didn't know if I'd ever see him again. I was afraid to ask. I got better work at the hotel, became a supervisor of the cleaning staff. And I was able to pay the rent out of my wages. I had my own place and I should have been happy. But I wasn't. I longed for Ben to return. After all the trouble I'd caused, I didn't think he'd want to see me again. I felt like my heart was breaking."

Hattie let out her breath slowly. Thinking that she was about to say something, Anya waited. "Yes?"

"Seems to me like he caused all the trouble for you. Not you for him. You were the one whose life was changed . . ."

"Yes. But, oh, if you only knew Ben, you'd know that he would never cause anyone trouble like that. He was horrified by what happened, kept saying to me over and over how sorry he was. How he didn't mean for it to work out that way."

"Still, you were the one who bore the brunt of it. And he probably had ulterior motives."

"Oh, no," Anya cried again. Then she looked at Hattie with a sly smile, "Now you sound like Clara."

Hattie averted her face. What was she doing? Did she really want to shake Anya's faith in Ben? If that was her goal, why didn't she just come out with the whole story? If not, why did she interfere at all? Yet she couldn't stand to have Anya feel as if any of it were her fault. The woman was so vulnerable, so willing to accept blame. Hattie could only imagine how she would react to knowing the pain she had inadvertently caused. "Well, maybe Clara wasn't entirely wrong, that's all I'm saying."

Chapter thirty-nine

"Wescott's General Merchandise and Dry Goods," came her friend's voice and the two worlds collided. Hattie pictured Fenston Corners, the store's cool dark interior, Will at the back meat counter humming and working, the rows of cans neatly aligned on the shelves, the vegetables and fruit on the side counter, and Athena, in a white apron and smiling, offering coffee and fresh muffins at the cashier's station. Suddenly, she longed to be inside her perfectly recollected scene. Or was Fenston also something she had put her faith in that might turn on her at any time?

She couldn't afford thoughts like that. She was very homesick and needed Athena's familiar, "That you, Hattie?" The greeting never failed to cheer her up. Today was no exception. Her friend continued, "I was hoping you'd call today. Everybody has been asking for you. I don't know what you want me to tell them."

"Everybody who?" Hattie asked, surprised at her own pleasure. She pictured the flow of Fenston people though the store.

"Well, Clem and Betty. And of course Tom. Eleanor and Eddie. And Paul makes it his business to stop in every day. 'Any word from Hattie' is now his opening line before he even says hello."

"How is Paul?" The image of her old friend came to mind. Paul was not good looking in a conventional way, but his face was strong and his gaze clear and intelligent. There was something so definite about the man. So sure of himself, so sure of what he was about. He didn't say much but you really knew where he stood on things. Hattie had always appreciated his friendship. He, like Athena and Will, was always there when she needed help.

"He says he wishes you'd come back. Fenston doesn't seem the same without you."

"Oh, really?" Again the rush of pleasure at Hattie's throat.

"Just yesterday he stopped in again in the late afternoon when Will was back from the produce wholesaler. They got to talking about the plan Paul had been developing to install a car wash machine beside his filling station. Will has been encouraging him, says if Paul doesn't do it, somebody from the outside will come in and do it for him. Paul just came right out and said: 'I've changed my mind. Don't think I'll be investing in something new here. Might even sell out and move on.'"

"Now why would he want to do that?" Hattie felt alarm, how could anyone so important to her as Paul just leave. Hadn't she lost enough already?

"Says Fenston's not the only place in the world. And it doesn't seem like the same place at all lately, that's what he said. Before I could stop him, Will started in teasing Paul, 'Think any of this has to do with Hattie's being gone?' Paul got real flushed and looked at Will like he'd like to pop him one in the eye. After a minute, he said, 'I guess Hattie's finding out for herself that Fenston's not the only place in the world too.'" Hattie felt a pang. So that's what they thought, that she'd gone away for a vacation or an adventure. The merry widow. Or maybe that she'd gone looking for a new place to settle down without a backward glance. Nothing could be further from the truth. She missed Fenston more every day and couldn't wait to get back. But for the moment, she couldn't. As if reading her mind, Athena asked, "You are coming back Hattie, aren't you?"

"Gotta go," Hattie answered.

Chapter forty

"For a long time after . . . Well, he just found the place for me, helped me to move in. He didn't desert me. He was kind. Like a friend. He helped me get the things I needed, groceries and everything. Helped me move enough of her things that I could feel the place was mine. Then he went away. I didn't see him again for almost two months."

Hattie wondered what her own life with Ben had been like during those two months. Was that the time they had chaperoned Alice's Girl Scout camp out at the lake? Was it when they had built the gazebo together and sneaked out of the house late one night to make love on a pile of blankets surrounded by the smell of fresh timber? Was it when they had volunteered to head up the food committee for the Fire Company Picnic and a thousand boxes of hot dog rolls had mistakenly been delivered to their house while they were in town? When they got home after only a half-hour trip, they had hardly been able to find the front door through the stacks of boxes on the porch. She and Ben had just sat on the floor amid the stacks and laughed.

"Little by little," Anya's voice jolted Hattie out of her thoughts, "the place began to feel like my own. I was still alone. But Ben began to come around now and then. We'd eat something, then maybe go to listen to some music. I don't know . . . a couple of years went by like that. I made a few friends at work, nobody special, but I went to the movies with them or out to eat. But mostly I was alone. And I didn't mind that. I worked on my English—took some classes. I was content, but nervous, of course, because I had no visa or green card I kept thinking that someday they would trace me and make me go back to Poland."

"Is that why you got married? Because you were going to get in trouble and sent back to Poland?" Hattie was struggling to understand.

"That spring, Ben seemed to be around more than usual. It was the third year I was in the house. One warm night we went over to the lake. We were walking by the shore just being quiet and happy. Two friends. Ben rented a little boat for an hour, and we rowed around the lake, just enjoying the cool air rising off the water and looking at the trees and talking a little about our childhoods and what we thought we wanted from life in those old times."

Again Hattie searched her memory to see if there was

anything she could recall about the summer of 1972, some rift between Ben and herself, some problem they'd had. Nothing remarkable surfaced, though she thought she remembered a party at the Rodiri's, a July picnic and parade, when she and Alice had been alone, as they had been much of the summer. In truth, it could have been the year before or the year after. Looking back, it seemed like they were alone more often than not. Was that how it felt at the time? Oddly, she really couldn't remember.

"I don't know how it happened, neither of us said anything, but that night after we'd come back from the lake. It was at the end of a long stay for Ben in those times, he'd been in town almost three weeks and we'd been together almost every day, mostly working in the garden after we finished our jobs. We'd often eat and go to the lake or for a walk and nothing happened between us. It was an ordinary night for us, but he told me he was leaving the next day.

"Every time he came I hoped the same thing, and nothing happened. He didn't seem to notice that I was a woman. I wondered that he didn't realize how much I was in love with him. I would have been shamed by that. It had been so long and nothing ever was said or done between us. I'd just thought it was impossible, that Ben didn't want the attachment. Maybe the kind of work he had . . . I didn't know. Or maybe he had been hurt once. But that night, when I had given up thinking he could love me and we could be happy, he just stayed. He climbed the stairs behind me and stayed."

The streetlight through the window lit Anya's face and animated her features as she returned to that night long ago, the night that would change so many lives. "Kasia must have been conceived that same night because Ben left the next morning for his work and when he came back two months later, I already knew I was pregnant. When I told him, he was sad and upset. I cried and cried too. I didn't want him to think that I had tricked him or that I was lying to him. After all, we had only been together one time. He didn't try to change my mind when I told him I could never do anything to stop the pregnancy. I was raised Catholic. Even though I didn't practice the religion any more, I still couldn't have an abortion. He said that he could not marry me. Because of his work, he wasn't free like other men. When he left, I didn't know if I'd see him again.

"But the next day, he came back and said: 'Okay, we'll get married.' So many times I'd taken out the half-finished wedding dress I'd made with a heavy heart, thinking I would have to marry Stan. Now the dress was going to be my wedding dress and I was marrying Ben. I loved him so, but I knew, even then, there would be a cloud on everything. That I would just have to take what I could get of him. I promised that I would never try to interfere with his work or keep him from it. And I think I kept the promise, though it wasn't always easy. That is, until . . ."

"Was that 1973?" Hattie couldn't help breaking her rule, asking a question.

Anya looked up curiously too, unaccustomed to any interruption in her reverie of recounting her life. "Let me think. Yes, it must have been. Kasia was born in February. February 1974. And that was the spring before. Late spring."

Suddenly a flood of images surfaced in the night air and Hattie sat pulverized by the memories that inundated her. Summer of 1973—one of the worst times of her life. And somehow it had not added up for her until that moment.

Chapter forty-one

The July heat had driven Hattie indoors from the garden and she had just settled in the kitchen rocker to read when Alice's car tore up the driveway. Before Hattie could make a mental note to complain about her daughter's driving, the door flew open and Alice dashed in, her face pinched around a scream, "Mom. Mom." She dove against Hattie's chest and buried her face as she often had as a child but hadn't for so long. As soon as she could control her sobbing enough to speak, she said, "Gordie's dead."

"What?"

"I was in the store with Aunt Athena. Some guys came from the Army. Took Athena and Will back into the house and shut the door. I could hear them talking, very low, like something serious. Then I heard Athena screaming. I came home to let you know."

Hattie was already on her way out the door.

"I'll drive you," Alice added. Hattie stopped for a minute, thinking that she'd rather go alone. But then who would be with Alice, the little girl who had just lost her best friend. Throughout childhood she and Gordie had been inseparable. When he left for the Marines, Alice cried for weeks. Now Gordie was dead.

The scene at Wescott's was chaos. Most of the people in town had convened and Athena and Will were being showered with questions. Athena sat on her stool behind the counter of the store, her usual station. Sharp-tongued, witty, Athena couldn't utter a word. Each time she opened her mouth to say something her voice broke. Will stood behind her, his eyes flat as dimes, trying to give his neighbors some information. Immediately, Hattie shooed everyone out of the store, then led Athena and Will back into their living quarters, nodding to Alice to lock the door and put up the closed sign.

When the phone rang, Hattie was ready to give the caller hell. But it was Clem Tomkins, the chief, saying that if Hattie would give any information to him, he would see to making the necessary arrangements. For the first time, she was impressed with his insight and professionalism. "Nobody wants to bother Will and Athena and Al, but you know how this town is, your business is everybody's business. For the good and bad of it. If folks can help, they will. But they'll want to find out what's happening. Human nature, I guess. You live so close here . . . Well, you just get any information to me and I'll make sure it gets passed on."

Grateful that she wouldn't have to play watchman, Hattie went back into the kitchen where Will and Athena were still sitting as she had left them, two human rag dolls, shocked into oblivion.

The details of Gordie's death emerged over the next few days. The irony would stay with them forever. When Gordie enlisted, Hattie thought Athena would lose her mind. Seventeen and never been out of Fenston, Gordie went right to combat in Vietnam after basic training and infantry combat training. The only time Athena seemed herself was in the day or two following one of her son's letters. Even Al, her older boy, the type who always did everything right and could be counted on not to cause worry, couldn't bring Athena out of it. Later Hattie couldn't help thinking that Athena must have had some kind of premonition about what was in store for Gordie.

When the cease-fire was declared in January, everyone breathed a sigh of relief. Gordie had only to finish his time as a guard at the embassy and he'd be home. Six months later, he was dead, the victim of sniper-fire while he stood his post.

When Ben called that night, as he usually did, Hattie told him what happened, her voice creaky from overuse and emotion. "It's the worst thing that I can recall happening in Fenston. Oh, God, Ben, you couldn't imagine Athena's face. It's as if someone hit her hard on the back of the head and dislodged her senses. I don't know what to do to help her."

"This is terrible. Oh, God, I can only imagine what they are going through. How's Alice taking it?"

"Not good. She's not saying much, but has locked herself in her room playing all her records from high school, the music she and Gordie always loved."

At the start of the conversation, Hattie assumed that Ben would come home right away. But as they talked she realized it hadn't occurred to him. Hattie caught herself blinking. Finally, when she felt the conversation winding down and Ben had still not mentioned coming home, she said, "I don't know how else to say this. I didn't think I'd have to ask. Ben, I want you to come home."

"I wish I could. It's just not possible."

"You're needed here."

"I can't just drop everything and come."

"Then do it. I've never asked you before. Not even when I was desperately in need myself. But this time it's about our daughter and our closest friends." She felt the tears edging into her voice, not sure if they were tears of sorrow about what had happened to Gordie or tears of frustration that her husband was not doing what she asked.

"You were a Marine, Ben. I'm sure your being here would mean a lot to Will and Athena." She heard her voice become shrill, wheedling.

"But I just left. I was home for the better part of six weeks. I just can't."

"Who knew something like this was going to happen. Don't they understand that emergencies come up?"

"I'm sure you're doing everything that can be done. I just can't come, Hattie." And she heard the dismissive finality in his voice. "I'll spend some time with Will and Athena when I get back. I promise."

Knowing that she could not change Ben's mind, and that she risked his anger if she continued, Hattie held herself back from saying, "And your daughter?"

Waiting was the hardest part, knowing that Gordie would be coming home for the first and last time. Each step of the process they were informed of the body's whereabouts. If they had wanted to, they could trace it on a map as he moved toward them, from Saigon to Danang, then to the Graves Registration unit in San Francisco, then home to Fenston. The silver casket, accompanied by a Marine escort, arrived three weeks after the phone call.

Throughout this period, Hattie did her best to hold Athena together and to comfort Alice who was mourning Gordie by writing raging letters to all public officials and snarling at anyone who came near her. That afternoon in late summer when they stood on the hillside and cried into the blue sky over the loss of a sweet, young boy, Ben had still not returned.

When she recalled that summer, the pain of knowing that Ben was not with them through such an ordeal and could not even be summoned, passed through her body anew; a deep shudder ran up her back to the base of her head as strongly as it had at the time. And suddenly so much of what she had not been able to explain to herself was completely clear, the way she came to realize that she and Ben were not the inseparable unit she had counted on. Their life together was not, probably had not been for a long time, central to him.

After that summer, he would continue to come and go from Hattie and she would continue to close her eyes to her own feelings of diminishment and abandonment. It was so simple—this unspoken agreement between them—that she had never even told herself about it. The pain of that conversation had scabbed over in her heart and become so hidden that she herself had forgotten it was there. Just like she had forgotten the summer of 1973.

Another shudder of shame and recognition shook her. Anya heard it.

Chapter forty-two

"That winter Mrs. Morris died. Her nephew arranged for me to have the house. She had wanted it that way, wrote it down in her will. The nephew came here and told me. I couldn't believe it. All I had to do was to pay the taxes and the house was put in my name. Mr. Morris went through her papers and drawers. I think he took a few pieces of jewelry and some cut glass dishes, really the only good things in the house. Then he told me I could have whatever I wanted and to give the rest to the Salvation Army. Ben and I boxed up all her personal things, her clothes and all, except a few dresses she had in her closet. I kept them to remind me of her, cut them apart for the material to add to the box of cloth, to cancel out the meanness of Clara's fabric. The rest, well, here it is." Anya shrugged and looked around the room as if what she meant was self evident.

"I had always thought that someday I'd have new things. I imagined Ben and me picking out a sofa, a peach-toned soft fabric sofa with loose pillows, and I dreamt how I'd sit there on it at night, and Ben would come in the room and sit beside me."

Anya was silent for a few moments, as if forgetful that Hattie was even sitting there. She closed her eyes. When she spoke again, her voice was full of tears, "More than anything, I imagined lots of afternoons on the lake. It was our favorite thing and once Kasia was born, we took her too. From the very start, she loved the boats and we would put a little life jacket on her and put her in her baby seat between us and go." Anya sighed, floating on the stream of her own memories. Hattie lost herself in them as well, only rousing when Anya concluded, "Instead, well, you know what's happened . . . I'm still here after all these years, no new sofa in sight and Ben missing. Like the old fisherman's wife, I didn't know that I should wish only to hold onto what happiness I had."

Hattie nodded. Her own new grief held its tongue.

Chapter forty-three

That night when Hattie went upstairs, all she wanted was a long, hot bath. While she had been sitting there listening to Anya's story and reliving her own, she had felt herself grow cold and stiff with dread. She needed to escape, to be by herself to think things through. First, she went into the bedroom and flopped down on the bed. The cabbage-rose wallpaper engaged her, as for a time she again counted the bouquets up one side of the wall. After she had finished counting the entire room, she jumped up and began to pace. She felt a terrible pain. Was it her heart? Was this the heartsickness she had heard about in those novels, the heartsickness she had always discredited as self-indulgent crap? She put her hand to her chest and felt around. Yes, the pain was there, a completely physical pain to match the horror of what she was finding out. The pain matched the terror as her mind struggled to absorb this new knowledge, then stepped away from it.

Dear God, she thought. Why had she come? What did she think would happen? Athena had been right all along. She had opened a Pandora's box and now she was going to suffer. Had she really imagined she'd find some shallow, stupid woman, some floozy that Ben had taken up with to amuse himself through some middle-aged male craziness she didn't even know he was feeling, a little distraction while he was on the road? That would have been painful enough, but it might have been a pain Hattie could accept and go beyond.

All the time, she had been convinced that nothing that she could learn or imagine would take away from his real life with her. Now she knew that was not true. Ben had been with Anya in the drama of their life together, rowing on a lake, conceiving a child, moving furniture.

Anya, this innocent, sweet, decent person. This woman who had obviously loved her husband, their husband, and the solidity, the reality of the life they had shared. The weight of all the shabby furniture, the lovely, cared-for garden, the simple pleasure of their time together rowing around a city pond in a rented boat—the joy that Anya took in all of it. Hattie found it impossible to take it all in.

She paused in her pacing and went to the window. Something more was coming to her. Something she had never before considered. What was her role in all this? What had Ben looked for that she couldn't give? It had been enough, up to this moment, to think that he had been disappointed and frustrated that she would not move with him. She could perhaps understand his using that as justification. But tonight, hearing the continuation of Anya's story and recalling the pivotal summer for all of them, Hattie had turned cold at the thought that Ben had returned Anya's love. And where did that leave her? She realized that the certainty she had always had of Ben's love was a delusion. Imperceptibly she began to open her heart to Anya and yet she didn't close it to Ben and his memory. That searing pain was with her still.

Not wanting to see Anya or Kasia just then, she waited until they had both used the bathroom and were in their rooms to draw a tub of scalding water. Then she entered the bath and lay back quietly in the old claw-foot tub, savoring the initial discomfort of the hot water. The bathroom, like the rest of the house, was very clean. Clean and faintly European, though it took Hattie a while to think just how one got that impression—the white lace curtains, the small wooden box of soap. Of course, it all made sense to her now. The lovely stenciling, the exquisite choices of scraps of dishes, how could that have squared with all that ugly wallpaper and furniture? Anya had made her small mark here and there; she had done as much as she could with very little money and a lot of old junk. She never did get a peach sofa to sit on in the evenings with their husband.

Through the window Hattie could hear strains of music, accordion mixed with salsa from two different houses somewhere along the alley. That day she had seen the woman with the bird tending flowers in her backyard, the huge white bird in his cage near her. The woman had lifted the bird out and he preened for her, holding steadily onto her crooked finger. Hattie thought she could hear the woman speak to him. She didn't only say things like "pretty boy" and "hello" and "come on out, sweetie" but other things. She spoke in a low voice, like she would at night to a lover, and she spoke of things that she was desperate to share—the stings of her life she could not trust to anyone else.

Hattie now realized that she would never tell Anya her secret, though she'd imagined telling her many times. Maybe Anya would say once too often how Ben really had a knack for lighting the small antique grill on the back porch or figuring out how to work the television or how he liked pot roast stringy, the carrots and potatoes and onions falling to a sweet mush at the bottom of the pan and Hattie could see herself look across the table and grab up Anya's hand and say "I know."

And she'd look at Hattie as if maybe she had told her that before like that's how she knew. It was easy to imagine blurting it out, but Hattie couldn't let her mind go beyond how Anya would look after she had told her. Already Anya's face had a kind of bashed look, like someone had taken it when it was hot and not quite formed and stretched the edges of it around her mouth on the left side. It was almost as if her expression had run like ink across a wet page. She could hear Anya say, her voice full of wonder and pain, "You know?"

And then, since she was already into the cruelty of it, she heard herself say, "Yes, I've known since the beginning and before that I thought I knew who he was. I was making his pot roast years before you set eyes on him. He was at my table nibbling under my skirt, the lace slips of mine he'd ruined and the curtains—how many times they've billowed around us in the sweet country air. How he'd get out of bed after we had good sex and strut around the room, master of it all, me and the house and the farm and the town. Wouldn't you think that would be enough for him? For anyone?"

But what would be the use of it? Causing Anya pain wouldn't cure her own. And somehow seeing Anya and Kasia suffer any more than they already had would hurt her too. As Hattie's body relaxed in the water she leaned back and thought of the nights in Fenston when she was alone, nights she thought Ben alone on the road. Peering around the edge of the window, the full moon becalmed her. Even though it was the first harvest moon she'd ever seen anywhere but over the ridge between Fenston and Crystalle, it was the same luminous presence whose steadiness at least would not desert her.

Chapter forty-four

They'd make an outing of buying school clothes. Hattie and Kasia left early and headed for the new shopping plaza at the edge of the city where some good outlet stores had recently opened. At first they seemed to walk aimlessly. Hattie was drawing on her experiences shopping with Alice, which told her she should not offer or suggest, but follow along waiting for Alice to get excited about something. Normally it didn't take very long before they were in the dressing room with armloads of outfits for Alice to try on.

A half-hour of circling the store and Kasia had not even stopped to fondle a sweater. She seemed unsure of what to do. Finally, Hattie took charge, "Look at this, Kasia. Do you think you'd like a skirt like this? I think blue looks very nice on you with your eyes." Hattie judged the child positively relieved as she eagerly held the shirt out in front of her. The sales clerk who materialized at their elbow said, "I'd say a size 8 seems just about right." Kasia smiled at Hattie's next choice as well. And the next.

"Don't you have an idea of what you'd like, dear? I don't want you to take things just because I like them."

"Oh, Hattie, they're so pretty. I'd like any of them." Suddenly, the child's mood shifted.

"Then why the worried face?" Hattie asked, having noticed Kasia's expression.

"Nothing. But . . ."

"But?"

"Well, Mom was worried that you'd spend too much money. She says we need to get along on a little less for a while, until Papa comes home."

She bent to look into the child's face. "I don't want you or your mom to worry about that. I'll pay and when your father gets back, we'll work it out. Okay?"

"Okay," Kasia replied, but her small face didn't reflect complete conviction.

"Trust me. It will be okay." And Hattie took the armload of clothes they had collected and led Kasia to the dressing room. Every outfit she put on fit perfectly and looked lovely. And Kasia was thrilled. If they had little personality in common, Kasia and Alice had the same coloring and body type. Hattie noticed the long straight legs and graceful body. Like Alice, Kasia's feet were long and narrow and she had the natural poise of a dancer. "Have you thought about taking dancing lessons? Ballet or jazz maybe?"

"Oh, I don't know. Usually I don't have time to do the after school things. It's too hard to get the rides. Mama doesn't drive. When I get older and can take the bus alone, I can be in something."

"Yes. Well, maybe dancing isn't the thing for you. But . . . you should at least try it." Hattie was struggling with herself. How much could she intrude into their lives? How much did she dare suggest to Anya and Kasia? She wished she could just do more, like volunteering to pick up Kasia from the after school activities. Trying to help them without their realizing how much she was helping was hard. Anya had been sick in bed for a few days, "The flu," she said, refusing Hattie's offer to help her. It seemed amazing to Hattie that Anya had been able to do the hard work in the motel just a few years earlier; now her strength seemed so limited and she always seemed tired. Hattie had easily convinced her to let her take Kasia shopping.

After the dresses, they got a new pair of shoes for school, new sneakers, a heavy jacket, a hat and boots, underwear and socks. Hattie had helped Kasia go through her drawers to make a list of what was needed. She realized that the child had almost nothing that fit. How could she go back to school without clothes? The little jet of anger at Ben for leaving them in this situation flared again.

It was clear that Anya was running out of money and just hoping that Ben would return. What would have happened to them if Hattie had not come along?

As she was paying for the clothes, Hattie was aware

of Kasia's movement at the front of the store. The little girl was standing very quietly looking closely at the display of Girl Scout uniforms and paraphernalia. She signaled to the clerk to wait, and she walked over to Kasia. "Girl Scouting, now there's a great pastime for girls." A clear picture of Alice in her Scouting uniform rose before Hattie.

But it was Kasia who beamed up at her, "Yes. They have it across the street from the school. In the church. The girls get to wear their uniform to school on Thursday. All the scouts."

"Is that something you think you'd like, Kasia? Being a Scout is great fun, you know."

"I'm too young for Scouts. This year I'd be in Brownies. Next year, I'd fly up. That's what they call it when you finish being a Brownie and are old enough to be a real Scout." Slowly she moved around the rack until she found the uniform for Brownies, a size 8. "What else do we need to be a Brownie?" she asked the clerk, remembering the beanie and sash and badges of Alice's youth. When all the elements were assembled, she said, "We'll take it. I'll tell Mom that I'll arrange to pick you up on Thursdays." Kasia's face glowed with delight.

When they left the store, Kasia insisted on carrying the bag containing her Brownie uniform. Hattie carried the worry that Anya would resent her making such a decision without consulting her. But there it was. She'd done it on instinct, knowing how few pleasures Kasia had had lately. If she wanted to be a Brownie, Anya would just have to understand.

Hattie was surprised by how much she was enjoying the outing. Once she had Kasia loosened up and talking, she could hardly shut her up. Hattie heard about the personalities and clothing of every girl who had been in Kasia's class last year. Over a lunch of toasted cheese sandwiches and chocolate milkshakes, they talked about what Kasia should do if someone teased her about her big feet again. Last year one of the boys had given her the nickname canoe foot and she had cried more than once at the taunt.

On the way out of the mall, Hattie detoured into a toy store. "Just checking to see if they have my favorite game," she said. Up and down the aisles they went and emerged with a new lunch box and pencil box, tablets and pencils for Kasia and a brand new game of *Clue* for Hattie.

The heat from the parking lot blacktop in the blazing fall afternoon sun hit them as they walked out of the mall. While they were inside, the temperature had jumped back to summer. They sat in a stupor while Hattie got the car running, opened the windows to air things out. When the air conditioner came on, she closed the windows and drove off. Kasia was quiet and Hattie glanced over to see if she had fallen asleep, but her eyes were wide open and she was staring as if she saw something unpleasant but unavoidable. After a few moments, Hattie said softly, "Kasia, is everything all right?"

"I love everything we got. I never went shopping like that before, buying so many things."

"So why the glum look? You should be happy now, looking forward to school."

"I am. And Brownies. I can't wait. But . . ."

"But what? Is there something else you need for school?"

"No. It's not about that."

"Well, then, what gives?" Hattie tried to keep her eye on the girl despite the traffic she was navigating. Finally, she pulled off into a drug store parking lot. "Kasia, what is it? You can tell me and I'll try to help."

"You know, Hattie, he's not coming home. Papa has gone away and he'll never come home. Just like Mama's father, he's gone." The child looked up almost begging Hattie to tell her she was wrong. Hoping that Hattie, the buyer of new clothes and provider of memorable entertainments, would be able to solve this terrible problem, Kasia wanted reassurance.

Hattie choked back emotions. Unable to speak, she held up her arms and Kasia slid into them and buried her face in Hattie's chest. For a moment, time stopped: Hattie rested her cheek on Kasia's head, stroking her golden hair and smelling the faint mixed scent of shampoo and childhood. Hold onto the moment, she told herself, as she murmured and patted. Kasia continued to sob for a few minutes then said, "He's not coming back. I just know it. And I'm not sure Mama does. She's sick and I'm afraid to tell her that he's not coming back."

Finally, Hattie said as much as she could, "Darling, no one knows the future. No one. But you know that your father loves you and if he possibly could he would come back right away. And you have your mother and me . . ."

Hating what she was about to do but recognizing that she must do it, Hattie tried hard to formulate her question so that it didn't appear to Kasia that she was being pumped for information. "Does anyone else come to your house?"

The child looked at her, confused and questioning. "Besides Papa?"

"Yes. Besides your father. Does your mom have any relatives?"

"Only Uncle Piotr. And he's in Poland. He doesn't come to see us. But . . ."

"But?"

"Uncle Piotr wrote to Mama. But she left the letter on the table and didn't open it."

As casually as she could Hattie asked, "And do you remember when this was. When she got the letter?"

"Before you came. Before Papa went away for good. I think it was in the winter."

"Last winter?" Hattie tried to control the excitement in her voice. Maybe there was someone else who could be called on. She recalled Anya's story about Piotr. But if he had been trying to make contact with Anya, maybe he had changed. Until just that moment, she hadn't realized just how frantic she felt about what was happening at 321 Gordon Street or how trapped and responsible.

"Yes," Kasia said. "I'm pretty sure it was last winter. I could read the printing and knew the letter was for Mama. I knew by the paper it was a letter from a far away place. And I read the stamp," she said, her voice full of pride at how clever she was. "We learned about stamps in school."

Chapter forty-five

The familiar box was open on the table before them when Hattie realized how her own mind had tricked her. An impulse. Maybe to keep up the momentum of their connection, perhaps in anticipation of the fun they would have playing, but before they left the mall she had wanted to get something that she and Anya and Kasia would all enjoy. *Clue* was a game she recalled from Alice's childhood as a pleasant evening's entertainment where the three of them would struggle to uncover the place, weapon and murderer. She had pulled that game from the array of boxes both familiar and new since her last round of game purchasing some ten or more years earlier. Now the three were perched around the old square coffee table waiting to find out if Mr. Mustard had indeed used the candlestick in the pantry. In her sweat pants and fuzzy slippers, Anya looked like a child, perhaps a few years older than Kasia. Her blond hair was loose upon her shoulders, softening the pinched, gaunt face. At her mother's feet, Kasia perched on a hassock engrossed in the board and trying to hold in mind all the variations of human folly.

It was Hattie's turn, and she wanted to get back to the billiard room. Eagerly she tapped out the squares of her turn but still didn't have the right answers. Suddenly the irony suggested by her unconscious choice amused and amazed her. Would she ever get to the place where she would have the answers she needed? And since there was no way anyone could be a real winner in this complex situation, what would success involve anyway?

When she had first set out on her odyssey, she thought it would mean that she would find out what Ben's life had been like away from home. Never in her wildest thoughts could she have foreseen what had happened to her in the few short weeks she'd been in Hartford.

Later, her quest had increasingly come to resemble the end of a difficult and tortuous puzzle. Hattie felt that if only she could fit all the pieces together, she would be able to solve some kind of riddle, figure out the tricks of this complicated life. While she was still being confronted daily with things she didn't know about Ben and Anya's life together, she had long since abandoned trying to solve the puzzle of human relationships. And she was gradually coming to understand that knowledge in itself would not make her free. Would anything?

Now she understood her own behavior as the key to what she needed to learn from the events since Ben's death. It was up to her to take in this awful situation, some of it of her own making (at least in as much as she didn't share what she knew), and then to somehow do the right thing.

But it went beyond that, she thought, as she looked across at Anya and Kasia, and felt an immense wave of tenderness and joy, a bond to this woman and child that she could not even explain to herself. She knew, with every fiber of her mind and body, that she had to honor that ineffable sense she had of their having been entrusted to her as a way of allowing her to understand something important about herself.

Anya looked over and said, "I don't think we've had this much fun in a long time." Then she nodded toward Kasia, "We could all use a little more of it around here. Thank you, Hattie."

Kasia lifted her head from the board's deep hold on her imagination and echoed her mother, "Yeah, thanks, Hattie. This is really great."

Hattie smiled. For however things would turn out, she knew that she had taken Ben's other wife and child into her heart and they had become her family.

It was her turn and Hattie tossed and tapped out her steps, gave her guess and understood one more thing about who had done what, where and how. If this other, more complex puzzle weren't her own life, she might be able to think of herself as some determined, talented detective unearthing the path a life took before it made a fatal error in judgment. Could she simply chalk up everything that happened to Ben's mistake of inviting a young woman singing in the hall of a motel to hear some music? And that one gesture, given the person Ben was, had inevitably lead to all of his other kindnesses to Anya, his sparing Hattie, his leading this strange double life.

Could it be that what we think of freedom or free will is only free for that one fatal choice? And after that our own personalities take over, she thought, and after that our routines, and suddenly we're in the track of a course that we cannot escape.

Chapter forty-six

After their shopping excursion together, there were many discussions about how to fix Kasia's hair for the first day of school and which of the five new outfits they had bought would be worn. Kasia spent hours rearranging the new supplies in the tiny compartments of her new pencil box and filling and pouring her lunch milk from the new E.T. lunch box thermos. She worried aloud that she had forgotten how to do her math problems from the previous year and took out some old papers to remind herself. Once school started, Kasia often waited until Hattie came into the kitchen after work to begin her homework, as if she needed contact with Hattie to verify that she was capable. Hattie sat watching the little girl gnarl up her forehead around a problem then relax as the solution floated out of its hidden spot in her brain. "See. I didn't forget," Kasia cried. "I just didn't remember." Hattie laughed at this paradoxical truism, one of many she recalled hearing from a child.

In the late afternoon sun's trick of light, it could have been her other life. It might have been twenty years earlier when Alice was that child. Unaccountably, a prayer came to her for Kasia, for the life the child would have ahead of her. Hattie felt such sorrow and tenderness for what Kasia would have to cope with in her life. It was more than just having Ben disappear and Anya being so sickly and distracted. Kasia and Anya lived in such isolation.

Coming from Fenston, she knew she had a different attitude about neighborliness than city people. Even so, she could not get used to the fact that people would come and go, sit side by side on their porches and seldom say a word to each other beyond a brief hello. Weren't they curious? She herself wanted to find out about the people next door. But days went by and the people seemed to change so often. She'd just get it in her mind that she would speak to the woman hanging clothes across the alley and then the woman would disappear. The next day someone altogether different would drive a car into the yard and begin working on its vital parts. The only steady presence, the constant but unreachable point amid people who came and went, was the old woman with the bird. Despite her curiosity about the neighbors, especially the bird-woman, for that is how she had begun to think of her, Hattie felt herself slipping into the same pattern, nodding politely and exchanging a courteous hello, but nothing beyond that. By mid-October she didn't even notice that it had happened.

Chapter forty-seven

Later Hattie would recall that for a long time she had had the uneasy feeling that there was something wrong with Anya, something more than allergies, more than depression and its resulting fatigue, more than worry over what had become of Ben. She'd think back and wonder that she didn't make more of an effort to find out what was going on. But her focus was on Ben's life and trying to understand what it had been like for him here with Anya and Kasia. She didn't let those other thoughts filter into her consciousness, though ironically they would come to play a large part in solving the mystery that surrounded Ben.

Often during the day as she went around the city, she thought about Anya and Kasia and their situation. If she didn't tell anyone what she knew she'd go mad. But whom could she tell? Not Anya. She'd already allowed herself to be innocent so long and had accepted so many of Anya's confidences that to tell now would seem the worst kind of betrayal. Anya had already had enough of that. And she couldn't tell Athena. Bad enough, the times she'd called all Athena had wanted to hear about was when she was coming home. She'd already blurted out more than she'd intended to and now she regretted it. Athena simply couldn't understand what Hattie was doing, why she had come and why she stayed. Small wonder. Hattie couldn't understand it herself. Although Hattie missed Athena very much, she knew that she didn't want to risk any more revealing conversations with her.

Kasia grew sadder and sadder. Hattie recalled when Alice used to get into those moods; how she'd feel helpless waiting for her daughter to tell her what was wrong. How much did Kasia understand about what was happening? Where did she think her father had gone? Where did she go in her mind when Hattie caught her looking around with that lost expression? Hattie wanted to help, but didn't know how.

Toward the end of October, Anya seemed more depressed than usual and unable to shake off a long bout of flu. The fatigue, the shortness of breath, the pinched, thin cough, were hanging on. Hattie lay in bed thinking over some of the events of the last days. Then, as had happened so often to her, she slept easily but woke and looked at the clock to see she had only been asleep for three hours.

Suddenly the dream that had awakened her flooded back. Ben. God, would she never rid herself of him? The room, the whole house smelled of him. Was the dream continuing? She wasn't sure whether she was awake or asleep. Ben stood naked over her bed speaking to her with his own voice but with Anya's heavy accent, the words rolling from his mouth as if he were a waterfall of sound she couldn't distinguish. His face was suffused with light and in the dream, if it was a dream, Hattie knew that she should be terribly angry with him, but couldn't remember why. She didn't feel, as she had each moment since she found Anya, the betrayal sitting heavy as a stone in her heart. Aroused, she saw the pendulum of his sex, felt it rub along her arm as he leaned over her. His words. She realized he was singing, the song before sex, "And a wayward wind . . ." plaintively came from Ben's lips, his voice in Anya's accent gradually becoming intelligible as Hattie relaxed into her own arousal.

Despite her anger, she wanted Ben to make love to her; she felt her love for him as some hunger almost outside herself. She tried to move her arms but couldn't, she couldn't reach out for him. He stopped singing and now in his own voice began telling her over and over again, the words becoming clearer as he spoke, that he should not have had to die, what he had done was not so terrible. He had just become enmeshed in something. Couldn't she understand that? What else could he have done?

The pressure of his scrotum on her arm diminished and she felt tears sear the edges of her eyes. Suddenly she was aware of the room again though she continued to lie there, feeling heavy and full as after sex. The relentless noise of the city around her and the weight of quiet rooms down the hall registered. Ben had transferred something to her, something she didn't want, but couldn't refuse.

She must have slept again because she awoke at seven to Kasia's small noises in the bathroom. Hattie lay there holding onto the dream, trying to sort out what had happened to her during the night. She touched herself and thought she even smelled Ben in the bed with her. She dozed again and woke with a clarity of purpose she fully understood. Relieved, Hattie finally knew why she had come: Ben had sent her.

Chapter forty-eight

The next day, the last Sunday of October dawned bright and warm. Lying in bed, Hattie comforted herself by thinking about the beauty of late summer in Fenston. In her imagination, she walked back to the edge of her land, where the orchard, surrounded by its stone wall, gave onto acres of wilderness. The apple trees were heavy with bright colors and the scent of late grasses rose to her. The picture was comforting as she felt the warmth and heard the soft clear syllables of a grosbeak.

Looking more rested and healthier than she had in a long time, Anya was already in the kitchen making breakfast for Kasia when Hattie came downstairs. They both smiled at her and a wedge of light from the window fell across her chair. She slid into its warmth. "What a gorgeous day."

"Yes," Anya and Kasia said almost as one and with the same inflection. As Kasia moved around the room, her hair caught and held the golden light.

"Don't you two ladies think it's about time for an outing? We've been sitting around the house for weeks. Let's just get in the car and go someplace."

"Where will we go?" Kasia squealed, instantly alert and hopping up and down in excitement.

"I don't know my way around here too well. But rumor has it that there's a lake not too far from here. Maybe we can find our way there." She looked over at Anya who was at the sink with her back turned. In the set of her shoulders, Hattie couldn't read any reaction.

"Mama, Mama, could we?" Kasia was almost shrieking now. "Maybe we could go out in a boat, like we . . ."

"I don't know. It seems so far. I don't know," Anya said finally, the accustomed weariness returning to her voice, after Kasia rushed over to her imploringly.

Immediately, Hattie realized what a blunder she had made. How could she think she could make up to Anya and Kasia for Ben's absence by taking them to one of their favorite places, the place they had all enjoyed as a family? The lake would only make them sad. And after everything Anya had told her, she knew she'd be bringing depression down on herself as well, as she pictured Anya and Ben on that fateful night, rowing peacefully along on a course that would change all their lives.

Thinking quickly, Hattie added, "But there's probably something else we can do too. I also hear there's a wonderful zoo not very far away. I haven't been to a zoo in the longest time. I want to see the lions. What about you, Kasia? What's your favorite animal?"

"The seals! The baby seals! In kindergarten we went to the zoo. It's cool. Oh, Hattie, you're the best."

She felt a flush of pleasure at Kasia's remark, but registered just the slightest change in the set of Anya's shoulders. She looked toward Hattic with a mixture of gratitude and something else. Maybe resentment, Hattie thought. But how could that be? Anya's tone implied a lack of enthusiasm but she agreed, "The zoo sounds fine. Why don't we see what's left in the garden to pack for a picnic lunch?" As they readied for the outing, Hattie went back again and again to Anya's complicated expression.

When they got there, Kasia had raced ahead from one area to another determined to see everything. After Anya tired, she sat on a bench in the shade and Kasia dragged Hattie back to the seals. And one more time to the bat house that had fascinated both of them. They stood in the bluish light looking at the tiny dark figures hanging upside down in clusters like some kind of gruesome bruised fruit. Kasia skipped in delight when they went back into the sunshine to meet Anya and go home. As Hattie backed the car out of the parking space, she looked over at Anya who seemed distracted and exhausted.

Chapter forty-nine

Again Hattie had fled to the bathroom to escape Anya's words: "Ben loved Kasia so much. I don't know how he could just abandon her. Even if he didn't love me anymore, he couldn't have stopped loving her. I just don't understand. He left May 15. Just drove away like it was an ordinary business trip, just like always. Packed his suitcase, folded each shirt, wrapped his shoes and put his shaving kit together, and left. Before he went, he said this time it would be different. This time when he came back, he would be back for good. He seemed so optimistic about getting a new assignment closer to home. He said he would just tell them that he had responsibilities now, that he needed another kind of job. Then he just left. Oh, God, how could he do that?"

They were standing in the kitchen unpacking after the day at the zoo when suddenly Anya, sad and preoccupied all day, began to cry. After all the weeks of her bravery, her confidence that there was some explanation for Ben's inexplicable absence had evaporated, and she broke down. Hattie instinctively put out her hand to touch Anya when she realized the woman was shaking all over, not just with the tremors of crying, but deep shivers convulsing her entire body. Identifying, Hattie felt grief like an undigested meal sitting at her own center as she watched Anya's anguish.

The woman's wispy hair fell over her face as she covered it with her hands. Hattie thought again that she had never seen anyone so vulnerable. Anya's shoulders were almost as narrow as Kasia's. Looking down, Hattie saw her own average, size seven feet, huge next to Anya's. As Anya sobbed, Hattie felt her own throat tighten as she was overcome by tenderness. Murmuring soft syllables, she held Anya patting and shushing her as her own tears started. They stood in an embrace until their tears subsided.

"But you don't know. He may have been detained by his work. Didn't you tell me he was often away for long periods?"

"Yes. But no matter what, he always called me, always. He called me from the road that day, a little earlier than usual, around 4:30. Now it's been four months and not a word. The worst part is that there is no one I can call. No work number, no one to contact, nothing."

Curious, Hattie asked, "And why's that?"

"Well, I'm not really supposed to tell anyone. But I guess since it's you it's okay. And besides with Ben gone so long what does it matter. Ben had a very important job for the government, a secret job. He made me promise never to ask about it because he couldn't tell me anything. Of course I didn't."

"A secret job. I see," Hattie responded.

"Yes. And he was trying to get a transfer to a different job. He wanted to be around more now that . . ."

"Let's just sit and have some tea. You're really tired out. Tea will fix you up." Hattie spoke with all the cheer she could muster, amazed at her own voice and how the words seemed to come of their own volition. She was amazed that she could speak like this without displaying her emotions, which at that very moment she was experiencing as a continuous kicking in her abdomen, a hyena of grief and fury struggling to get out.

She guided Anya to the table and set out the tea things, all the while struggling to hold onto her own composure. She refused to let her mind process May 15. She held the date like a knife blade, away from herself: May 15, May 15—not sure how long she could sustain the tension before she just let it fall and pierce her heart.

A half-hour later, Kasia came in from the garden. By then Anya had stopped shuddering and smiled at her daughter with unclouded blue eyes, "Come, Kasia, let's have a quick snack, then bed. It's been a big day."

As Anya busied herself with her daughter's cookies and juice, Hattie dashed to the bathroom, carrying with her this latest terrible revelation. Hattie didn't have Ben to herself even on the day of his death. Ben had called Anya for the last time less than an hour before he arrived in Fenston. Somewhere along the road on his way home to her, he had stopped and phoned and reassured Anya that he loved her and would soon be with her and their daughter again. She thought of Ben packing his bags here in Anya's house, preparing for a trip to Fenston, as if this, not his home there with her, were his real place in the world.

He was on his way home to her to confess what he had done and to leave her, for surely that's what he had intended when he told Anya that he was going to get a different job, one that allowed him to be home.

But something didn't feel just right about it. Why after all these years of his double life would he want to change things? He had been getting away with a life that was the stuff of mysteries and obviously relishing it. Suddenly he wanted to give it all up, her and the farm and Fenston and Alice and everything their life had been about. Would he really want to live here all the time with Anya and Kasia? Hattie could hardly believe that. Ben was a lover of the small luxuries their life afforded. Since her arrival at Anya's door—seeing the shabby conditions they lived in—Hattie could hardly conceive of Ben living here even part-time.

Gazing out of the window at the garden, Hattie convinced herself that she could not go on with the charade any more. She would just leave. She had found out what she needed to know, and now she could just go back home and deal with her own emotions. If she continued to hold her grief and fury inside, she felt she would explode. And what could she even hope for if she stayed?

There would be no conclusive answers to anything. The only one who could explain Ben's actions was Ben. She knew that if she returned to Fenston, time would heal her. Surrounded by all her friends and belongings and the familiar views and the solitude of her woods, she would come to terms with the truth about Ben. And then she might be able to get on with life.

Chapter fifty

Later, she would think it was her desire to find out one last little bit about Ben or that fate had driven her to it, but whatever the case, Hattie stood in front of the bathroom sink looking at the green vines and pink flowers that Anya had stenciled on the wall around the medicine cabinet. Only knowing Anya's present lack of energy and enthusiasm, Hattie could hardly imagine her perched on the sink executing the delicate and tedious work.

Then she did something she'd never done before; without even thinking, she reached up and twisted the small metal tongue and opened the old wooden cabinet. Ben's presence was in evidence in the form of a small bottle of Canoe, his favorite scent and a vial of his sinus medicine. The rest of the shelves were given over to a range of prescription bottles, more than a dozen of them, all for Anya Darling. Hattie fingered one after the other, none of the names of the drugs were familiar to her, but something came into her mind—Anya's deterioration. And then something else, the small piece of paper, which had begun her odyssey. The doctor's name matched the name on the many vials of medicine she found inside the cabinet.

Chapter fifty-one

"Time has speeded up," Hattie blurted out as soon as Athena answered the phone.

Usually it gave Hattie comfort to think of Athena in the store at Fenston Corners, picking up the old-fashioned rotary phone she and Will refused to get rid of. Often she'd hear snatches of conversation from her old neighbors as they shopped, and this fortified her connection to her former life, a connection she very much needed, as her real life was beginning to seem less and less real every moment. Today she was so distracted she could hardly keep her mind on what she was doing.

"When are you coming home, Hattie?" Athena said in an uncharacteristically short tone. "All manner of things are going on here and you're needed. Tom had to go into the hospital for tests. And Eleanor's kids are running wild. I wish you could talk to her about it. She's driving me crazy coming over at all hours of the day and night and wanting me to tell her what she should do."

Hattie smiled at her mental image of the whole town of Fenston holding its collective breath until she got back.

"You're just trying to get me to come back by emphasizing duty. And I know it. It won't work. I'll come back when I'm finished here."

"What does that mean?"

"When I've found out everything I need to know about Anya and Ben."

"I'm telling you, you're charting a dangerous course for yourself and for them. How many people are going to get hurt till you know what you need to know? And the main one, I'm afraid, is going to be you."

"I didn't call for a lecture, especially one I've heard before," Hattie shot back. "I promised I would call and I have, but I'm not going to stand still for your opinions unlimited."

Athena backed off and changed her tone, "Okay, so what's going on there?"

"I found out that Anya has no idea where Ben is. She didn't know he was married. Or anything."

"What did she know?"

"Can you believe he told her he had a secret job with the government? Had to be strictly confidential, something like the FBI. That's why he was gone so long at a time. And why she couldn't know whom he worked for exactly or how to get in touch with him; that's why he gave her cash to run the house rather than a paycheck. He kept all his Harden stuff in the car, just like he did at home. Remember how he always used to say his office was in the trunk."

"Oh, my God! I can't believe Ben doing something like that."

"So far, I figured out that he just went from one lie to the other, inventing a cover-up as he needed it. And the money they lived on; I guess that was his expense account. I'm surprised he never got into trouble with Harden over it."

"Seems incredible. Ben turning out to be such a bum. Who would have credited it? What kind of a nitwit is she to believe that stuff, anyway?"

"He was her husband and she believed him just like I did."

"Her husband?"

"They were married, Athena."

"Hattie, what in God's name do you mean? He was your husband."

"Yes, but they went through a ceremony and they had a license. For all she knows he's her husband and only hers."

"Now let me get this straight. She thought she was married to someone who had a secret job and she had no way of getting in touch with him for weeks on end. And she didn't think anything was strange about that arrangement? And neither do you?"

"Well, of course I do. But maybe that's only because I know what I know now.

"There's a name for Ben—bigamist. And not much else you have to know about it."

"Everything isn't always that clear. Now that I've found out what he did, I have to stay here until I figure out why he did it. I know Ben, or thought I did. I have to try to understand what happened."

"He did it. I don't know as there's much more to it. What could explain a thing like that, short of simply losing his mind? And, her, like I said, she must be some kind of nitwit herself to have believed him."

"No more than I was, I guess, when Ben would be in New England for a month or more straight without coming home. When I think about it now, I can't believe that I didn't suspect something. Athena, this is the 1980s; people go to China and back in a month. Not just a few hundred miles away."

"Yes, I have to admit, you didn't have your eyes open either. Or if you or anyone else sensed something was wrong we just closed our eyes to it."

"Are you saying you thought something was wrong?"

"Not thought, exactly, but every once in a while, I'd get this strange feeling about Ben, like he was there but not there, if you know what I mean. Not anything in particular that he did, just how he acted sometimes like he was not paying attention to what went on around him in Fenston, like it didn't matter."

Athena's words stung Hattie and she was baffled by her own feelings. Why would she feel protective of Ben after all she had found out? How could she still care for him? But the truth was that though she was furious at him, she had not banished him from her thoughts and feelings. And she didn't like Anya being referred to as a nitwit either. Finally she said, "I'm in such a state right now. Half the time I wish he could come back to life so I could kill him for what he did to me; the other half of the time, I want to kill him for what he did to her. And then I have these periods where I envy her that she doesn't know he's dead."

There was more but Hattie felt too ashamed to admit she'd like to pretend that he might walk back into her life too. Ashamed to almost think she'd be willing to go back to having her share of him and letting Anya have hers.

"Think of what you're saying. He cheated on you, left you alone all the time, and now you find out he had another wife somewhere else." Athena was almost screeching into the phone.

"And a child," Hattie added softly.

"What are you saying? They had a child together? This is impossible . . ."

Hattie cut her off before she could finish, "Athena, it sounds busy in the store, I'll let you go. Call you again when I can." And Hattie hung up before her friend could protest.

Chapter fifty-two

In the little cubicle in the studio where they recorded for the blind on Park Street, Hattie had worked her way through *The Three Musketeers* and *Pride and Prejudice*, neither of which interested her very much. But Mr. Miles would meet her at the door, never failing to compliment her on her dedication and skill at reading the dialogue. Something about the work made Hattie very happy. For the first time since she had quit her job to marry Ben and keep house in Fenston, she was doing something unrelated to a woman's daily chores. Often she imagined a blind person groping along a bookcase of Braille-embossed cassettes and settling back in a chair and smiling as Hattie's voice unveiled a mysterious and delightful world.

When she opened the cover of *Sister Carrie* and read

the first few pages, she knew it was a book she'd love. As she read, she thought about the lives she and Anya and Kasia had, how they had come to be joined by fate or chance or misfortune—whatever you chose to call it, it was certainly an odd collision of souls.

Mr. Miles stopped by her booth twice one afternoon and smiled in at her through the small window. The first month that Hattie read, despite her declaring that she was married, he continually asked her out for coffee and tried to detain her on her way out of the studio with long conversations. Firmly but politely, Hattie refused the invitations and moved the talk away from the personal. Finally, it appeared he had given up the flirtatiousness. As she left the building for the day, he motioned her aside.

"Just wanted to let you know I found someone. Janice. She's wonderful. A widow. About our age. She had almost given up on meeting someone and then we bumped into each other in the Safeway. It just happened." Hattie pictured the two—carts full of vegetables and canned goods—careening into one another, and, after an embarrassed exchange of apologies, starting up a lively conversation.

"I'm so glad for you," she said, meaning it; and glad for herself, too, that Mr. Miles would be less talkative when she worked.

When she left the center that afternoon, Hattie drove through the lovely neighborhoods of West Hartford. The beautiful houses set back on manicured lots reminded her of her own home in Fenston.

Turning onto another street of expensive homes, the

luxurious life it reflected made her wonder what kind of life she would have had if she had come to Hartford with Ben all those years ago when he had wanted her to. Would they have lived in an area like this? Surely, they would not have lived anywhere near Gordon Street.

Back at the little row house, the wonderfully warm unseasonable weather would call them into the yard in the evening. Hattie and Anya were working in the garden and Kasia playing nearby with Mickey, one of the neighbor kids, when Hattie asked the girls if they knew how to play statues. Both looked at her with delight and interest.

"Come here," Hattie said, taking Kasia by the arm and slowly twirling her in a circle. "Now when I let go of your arm, you let your body move through the air and when you stop you must stay absolutely still where you land."

Kasia and her friend Mickey were enchanted. Over and over, Hattie twirled them and let go as the girls spun and stopped in the lovely ballet of a summer evening.

"That was so neat," Kasia said, when Hattie finally pleaded fatigue and went to sit on the porch steps to catch her breath. "How do you know all these games?" Kasia asked. As it had gotten too dark to work in the garden, Anya joined them on the steps. She looked inquiringly at Hattie too.

"You remember my telling you about *my* little girl?"

"Yes," Kasia said, "Where is she?" The child looked at Hattie as if she could miraculously produce the other child.

"Well, strange things happen, you know. Little girls have a way of growing up right before our eyes. Just like you are doing now. That's what happened to her. One day she was a little girl with blond hair and with gaps between her front teeth and with dirt on her face and hands. She liked to play in the woods with her friends. They'd come into the kitchen and I'd make them picnic lunches to take with them when they set out for an adventure. Peanut butter and banana sandwiches and a kind of punch they liked to call bug juice. Now she's a nurse out in California."

The old games that Alice and her friends enjoyed in the backyard in Fenston played a time trick on Hattie. It could have been last week when she looked out the kitchen window to check on the children. Time complicates things so, she thought. How can you explain to a child how slowly it passes and how quickly it is gone? It could have been the same summer twilight evening that Alice's friends dotted the back meadow with their lithe and glowing statues. Now here was Kasia.

"Your girl, what's her name?" Kasia asked, drawing Hattie back.

"Alice. She's twenty-five. All grown up and off on her own." Hattie looked at Alice's little half-sister, wondering again if she had the right to keep their existence away from each of them. What would it mean to Alice to know that she was not an only child? Would it cancel out the hurt that her father had lived a secret life away from them? Hattie second-guessed her decision once again, but came up with the same conclusion.

"Did you have a husband too?" Kasia asked.

Anya, who had been sitting behind Hattie on the stoop steps and listening quietly said, "Now, Kasia, you're asking too many questions," the edge to her voice telling Kasia that she was going too far.

"I don't mind. It's a natural enough question. I guess you're both curious about it. Yes, I did have a husband, but he died. Quite unexpectedly, he died." Hattie considered what she'd say if Kasia asked his name too, but both Anya and Kasia flinched at the knowledge that husbands could suddenly die. Ben was palpable among them.

"Sorry," Kasia said, her long face reflecting her sadness.

"It's all right. I don't mind talking about it. I guess we just never got around to it before. Things like that happen. And the people we love are with us always. We just have to go on."

After Mickey left, the three sat in silence, each immersed in her own thoughts, and accompanied only by the sounds of the Indian summer night. City sounds, but somewhere in the grass at the edge of the alley, crickets shrieked their last wild lament. "Hear it?" Hattie asked quietly.

"What?" Kasia whispered back. "The crickets?"

"Yes."

"I'll tell you a secret. One Alice told me when she was very small."

"Yes?" Kasia breathed eagerly.

"Keep your eyes closed and listen very, very hard.

When the crickets stop singing. Make a wish. If you wish hard enough, it will come true."

"Can I tell what it is?"

"I think with most wishes, it's better if you don't. Then when it comes true, it's all the better." Hattie looked over at the child, whose small face knotted around the possibility of wishes. Hattie's own thoughts ran in a familiar direction—if only this life weren't so complicated.

How was she going to help Anya and Kasia and was she doing the right thing by keeping Ben's secret? She wished desperately for some guidance, some way to know what the right thing was, now that she knew what she knew. Her mind drifted back to the summers of Alice's innocence. How close they were in those long-ago times. She also wished she could fix whatever had gone wrong between them. Being so present with Kasia brought her back to those lovely, lost days of Alice's childhood.

Chapter fifty-three

Walking through the neighborhood in the early evening, Hattie kicked her way through a path of oak leaves grabbing at her ankles like tiny hands ready to haul her into some fearsome darkness. The city air hummed. The television Kasia and Anya watched each night was turned up a notch louder to accommodate it. They all spoke a bit more sharply. The coffee perking hardly drowned it out. The hum seemed louder than it had in the summer, especially when she walked. Inside, with the windows closed and the furnace kicking on, the hot air gusts blasting through the old-fashioned rattling registers, it diminished.

Gordon Street, an island of small, row houses, backed and fronted on similar streets. On either side, housing projects rose tall enough to block the sun's early morning and late afternoon rays. Beyond the last building, she could see the tube of car lights crawling like a glow-worm beyond the bare branches and across the horizon. The leaves had absorbed much of the traffic sounds during the spring and summer seasons. Now bare branches seemed like fingers admonishing Hattie against her own thoughts.

It had become her habit to leave the house for an early evening walk, though she felt on a short tether, not wanting to go very far. Again and again she pondered the extent to which Kasia and Anya had come to depend on her, and how it had happened. Sometimes she felt frustrated and trapped, wanting to run away. But somehow, she just couldn't. As important as it had been for her to come to Hartford, it was equally important for her to see this thing through. She would leave when there was some stability for Kasia and Anya.

It had been years since her presence was needed so persistently. Alice had been a self-sufficient daughter. So long ago, Hattie thought, Alice's childhood. Alice and Ben had clowned constantly, while Hattie played the cheerful, appreciative audience. Had there been something missing between them, some glue other families had? What had gone so wrong that her daughter seemed more a stranger to her than these strangers; what had gone so wrong that her husband had reinvented family life without her? Why hadn't Ben wanted to have another child with her and why had he then fathered a child by someone else?

As she walked home, Hattie glanced from house to house, noticing the reflection from televisions and the muffled noise. Everyone on Gordon Street had settled in for the evening. Kasia, dressed in pale green, fuzzy pajamas, snuggled next to her mother on the worn green sofa. How alike they are, Hattie thought. Kasia, almost as tall as her mother, had tremendous composure for an eight-year-old most of the time. But just when Hattie had begun to think of Kasia as a miniature adult, the little girl shifted into a different mode, one Hattie recognized very well.

"Please, Mom, can I have one of these?" Kasia wheedled, showing her mother a picture in the Christmas toy catalogue.

After Kasia went to bed, Anya sought out Hattie in the kitchen where she was folding laundry. "Strange how people develop certain habits," Anya remarked. "When you go out at night, I can't help thinking of Ben. He had the same habit, 'Stepping out for a bit of fresh air,' he'd say. Ben always left the house after dinner. Walked or drove for a while and then came back. I knew it was a time he needed to be alone."

"Oh," Hattie answered conscious of her voice cracking. Conversations between them when Ben's name came up—even after all the time she had been with Anya and Kasia—still made her feel as if her throat would close. She was anxious to hear what Anya might have to say about Ben; yet afraid she would somehow betray the secret. And she was equally afraid that she wouldn't.

"Yes. He was never away for more than a half-hour. He'd come back and have changed somehow. Like he needed that time to get back to himself."

Hattie listened; all too familiar with Ben's evening routine; fascinated that it differed in no way from the one in Fenston. She knew, too, what was at the bottom of his activities. He had instructed Hattie to call and leave a message at Harden if he was needed, saying that was easier than having to try to track him down in one of the many places he stayed throughout his territory.

It was the rare evening he didn't call her just after dinner—a few minutes on the phone, a report of his work life, things he had seen or done during the day, a few questions about her, about the weather, about Fenston's latest doings, and then he was gone, his voice trailing off into the night. If she weren't home, he'd call again in the morning.

Now she knew that when he was with *her*, and he left the house each evening for his drive, he was probably heading down the highway to Winton or Crystalle where no one would recognize him and think it odd that he was using a pay phone. Now she knew his nightly ritual, his conversation with Anya.

Oddly, each scrap of information Hattie amassed about Ben's life with Anya made her all the more resolute in her decision not to tell about Ben. His *secret*, as Hattie had begun to think about it, was now her secret too. Inexplicably, she cherished their secret and almost hugged it to herself—as if it were a thing so precious she couldn't share it, even with Anya, to whom it also rightfully belonged.

Instead, she looked at Anya and said, "I've been thinking about how you've been so sick lately. Don't you think it's time for you to tell me what's going on with you? I mean I know it's your business, but I've been here watching and I care. I happened to see all the medicine in the cabinet upstairs. Won't you tell me what's wrong?"

Chapter fifty-four

"After everything I've told you about him, I can't believe you're suggesting I should get in touch with Piotr," Anya spoke softly.

It was the first time she and Hattie had disagreed on something important. The two women stood side by side at the sink cleaning peaches for canning. Hattie had stopped by the farmers' market earlier in the day and found herself with a bushel basket of late peaches. Foolish, she thought, how would three people ever be able to eat their way through a bushel of peaches before they rotted? Then it occurred to her to can them, and she and Anya got busy scalding, removing the skin and finally, expertly, halving the peaches with a thumbnail and removing the pit. As they worked Hattie recalled so many days of canning and conversation she had shared with Athena and Eleanor.

Hattie had put off suggesting they contact Piotr as long as she could. Anya's health was declining each day, and Hattie worried about what would happen to Kasia if Anya died. But there was no easy way to talk about those contingencies or Anya's doubts. Hattie drew in a sharp breath and said, "But you already said you were worried that Ben was gone forever."

"Well, yes, I do think that sometimes when I'm low. But then I think of Ben, how determined he was to be with us. It's confusing, but I have to believe he's coming back. He'll be here to take care of Kasia . . ." her voice much less assured than her words, trailed off.

"It has been so kind of you, Hattie, to help us. I don't know what we would have done these last months . . . Kasia loves you very much." Anya looked up into Hattie's face. "Me too. I don't know what I've ever done to deserve such friendship. But I'm grateful."

"Never mind that . . ."

"No, wait. I want to finish. All the way around, it seems like you've always been here and that you understand. But if you knew Ben, you'd realize he could never just leave us. He simply wouldn't."

As for Piotr, Hattie didn't know him either, or she wouldn't be suggesting that Anya contact him. He'd already abandoned her once; she didn't want to put herself and her daughter in that position again.

As Hattie and Anya returned time and again to the subject of Piotr, the tension between them grew. Anya's sorrow played out as venom against her brother, almost as if it were his fault, rather than Ben's doing that she was in this situation. Balancing her concern that Anya not get too upset and expend all her strength, against the urgency she felt to make sure there was some other responsible adult person in the situation, Hattie pushed on, "But he's your brother. He has a right to know what's happened."

"He gave up his right many years ago when he sent me to Stan and wouldn't let me come home. Then he showed up, didn't even give Ben a chance, demanding that I go right back to Poland with him."

"And you didn't want to go?"

"It was in the late summer, right after Ben and I were married. I was so angry with Piotr that I didn't even let on that I was pregnant."

"Anya, people change. Maybe he has. I'm only thinking that someone else should be here with you. What if I got called away?"

Anya's face hardened with resolve. "No. I don't want to take a chance. I'll figure out what to do. If you have to go, then you should. You don't owe us anything. You've been too kind already. Don't worry, it's not your problem."

"Yes, it is my problem. I care about you and Kasia. That's why I'm here. And I'm just trying to help you examine all the options. Sometimes someone else sees things more clearly."

Hattie's mind raced through all the possible arguments she could give. Not having time to express them all, she had to choose carefully. When the thought came to her, she held her hand out to Anya and said, "Think of it this way. However long you have on this earth or whether Ben comes back or not, that's still a pretty small family for a child. Children need all the love they can get. As far as you know, there are no relatives on Ben's side of the family . . ."

Anya nodded agreement.

"And the only family you have, the only close blood relative is your brother. Do you really think it is right to keep him away from Kasia? To keep him from knowing of her existence and her from knowing whatever love and support he can offer her?"

They had both stopped working on the peaches, and Anya grabbed Hattie's hand. As she thought about what Hattie was saying, a tremor of recognition of this singular and important idea she had tried to talk herself out of invaded her.

They stood for a moment facing each other in silence, though each knew what the response would be. Anya's eyes reflected a swirl of emotion. Gone was any hint of resentment as she exhaled a quiet, "All right. But I won't do it. You call him if you want to." Then as an afterthought, "And then we'll see if he cares, if he'll even come."

Chapter fifty-five

Hattie was out in the garden, checking on the few remaining heads of cabbage and squash when she heard the dim jingle of the doorbell and raced in to get it, thinking that Anya had returned from the doctor and forgotten her key. Peeling off the garden gloves and brushing her hair back from her face, she bolted up the steps and through the kitchen and dining room and pulled the door open to find Athena standing in front of her. For a moment, neither was able to speak.

"Well, I guess you know how much you've made me worry to drag me all the way here after you. At least you gave me the street address!" Athena blurted, before she burst out laughing.

"Aren't you something?" She looked down at Hattie's dirt-caked bare feet and knees. Hattie was still speechless, but she put her arms up as in surrender, then placed them on Athena's shoulders and drew her old friend to her, inhaling a whiff of cool fall air and the faint scent of early October nights in Fenston. Athena hugged her back, "You know I should be really angry with you, but . . . Oh, God, I've missed you so, Hattie. I couldn't stay there worrying what new pickle you'd got yourself into."

Suddenly, Hattie heard the clash of her two worlds. Tension shot through her. "It's good that you came when you did. I don't know how I would have been able to handle it if Anya were home."

"Doesn't she know you had a life before you showed up on her doorstep? I guess you'd just say I was a friend passing through. Or aren't you allowed to have friends?"

"Of course. But, well, I don't. I've been so busy trying to figure out what to do with this situation here. And Anya and Kasia are around." Hattie swept the room with her eyes and Athena followed as if they both expected people to materialize from the corners of the room.

"Where are they?" she asked.

"Anya has gone to the doctor, and Kasia is still in school."

"Oh? And you're here waiting for them to return. How sweet. Hattie, the waiter. They're going to put that on your tombstone. Seems like the same old record for you. First you wait for Ben. Now you're waiting for them. I just can't figure you out. What are you waiting for?"

"Stop it. You've just got here and now you're making assumptions, judging me. Can we say hello first?"

Athena answered Hattie's tentative smile with a grin. "I can't say I didn't have a heck of a time finding you. If I had driven around this city until I knew every street by heart, I don't think I would have picked out this place."

"No?"

"You didn't tell me that it was in such a . . . poor section. I don't know what I expected but certainly not this," Athena waved to include the house and street. "What was Ben thinking? I just can't imagine him here."

Those had been Hattie's exact feelings when she first laid eyes on the place, and yet she felt a little defensive when Athena uttered them.

When her friend looked up again, Hattie saw fatigue and distress in her eyes, and knew what it had cost Athena to drive all this way alone, unsure of what she'd find. Neither of them had ever driven more than an hour or so away from home alone. Now here they were; both had traveled what for them was an unfathomably long distance to solve the mystery of Ben's life.

"Why don't we go into the kitchen and sit," Hattie said. "I know I owe you some explaining after you've come all this way for me."

"I didn't come for you. I came because I was driving myself crazy and decided it was easier to get in the car and come than it was to keep worrying."

"Oh, Athena, let me just sit here and look at you. I can't believe you're here. But what did you tell Will and the others?"

"Simply that I was heading out to pay you a visit. I

didn't hang around long enough to play fifty questions with anyone. I think Will knows something is not quite right, but he wasn't asking and I wasn't volunteering."

While Hattie ran upstairs to change clothes and comb her hair, Athena looked around the odd little house, as if she half-hoped that Anya would get back and she could size her up. She walked to the hall table and picked up the same photo of Anya, Kasia and Ben that Hattie had examined the first time she had entered the house and many times thereafter. First Athena studied the woman's face, then the child's. Finally she stared into his smile.

"You trickster, Ben, see where it's got you. See what trouble you caused," she said softly to the oblivious face.

"We can talk in the car," Hattie said. "I wish you could stay here, but it's out of the question, with Anya sick and all."

"That's okay. I expected to stay in a hotel. I'll only stay a day, anyhow. But I couldn't rest until I saw you face to face and knew that you were all right."

Hattie left Anya a note that something big had come up with her job and she would have to work the whole day and into the night and many hours the next day, an explanation good for her own devices as Anya had recently asked her if she'd been neglecting her work to help out at the house. Hattie had murmured something about waiting for the next assignment and it being a slow time but sure to pick up soon.

Chapter fifty-six

Over dinner, Hattie had almost as many questions as Athena, whose presence brought on a wave of nostalgia. How had the summer been? The apple crop in her orchard? Had someone used the apples? What was the local talk? Rose, Athena's daughter-in-law, had had her gall bladder out and Athena got to spoil Al and Gary, her son and grandson, while Rose was in the hospital. Will had remarked that Rose's personality might improve without the gall bladder. Fenston was gearing up for the local elections, hotly contested races in the borough manager and School Board seats. The Fire Company had been called out twice when Robbie Rodiri was trying to figure out how to use the new wood-burning equipment he'd bought at a flea market.

Eleanor and Eddie had taken up camping and bought

an old Airstream trailer which they'd parked back at the edge of their own five hundred acres for a getaway, back by the old quarry Eddie had bought ten years earlier with the idea that there'd soon be demand again for flagstone and he'd be ready. Eddie's back was still terrible, though he'd doctored all up and down the valley from one clinic to another and no one seemed to be able to find the cause of the pain.

"Back pain is like that sometimes, hard to put your finger on," Athena said solemnly, but they both burst out laughing, Hattie practically having to hang onto the underside of her chair to keep from toppling to the floor with mirth. "That Eddie, he's a real Christian martyr," she said when she got her breath, then they both broke into giggles again. "Oh, God, poor Eleanor. What she's got to put up with. No wonder she's praying half her waking hours. Probably asking for patience."

Fall had tarnished the city, torn the leaves from the trees and yellowed the grass. Hattie drove along the river, wondering about the strange events that had unfolded in her life since the last fall, when she didn't even know of Anya's existence. Now she wondered if she would ever experience that kind of simplicity again. Would she ever look at something and trust it to be what she perceived?

They lingered over coffee until they were the last people in the restaurant and the waiter began to hover. Athena told Hattie about something that had taken place in Wilkes-Barre, in the next county over from Fenston. After a domestic altercation, a prison guard had gone on a shooting spree and killed thirteen people, some of them members of his own family. The women shook their heads over how suddenly tragedy could strike and how lives can be so easily ruined.

The next morning, Hattie was running late when she showed up for Athena. Breathlessly, she rushed to park the car and impatiently pushed the button on the elevator, jabbing at it again and again, as if to get it to respond to her sharp summons. Athena was reading *Better Homes and Gardens* when Hattie arrived.

"I thought you were going to stand me up," Athena said when she answered the door. Instead of her usual blue jeans and polo shirt, both days Athena had worn a denim jumper with a sprigged cotton blouse and penny loafers. Her hair was pulled back neatly into a ponytail and held by a silver clasp. Immense waves of gratitude and affection for her friend washed over Hattie. The room looked almost uninhabited, as Athena had made up the bed and her small suitcase was repacked and waiting by the door. "They want checkout by 11."

"I'm sorry I'm late. Anya didn't have a good night, so I got Kasia off to school before I came. You know eight-year-olds—she dawdles if I don't keep my eyes on her."

"I know eight-year-olds, all right. What I don't know is what in heaven's name you're doing with this one."

"What do you mean?"

"This beats it all. You find her, them, then you move into the house and now you've become some kind of an honorary aunt, or a nanny to your husband's illegitimate child. And . . . I'm afraid you're going to let yourself get too attached. Then where will it lead? You'll suffer from it and you don't need any more of that."

"You don't understand. They're so alone. They don't have anyone. Ben just left and they don't know where he is or why he hasn't come back. I . . ."

"And you're getting more and more drawn into this thing. When will it end? Do you intend to tell her at some point? Is that why you're hanging around?"

"She's such an innocent, sweet person. No, I don't think I could tell her—I don't think I could ever let her know. Why would I? What good would it do?"

"It might make you feel better. Remember. That was your initial reason for coming."

"I know it was. But I didn't know Anya then. Then I didn't understand the situation at all."

"And you're telling me you do now?"

"Well, no. I don't. But I just can't leave them."

"Hattie, you're not fooling yourself that you and she are friends, are you? If it looks like friendship, just think about how she'd react if she knew the truth, knew why you'd come. She'd hate you for not telling her about Ben, and for not being honest about who you are and why you came. Do you think she'd forgive you for tricking her like that? Do you think she'd want you around her child?"

Chapter fifty-seven

"It may come as a shock to you, but I've already told myself everything you're saying. I've been very close to leaving a few times already. And I will. Without telling Anya anything. I just have to figure out how to set up a few things up for them."

"What do you mean?"

"They're penniless. But for the rent I pay, I don't know that they could eat." Hattie's tears splashed against her cheeks, before she even realized she'd been crying. "What we had, Ben and I, we made together. They should get something." Hattie wrung her hands. "I'll have to figure it out.

"I don't want to be here either. Oh, Athena, it really hurts—every day—to be reminded of what Ben did. The loneliness of being the only one who knows he's gone. But foolish as it seems, and I know it does, I just can't turn my back on them."

Athena gathered her friend in her arms, patting and shushing her. "I've known you long enough and well enough that I can be sure of your doing the right thing for everyone. I wish there was some way I could help."

"Me, too. The only thing I can think of is for you to keep an eye on things at home. I never thought I'd be away this long."

"Of course I will."

"How's Paul?" Hattie asked, drying her eyes and changing the subject with a brave smile.

"Forgot to tell you. He's all but decided to leave. Closing up the shoe repair shop and renting out the service station."

This news hit Hattie very hard. "I can't believe it. I never thought he'd leave Fenston, even when he threatened to. Where will he go?"

"Says he doesn't know. Travel around for a while."

Suddenly a chill went through Hattie. "You don't supposed he'd try to find me, do you?"

"I don't see how he could. Anyway, I think he's headed out west."

Hattie was surprised at how sad she felt to think that Paul would leave Fenston. Maybe the place wasn't as special as she had made it in her mind.

They emerged from the hotel into a beautiful fall day, the air crisp and the city swathed in energy and color. Hattie and Athena walked along, talking and not talking. They window-shopped and stopped for coffee, each aware that the visit was much too short, and feeling the wrench of separation again.

"You know, it's as though I'm in the middle of a great swirling that started with Ben's death, events that seem somehow to have to take their own course. The best I can do is play my part. I'm just hanging on trying, from day to day, to figure out the best thing to do for everyone."

"I know, dear, I know. You'll do the best for everyone and think of yourself last."

"How could all this have happened? It would be something else if we led some kind of soap opera life. But Ben was just an ordinary guy. We had an ordinary life. How could there have been so much going on that nobody knew about?"

Athena sighed and reached over and took her friend's hand and steered Hattie to a place along the river where there were benches and a view of bicycle trails below.

"I think I know what you mean. Life drifts along for so long that you're lulled into thinking it will always be that way; that the future will be as steady and sure as the past."

"That's it, yes. And when something happens, you don't expect the ways it will radiate out and you don't expect it to change so many lives. If I'd ever thought of Ben's death ahead of me, I guess I would have anticipated missing him in so many ways. Instead, I have all this other stuff to deal with. I've still not had a moment to do what

I always thought mourning should be about. Instead I've just had to follow my instincts in this bizarre situation; I'm fumbling in the dark." Hattie paused, as if deciding whether to continue. "Now, there's something else," she said.

Athena leaned closer.

"The other day, odd that I had never looked there before, but I found something. In the medicine cabinet. All kinds of heavy-duty medication. I'd noticed that Anya was sick a lot, coughing, short of breath, and so fragile, her body seems like a twig about to crack. I also saw other signs. Do you remember Mr. Midgers—how towards the end he had blue around the mouth sometimes, and blue hands. I suspected for a while before she told me. Heart problems."

"Oh," Athena questioned. "Serious?"

"Very."

"Oh my!"

"It's strange, but at first after all Anya told me about her life, I felt funny asking her. I kept hoping that she'd tell me what was going on. I think she wanted to but didn't because she didn't want to seem more pitiful than she already was. But, finally, one day last week, when she seemed particularly tired and drawn, I just came right out and asked her what was wrong with her and when she was seeing the doctor again."

"And?"

"She seemed relieved. Looked up at me as if she were grateful that I'd asked. 'Next week,' she said. But her voice was tense. For a minute she didn't say anything else. I waited. 'For all the good it will do,' she said. Then it all came out. Once she got started, I think she couldn't wait to tell me."

"And? What did she say about all the medicine?"

"She has a very serious heart condition. Evidently she had rheumatic fever as a child and it wasn't treated. It was just after the war, and there was so much chaos. She had been sick most of the winter, but when the spring came she seemed to get better. Anyway, no one suspected and she seemed all right. But years later, when she was pregnant, the problem resurfaced. Then it became clear there was damage to her heart, and there was nothing to be done for it. Since then, she's gotten worse. Now it's a matter of time, months at the most. Maybe weeks."

"Oh, God," Athena said, suddenly sorting through the events of the past few months. "And the doctor's card?"

"Yes. Dr. Downs is her cardiologist. And the rest of it fits together. That's the reason Ben told her he was going to get another assignment. He had come back to Fenston to tell me the whole thing and leave me so he could be with them. I'm guessing, of course. But it stands to reason. It was the only thing he could do. Even if he could somehow keep up his double life through Anya's last illness and death, there was Kasia to consider. He'd have to be responsible for her. He could hardly show up at home with this unexplained child calling him Papa."

Athena moaned, "I've never in my life heard anything so complicated and awful."

"So here I am. With Anya dying. No one to care for

Kasia and no real claim in the situation. You know what you said earlier about trusting that I'd know what to do? Well, I don't. I feel the way Ben must have. He passed his secret on to me and instead of taking it out into the open and trying to find an honorable way to deal with it, I've let it grow and strengthen. Now I have a real situation on my hands."

"What will become of her child? Wait. Didn't you tell me that Anya had a brother in Poland?"

"Yes. But she hasn't spoken to him in years. She has only bad feelings about him. Apparently he tried to pawn her off on some lout, and she rebelled."

"It's something. You have to talk to Anya. Try to impress on her that Ben may not come back and that you must get in touch with her brother."

"I'm way ahead of you there. Actually, I already have talked to her. When she finally gave me her permission to call, I had no trouble finding him. Seems he'd been there the whole time, in the same house, at the same address. I called expecting to have trouble communicating . . ."

"Now you speak Polish?" The humor had returned to Athena's eyes.

". . . and as Anya said he speaks English very well. I explained what had happened with Anya's health and that Ben was gone. Then I told him that there was no one to care for Kasia." Across two continents, Hattie had felt Piotr's shudder. "It was clear he didn't even know the child existed. He said he'd come at once. What he didn't say was how long that might be."

"He's Kasia's only living relative?"

"Except Alice."

"Except Alice."

"Don't think I haven't gone round and round with myself some nights wondering if I have the right to keep the knowledge away from Alice and Kasia that they have a half-sister. I've tried to examine my own motives for telling and not telling. But somehow, I just can't do it. It would involve too many other revelations that I don't think either of them needs right now."

The wind had picked up on the river as the mid-afternoon sun shifted and slipped behind a building. Athena shivered and wove her arm through Hattie's.

"I think you have enough to worry about right now without trying to solve the whole mess. If her condition is as bad as she says, you don't have much time."

"I've been sitting here dreading the moment you'll have to leave. But I want you to get on the road so that you'll be home by your bedtime." Before they stood up to continue their stroll, Hattie stared at Athena as if memorizing each feature of the face that she'd known through all its changes since adolescence. "I can't believe you came. What a blessing to open the door and find you there. And I didn't even know the half of how I needed it."

"Oh, my God, I almost forgot. I can't imagine how. Alice called me the other night. Wanted to know where you had disappeared to . . . Evidently, she's been frantically calling you on and off for weeks. Doesn't sound like things are as rosy in California as she thought they'd be." Athena handed Hattie a slip of paper.

"Maybe you should give her a call. She left her number."

"What did you tell her?"

"I didn't know what to say. I mumbled something about your needing a change, about your visiting some people in Hartford. She sure was surprised at that."

"Aren't we all?" Hattie laughed.

"I'm glad you can have a sense of humor about it. I've been worried sick. When will it end, this mess you've gotten yourself into?"

The two friends were silent, each unable to answer that question. Just as Athena turned to go, all the misery that had been on Hattie's heart since Ben died burst from her. She sobbed and sobbed. Oblivious to the comings and goings of a busy corner, the women hugged each other as Athena patted and murmured to soothe her friend. Eventually, Hattie pulled herself together and was even laughing again, as they walked slowly back to the hotel and Athena's waiting car.

Chapter fifty-eight

Always a quiet child, Kasia had become almost silent, examining the world through her large anxious gray-blue eyes. On the evening of parent visitation at school for report card night, Anya didn't felt well enough to attend, and Hattie went in her place.

Perched on the tiny seat, along with the other parents of Mrs. Aimey's second grade, Hattie studied the blackboard, which was covered with paper cutout leaves. Inside each leaf, on a sheet of lined paper, a child had written a short paragraph of self-introduction.

The room was colorful and bright and Mrs. Aimey, in her navy jumpsuit and silk blouse and tousled hair, was eager to talk about what the children had been working on. Each parent or set of parents went up and collected their child's report card. When Hattie's turn came, and she said Kasia's name, Mrs. Aimey looked up at her and smiled, "Are you Mrs. Darling?" And Hattie choked back an automatic yes. "No, I'm a friend of the family. Kasia's mother is ill and I'm filling in for her."

"Oh, dear," Mrs. Aimey said, her sweet round cheeks forming a pout. Hattie realized at once she should have lied and passed herself off as Kasia's mother. All these months of deceit, she thought wryly, should have made lying come more naturally. "Not related? Have you brought some kind of authorization from the mother? We're not supposed to give out information about students to anyone but a parent or guardian."

"We, we didn't know. Her mother was going to come, but she got sick. Maybe you could call . . ." Hattie suggested, embarrassed that she was holding up the line of other parents.

"Yes. That's what I'll have to do," the teacher said, as if one more complication, one she could and would overcome, had just been added to her day.

"Please go down the hall to the office. The secretary will place the call and verify that Mrs. Darling has given you permission to accept Kasia's report card for her," she said officiously, anxiously peering over Hattie's shoulder at the real parents behind her.

When Hattie returned carrying the secretary's verifying note, the last parents were with the teacher. Hattie stood and waited, reading the assignments on the board. Kasia's had said, "I'm Kasia. My mother is from Poland.

We live on Gordon Street and my uncle is coming to visit us. We'll have special tarts when he comes. We have a friend who lives in our house and teaches me to play *Clue*. It's my favorite game."

"I had hoped," said Mrs. Aimey earnestly, after examining the paper and putting it carefully in her desk drawer, "that Kasia's mother would be here, but since I now have the slip, maybe I can talk to you and you'll let her know what we've talked about." Hattie stood in front of her, feeling like a school child who had forgotten something important and had been called to the office.

"Kasia is a bright little girl. And her work is always good. Her homework is complete and she's prepared in class. But I've seen enough children to know that there's something bothering her. She's in a kind of fog most of the time. If she weren't as bright as she is, she'd be lost. Is there something wrong at home?"

Hattie hesitated. "Kasia's mother is quite ill. I'm sure she's worried. But Kasia is a quiet child to begin with. I imagine she's more so now."

"Maybe I should have the school social worker talk to her. Of course, a parent will have to sign the permission." She inspected the contents of her orderly desk and handed Hattie a form. "Here, please have Mrs. Darling sign it and mail it back to us. We'll make an appointment for Kasia as soon as we get it back."

Hattie was amazed to think that there were actual social workers in the schools. But of course, things had changed a great deal since Alice was in grade school.

In Fenston, when Alice was growing up, the whole town knew each child. If anything even started to go wrong, the parents would get a call from a neighbor. When Alice and her friends were lighting matches down by the lake one spring, fascinated by the danger and power of fire, Hattie and the other parents were visited by Clem and the chief of the Fire Company. After the adults had spoken, the children were called into the room and shown a movie about how easily a small fire could get out of control. Contrite and fearful that Hattie would give her a stiff punishment, Alice sobbed as Hattie put her to bed that night. Ben, of course, was away at the time. When Hattie reported the incident in one of their phone conversations, he made light of it saying, "Kids will be kids." Hattie had other ideas. She thought that everything children did or said should be taken seriously. In Kasia's case, it was everything she didn't say that Hattie worried over.

"That's good. Kasia needs all the support she can get."

"The father. Is there a father in the home?" Mrs. Aimey asked. But her expression suggested she already knew the answer and sighed when Hattie shook her head. "Poor little thing," she said. "I'm glad you came. I'll do my best here. And of course, the social workers are professionals, used to this sort of thing. They're good at helping troubled children. You wouldn't believe some of the complicated situations they've had to deal with."

Hattie suppressed the bitter laughter welling inside her—of course she'd believe it! She imagined herself saying to the picture-perfect Mrs. Aimey, "Let me tell you about complications!" And, she thought to herself, who could have more cause to be troubled than Kasia.

Chapter fifty-nine

"That man," Piotr spat out the words, his whole face slowly twisted with pain and rage.

"First, he ruins her life. He gives her a baby and is never around. Now he leaves her altogether when she is sick." He fumbled for a moment, summoning words in an unfamiliar language to express his strong emotion. "Ach, and look at this place. Anya. Where is she?"

"Resting now. She gets tired easily. She'll be awake by the time Kasia gets home."

He had been standing with his suitcase in his left hand. Suddenly but quietly, he placed it on the floor. He was as large as Anya was tiny, but they shared the same coloring and facial features. He bent to open the suitcase and took out a small package wrapped in tissue, which he carefully undid to reveal a lovely old doll dressed in traditional Polish peasant costume, its long blond braids slightly unraveled. "This was Anya's. I found it after she left. All the time I kept it with me—to think of her. Maybe the child would like it . . ."

"She'd like it very much. And I think Anya would like to see it too."

"*Czas leci. Czas leci,*" he said, staring down at the doll in his large hand.

"What?" Hattie asked.

"I think you say time flies. The doll is the only thing that has not changed in these years. I remember when Anya was the little girl who played with it."

Piotr Sikorski was the sort of man who looked like someone you knew. Comfortably dressed in neat, expensive clothing, he reminded people vaguely of their brother, uncle, teacher, friend, but always someone kind. Hattie couldn't help wondering, as she stood with the door open facing him, what Anya could have been afraid of in this gentle man. He was a tall man who walked with his shoulders slightly bowed, as if he didn't want to impose his stature on those around him. His accent, though much stronger than Anya's, had the same emphasis, and for Hattie, the same charm. Despite all the reservations she had had about his coming, Hattie felt comfortable with him at once.

"Is the child at home?"

"Not for another hour or so." Hattie answered. "She has Brownies after school today."

"Brownies?"

"A kind of club for little girls. I . . . I mean we, thought it would be good for her to get out of the house and mix with other children. To play." He looked at her politely but curiously.

"That's good," he said, and his "*that's*" came out as "*thas*," slightly more pronounced than the manner in which Anya would say it. "The children, they need to play."

"Especially Kasia. She's been hit pretty hard by things around here."

"Things? Anya's sickness?"

"Yes, and her father being gone."

Another transformation of his features, Hattie couldn't decide what the emotion was until he reached into his breast pocket and removed a very white, neatly folded handkerchief. He removed his glasses and wiped the welling tears from his eyes before they coursed down his face. Piotr's gestures were slow and deliberate, completely lacking the self-consciousness she might have expected from a man crying in front of a total stranger. He cleared his throat and looked at Hattie almost imploringly and after a moment asked, "How bad?"

"Very bad, I'm afraid." But I haven't actually talked to the doctor. I'm not a relative. I thought I'd just wait until you . . . I was relieved when you said you would come."

"Of course I'd come. A brother would come."

Hattie said nothing, but her glance must have.

"I know that Anya probably told you the whole thing.

How I wanted her to come here to be with Stan. So yes, I did a bad thing. But I did it because I thought it would be a better life than there could be with me. I didn't have a very good job at the time and I wanted more for her than what I saw would be possible there." Hattie was touched by the sorrowful, kind, gentle expression of his face.

"I convinced myself that it was best for her to be in America. I probably did the wrong thing. In Poland, we were raised to perform our duty. In love, well, we showed that through duty, too. I felt I was doing my duty to her.

"But I must be honest now. I wasn't able to be then, because I couldn't face the truth myself. It was more than wanting something better for her. I was selfish and didn't want to have someone dependent on me. Do I admit that too? I admit it.

"When she ran away from Stan, I tried to find her. Two years it took me. She hid herself because of the green card. I hired someone to look. I came myself and searched everywhere. Finally, she was located. I wanted to take her back. Now I was earning more and I could take care of her well. She would have the best."

Again, he looked around the shabby little house. "She refused because *he* had already taken over her life. After that first time, when I argued with him, she didn't even want to see me. I left. At least I knew that she was safe."

Hattie sighed at the sadness and the emotion of Piotr's story. More missed connections. How often people failed each other even when they tried their best.

"But I always loved her, even if she didn't want to

know it. And I think I always thought I would have time to show it. I thought that eventually she wouldn't have to be mad at me. And we'd be together again."

Hattie felt such an immense wave of tenderness that she almost reached out her hand to touch him. "Now this . . ." he broke of with a wrenching shudder, "before we even had time . . ."

Hattie held back. Overcome by her own emotions, she cleared her throat and said, "She'll be getting up soon. Let me run upstairs to see if she's awake. Then you can go up."

Chapter sixty

Anya was lying on her side in the darkened room when Hattie opened the door softly and tiptoed inside. "I thought I heard Piotr?" Anya's voice was soft and husky at the same time, a voice full of tears.

"He's come and he wants to be with you."

"I knew it was him. I couldn't hear the words, but the sounds were full of him. I woke up to it, realizing how I'd not let myself think about him in a long time."

"How do you feel about seeing him now?" Hattie wanted a little acknowledgement that she had been right to insist on calling Piotr.

"He's here. He's come all this way to see me. Now I know for sure I must be dying. What else would bring him?" Anya laughed, but there was an edge to her voice

Hattie did not associate with Anya. "You know he always felt he needed to control me. Now I'm sick and have no choice. I guess he'll be making the decisions."

"I don't know what happened between you. Only what you've told me. But he seems a fine person and he came. So that's something. I think he has lots of regrets about sending you here."

"Good. I hope I'm not the only one with regrets."

"Oh," Hattie said wonderingly.

"I was lying here thinking about those evenings on the lake with Ben. How happy we were. But was it worth it? Maybe I should have stayed with Stan or gone back with Piotr when he came looking for me that time. Oh, God, I don't even know what I'm saying. Then I wouldn't have Kasia. Then I would not have had Ben for twelve years. I can't think my way around this. Where has Ben gone? And why? Am I to spend my remaining time on earth regretting my happiest years?" Anya broke into sobs.

Torn by her own emotions, Hattie rushed to comfort Anya. "You can't see into the future. But your brother's here. He's come all this way to see you. And Kasia will be home from school in an hour. Why don't you try to concentrate on the blessings this day holds for you and forget the rest?"

"I can't forget. But you are right. I can at least have the ones I love in my life."

"Here," said Hattie, offering Anya her hand. "Let me help you." Weightless, thought Hattie. There's less and less of her each day. Someday, she'll disappear completely. And the rest of us will follow.

"Hattie, thank you. You were right that he would come. Maybe you're right about other things, too. I get so confused. Thank you for helping me see what's there and not to focus on what's just in my mind."

Hattie smiled. "I wish I could claim that ability. I'd do it for myself sometimes."

"I'll go into the bathroom, then come downstairs. I don't want Piotr to see me in bed." And with immense effort, the tiny blond woman stood, went into the bathroom, and came back with her face freshly washed and her hair combed. At the dressing table, she dabbed a little lipstick on each cheek, rubbed it in with her finger and applied a quick slash on her lips. "Now, so he won't think me too haggard. I'm ready."

Hattie followed her to the landing. Anya turned to see if she was behind her on the steps. "No, Anya, I think this is for you and Piotr. You need some time alone, before Kasia comes home from school and without me. You two have a great deal to talk about."

Hattie waited until she heard Kasia's voice in the living room and then she went down to join them, finding Piotr and Anya almost unable to keep their eyes off each other. Anya's features brightened and the fatigue often so evident in her body seemed to have left her. She looked happier than Hattie had ever seen her. She continually reached out for Piotr's hand as if to verify his presence. Piotr's smile was contagious; soon Hattie, Kasia and Anya had caught it. His appearance had set off other waves, which would reverberate through each of them.

Chapter sixty-one

Piotr would stay in her room, and she would take the other twin bed in Kasia's room. Soon, Hattie would leave and Kasia could have her room to herself. Soon, it would be over. She would have done everything she could for Anya and Kasia, and she could go home. Since the evening she first called Piotr and he said he would come as soon as he could, Hattie had thought about nothing else. It was a reprieve, at last. She could turn the responsibility for Anya and Kasia over to him, a blood relative, where it belonged. Then she could pick up the frayed threads of her own life and hope that there was enough substance to create something whole and useful.

The first night Piotr was in the house, after Anya had helped Kasia bathe and had looked over her homework, sitting with her at the kitchen table, she had excused herself and went up to tuck her daughter in. He looked at Hattie and she felt the strength of his gaze.

"How is it you came here?" he asked, studying her face. "You say you've only been here a short while?"

"Since July, four months. Yes." She felt somewhat flustered as she spoke, as if her answers were very important and needed to be measured out.

"And how is that? How did you come? Were you friends with Anya before . . ." His voice was warm and kind but she saw his mind working behind what he saw, evaluating it and trying to make sense of it. He'd not be fooled for too long, Hattie thought. She'd better watch what she told him, as she understood he could very easily uncover her secret.

"It happened quite by chance. I got the wrong address. I was looking for a room to rent. Then Anya asked me to stay." The whole thing sounded as implausible to her as it must have to him.

"Incredible. You just walk up to the door and she asks you to stay?"

"Not quite like that. But something. We got to talking. And you know how it is, some people just click." Hattie felt her face redden. "Anya and Kasia and I just did."

"Click?" he asked. She saw that he was flushed as well.

"A kind of chemistry. You meet people you feel a bond with immediately."

"Yes. Things like that happen. Things very real but hard to explain. I've seen it many times and once or twice been lucky enough for it to happen to me." He looked at her with great intensity, searching her face. Hattie felt a small flicker inside herself, an unaccustomed though not an altogether unwelcome sensation.

He took her hand and a little shock went through her. He said, "I don't know how you came here, how to explain it and I don't even think I want to. But I'm glad you're here. And I hope you'll guide me. I want to do the right thing, but can't think how to do it, because I don't know what that is. Or even if there is anything I can do."

"We can put out heads together over it tomorrow. God, I can't tell you how glad I am you've come. I kept thinking that I wouldn't know what to do if anything happened to Anya. Kasia, well, she's not my child; I'm not even a relative. Maybe the state would come in and put her in foster care. How could I explain to her that a few months ago she had two loving parents and now she has no one and that she would have to go to live with strangers?"

"Thank God you called me. I don't know how we can ever show you how important you've been to Anya and Kasia and now to me."

His voice and manner were so gentle and kind. Hattie sifted through the men she knew and realized that she had seen a man cry for the first time in her life. Pain leapt into his face as he recognized that they were talking about Anya's death. Hattie realized that she had had months to come to terms with Anya's situation. Piotr had just found his sister again and now he was having to think ahead to his inevitable loss. She hastened to reassure him, "But tomorrow. We'll get on to all that tomorrow, and after you've slept and had some time we'll be able to sort it all out and figure out the best thing to do."

Perhaps Piotr slept. Hattie would never know. She spent the night thinking about what kind of man this was and how she could help him with the task he had ahead.

Chapter sixty-two

When Piotr returned from seeing Anya's doctor, he entered the room soundlessly and crossed to the sink, took a paper towel, wet it, removed his glasses and wiped his face slowly from brow to chin, then back. As he bent to place the towel in the trash, Hattie noticed the small dot of skin on the back of his head where he had begun to bald. She did some arithmetic: if Anya was thirty-seven and Piotr was fifteen years older, that would make him fifty-two. Six years older than she. A year younger than Ben.

Piotr's back was to her as he drew and drank a glass of water.

"What is it, Piotr? What illness does she have? Can't anything be done?" Even though Anya had already told her about her disease, Hattie wanted to hear it from Piotr, hoping that there would be some other information, something more hopeful.

After a moment, his face still averted, he said, "Three months at the most."

"Oh, God," she cried.

"More likely six weeks. And at the end she will be very, very weak."

"Yes," she said, though she didn't know why. The information he was giving her was not completely new. Her voice was soft around that one immutable syllable.

"She first got sick as a little girl. When the doctor asked me about it, I could hardly remember. But then I did. She had a sickness when she was as small as Kasia is now. We were very worried, but then after months and the doctor there not really knowing what was wrong, she seemed to get better. We didn't have the tests then and so we didn't know that the sickness had damaged her heart. It was like a little thing in there waiting to come back. Evidently, the doctor explained, when she was pregnant, it started the problem again and her heart kept weakening. Now there is nothing to be done. She will die when her heart just can't keep working anymore. Nothing anyone can do about it. I begged. Told them I had the money for the best doctors, could fly her anywhere they could help her. But they said nothing. Just looked at me as if we should have known all those years ago this would happen." Again, he wept openly, soundlessly, then dried his eyes on a paper towel.

"I'm sure they don't think that, Piotr. There was nothing that could be done then either."

"I keep reading these articles about the new heart surgery. Now they can take a heart out of someone who has just died and put it back into a person with a sick heart. I asked about it, but they told me that Anya's problem is not the kind that this operation works for. And even if it could, she's much too weak to survive it."

Hattie began to weep, too. "I know how awful it is to lose someone you love. And I know how terribly hard it is to think there's nothing you can do."

After a moment, he wiped his face again and cleared his throat as if to change personas, becoming the man who could again take charge of things. "Has the child been told?"

"Some. But I'm not sure how much. As far as I know, she's been told that Anya's sick. Certainly not that she is dying."

"*Kazda polprawda jest calkowitym klamstwem,* the old people would say," Piotr translated, "Every half-truth is a complete lie."

"Sometimes, half-truths and lies are told to protect people," Hattie said, smarting from having applied Piotr's saying to her own situation.

"And then they lead to more complications, don't they. See what a task the half-truth has set for us?"

"Yes," Hattie said softly.

"Someone's got to tell the child," he said as he turned to face Hattie, squaring his shoulders at the task.

Suddenly, a fury of emotions boiled in her. Before she could even edit what she thought, she'd begun, and all her sorrow and confusion came spewing out at him.

"The child, the child! Christ, Piotr, the child has a name! Kasia. Can't you at least use her name? Or does referring to her as 'the child' keep her from being real? Take my word for it, she's real. And losing her mother will hurt just as much whether you call her Kasia or the child. Especially after . . ."

Then she caught the bewildered expression on his face and realized how she must have sounded. "Forgive me. Oh, God! I don't know why I lashed out at you!" She put her hand on his arm.

"Hattie. It's all right. We're all upset. There is no way out of this sadness. We'll try to find the right way to tell Kasia. Poor little one." Piotr put out his hand to Hattie. "Maybe you and I can do this. She loves you. She trusts you."

Touched by his grace at her angry outburst, she looked up at him, "Let's do it fairly soon. No use putting it off. She'll have more time to adjust." She looked at him pleadingly, "And please forgive me. I didn't mean any of that."

"Can I ask you one favor? Don't even mention that man to me again. And yes, you're right. Knowing that beautiful child will have to bear the same loss that seems to have clouded Anya's life, well . . ."

"Of course."

"Oh, God, Hattie, how can I do this thing?"

He paused for a moment, then seemed to remember what else he wanted to say, "Him, he's responsible for this. This is his family. What kind of a man is he? Can you imagine anyone that spineless? He finds out that Anya is terminally ill and then he tells her he's going away but will be back and will stay with her. Then he disappears."

"How do you know that he knew? Anya refused to tell me anything about her illness for a long time. Maybe she was hiding it from him too?"

"Why are you defending him? It doesn't seem like you to take the part of someone so irresponsible."

"I just wanted to try to understand. To know for sure."

"I know that he knew because the doctor's secretary told me he called. He had a long talk with the doctor. He knew all of it. The whole thing. Then he disappeared."

"What?"

"He knew everything. The doctors had been pretty sure what she had, but they were waiting for the test results. He called the doctor from the road, away on one of his trips. The doctor told him everything. What the disease is like, how long, how much help she'll need, everything." Piotr paused, bitterness distorting his features. "So our hero disappears. He just deserts her without so much as a word of explanation."

Hattie couldn't meet Piotr's eyes. She looked around the room for something to focus on.

"And the woman at the desk in the office verified it. Ben had talked to the doctor the very day he left here. Anya hasn't heard from him since. Now what explanation could there possibly be except . . . ?"

Hattie took the weight of his condemnation of Ben upon herself. She felt it like a body falling into her arms.

Feebly, she responded with the only bit of information she could give, "Maybe he couldn't help it. Maybe something happened to him. He told Anya he was going to ask for a different assignment or look for a different job, one that allowed him to stay home."

"Anya would believe anything he said. Can you imagine a secret job that she could not know about? What kind of a story is that? Whoever, besides such an innocent like Anya, would believe that? And if you believe it too, you're just as naïve."

Her eyes stung at his innocent but hurtful reproach. Of course she *had* always believed Ben, just like Anya. "Piotr, surely you don't really think he'd deliberately abandon them, do you?"

At that moment Piotr's purposeful, angry face crumbled into grief. "I only set eyes on the man one time. And I didn't trust him. But she's my sister. I loved her and I should have taken better care of her long ago. Maybe I'm putting my own guilt on him. But she's dying. That's a fact. And he's nowhere to be found. That's a fact too. What else is there to think? And worse than seeing her so sick is knowing that she is tortured by thoughts of him. She can't even have a peaceful death. You tell me if there is anything that can be said in his defense."

Hattie wanted to say something more. When she attempted to speak everything she knew about the day Ben died was waiting to be spoken. Only she could explain that Ben had intended to do just what he had promised, that he had been about to make the changes in his life that would allow him to care of Anya and Kasia. That he had fully intended to leave Hattie and come back to Hartford and be the husband and father he could be. He had already begun to set the train in motion, but he died.

But how would any of it matter, except to hurt the rest of them and to condemn Ben all the more as his bigamy was revealed? In the half-truth and lie department she was complicit with Ben. She, the injured wife, and Ben, the well-intentioned bigamist. Her anger tasted like ashes.

But she heard herself say, "I know it's hard for you to believe this, but bitterness only hurts the one who feels it. Give up the anger you have against Ben. Make your energy take on something else. You have Anya and Kasia to think of now. Give all your emotion to them and the rest of it, all of the negative parts, will dilute themselves."

Piotr relaxed visibly at her words, "I know you're right. But you'll have to remind me from time to time. Anya and I have that in common too: we're good at holding a grudge."

"Did the doctor say anything else? Anything more about Anya's condition?"

"Only that he's amazed that she's been able to hold on this long. She's obviously been drawing on all her reserves of strength to wait for Ben to come back. For him to come and take care of Kasia."

"Piotr," Hattie said softly, "soon I'll have to leave here. I was waiting . . ." Then she saw his reaction. "No, not for Ben. But for someone, something . . . you, I guess. To come to care for them. I couldn't leave them alone. Now that you're here."

"Please. Oh, please," he responded quickly. "Don't leave right away. I need you to stay. We all do. I know how much you've done. I know it's asking a great deal. But we need your help. It can't be long . . . and Kasia loves you and trusts you. Don't leave her yet. She hardly knows me."

Chapter sixty-three

There was a respite, a few days of undiluted pleasure, of sitting around the house, with Anya and Piotr reminiscing about their lives in Poland, recounting for Kasia and Hattie how clever their mother had been, seemingly able to make something out of nothing. How Anya had a silk communion dress of such beauty that the other families gasped. Later, their mother had enjoyed telling them how the dress had been made of parachute fabric that she had traded eggs for. After all, who would want a useless, shredded parachute? They both paused in the conversation as if they saw their mother rushing in the door with her prize and could hear her laughter as she explained her coup.

"It's too bad she didn't get to see you, *Malutka.* You had a fine grandmother, a very wonderful *babcia*. She would have taken that blond hair in her hands, just like this," and Piotr reached over and grabbed a handful of Kasia's long beautiful hair and put it to his face. Rubbing the hair across his cheeks, he said in a voice imitating his mother's voice, soft but strong, "'Like wheat,' she would have said. 'Beautiful like the wheat growing in fields of sunlight in Poland.' Then she would go out to the edge of the roof by the porch where she gathered rainwater. She'd carry it in and warm it on the stove and wash your hair with the special soap she made. 'Rainwater and honey soap, that will keep the shine in your hair.'"

The child laughed and flushed with the attention from her uncle. Hattie noticed Kasia didn't move away from him after he released her hair, but sat close by his side, looking up at him from time to time. And Piotr had begun to call her *Malutka*, and sometimes, *Slodka Malutka*, which he told Hattie meant 'pretty little one.'

"Oh, Piotr. How you remember so many things . . . I'd forgotten the hair baths in rainwater and the smell of that soap, good enough to make you want to take a piece of it in your mouth. I'd forgotten so many things." Anya's face was filled with the light of memory. Hattie thought how beautiful she was—is this how she looked when Ben fell in love with her?

Other things Piotr knew better about, because he was so much older than Anya. He remembered how, after the war, after their father was gone, their mother would bake the lightest, sweetest *babka*, the top domed high, filled with raisins and gleaming, then take them in her big basket to the market. When she returned, she'd have enough to make two batches of *babka* and enough left over to feed them for a few days.

When Piotr saw Anya's garden, his eyes glistened. "Just like Mama," he whispered. "You can make something beautiful grow anywhere."

The next night was uncommonly warm for mid-November. They all bundled up and went out into the garden to look at the moon. Piotr had carried a chair for Anya and she sat quietly, but her eyes moved from Hattie to Piotr to Kasia and back again. Hattie and Piotr sat on the steps of the back porch. Kasia skipped around the garden, happy for this unusual after-dinner event. She began to sing, "Carolina Moon," Ben's song for evenings in the fresh air.

Hattie recognized it immediately. The sting she had felt when Anya or Kasia sang one of Ben's tunes didn't come over her this time. Piotr's arm was near hers and she felt the heat and vigor of his body. Ben's song seemed to come from far away and had lost its power to hurt her.

There was no doubt, it had happened to her before, almost thirty years earlier, but she remembered it so well, that arc of electricity between two people. The summer evening Ben Darling had walked into her life, she had felt it. And now. Hattie and Piotr had crept into each other's hearts amid misunderstanding and sadness.

At first Hattie tried to deny it to herself. When that was impossible, she tried to talk herself out of it. And when that failed, she thought of it as another complication in this whole scenario that she would have to deal with, almost as if she were continually being challenged with a new hurdle as soon as mastery of the previous one seemed within her range. Suddenly she had to fight with herself to keep her plan in mind. Very soon, she'd have to figure out what she could do to cure herself of the spell she was under, but for the moment, it was so pleasant.

Chapter sixty-four

As the weeks passed with Piotr in the house, Hattie felt the tension between them growing. She was aware of Piotr's presence every minute and tormented by her own attraction to him. On the other hand, she recalled how she had worried when Mr. Miles, at the reading center for the blind, seemed to be interested in her, and how afraid she had been that everything that had happened, Ben's death and her discovery of his betrayal, had destroyed that part of her which could respond sexually.

One evening, after Kasia and Anya went upstairs to read, Piotr sat in the living room near the fringed lamp, which threw odd shadows on his cheek and neck. Hattie made herself busy putting some things in the china closet.

"Can you come here and sit with me, Hattie?" he asked.

A small tremor of pleasure swept over her as she put away the last place mat and walked over to him. When she got home from her work at the reading center, she had changed into khaki slacks and a turtleneck for her evening walk. She wished she had worn something more feminine. Too late to think about that, or wonder whether her hair was combed. Something was coming.

"I don't know how to talk to you about this," he said. And this is certainly a very hard situation and therefore I may be misguided or mistaken. If so, please forgive me. But . . ." He stopped.

"But?" she asked, searching his face for clues. Did he suspect something about her? Had he continued to find her story implausible? She knew from her own experience and how easily she herself had located Anya that if he were really suspicious, he could find out about her in short order.

"But, I have this feeling." He gazed at her. "Let me start somewhere else. When my mother died, I thought it was going to be the end of the world. Then Anya left, and I thought it was going to be a good thing for me, and it turned out to be awful. I missed her so much. But maybe that turned out to be a good thing, because I worked so hard, all day and night, and something good happened for me in my business.

"Then I thought I should try to have a regular life. No matter how I looked for the right person, I couldn't. I'd been in love once when I was very young and she went away. I never had that feeling again, but I knew what it was, at least enough to know I didn't have it. I kept trying to will myself into that feeling with this one or that. But always the voice telling me it's not right, not the right one. Maybe I'm miserable by myself, but I thought to myself: why make two people miserable as I surely would if it was not the right person for me?

"Then this terrible thing happens with Anya. And I rush over here. The door opens and before I even know who you are, what a kind, wonderful person you are, I have it, the feeling. It was miraculous and unexpected. *Niema tego zlego co by na dobre nie wyszlo.*"

Hattie was once again charmed by the sound of Piotr's soft voice using the syllables of his language. She loved the sturdy sound of the Polish words and the wisdom and simplicity of the sayings. "What are you saying, Piotr?"

"What, you haven't picked up Polish yet? I guess we're not eating enough *pierogi*," he laughed. "It means there is no such bad thing that doesn't result in some good." He held up his hand and smiled, pointing to her.

"I've often found that the case. But it's usually hard to see it at the time," responded Hattie, thinking, then, about Ben's death. How long would she have gone on living that half-life, the dread and empty feeling around Ben's absences and lies which she had tried to stifle by losing herself in making her home beautiful? She recalled, as if from some very distant past, that fear that had made her unable to leave her home and familiar surroundings. Piotr interrupted her thoughts.

"I know what I'm feeling for you."

"Piotr. I . . . I . . . I mean. How can you be sure of something like that? We're all so overwrought . . ."

"Please, Hattie, if you don't feel it, you can say so. But don't try to talk me out of it. I know what I know."

"Okay," Hattie said, averting her eyes. Should she risk saying what she felt?

As if stealing her thoughts, Piotr said, "Now that I've put my heart out before you, can you please tell me if I can hope."

And for a moment, love seemed so simple. Hattie forgot about how she had gotten there, how tortured and convoluted her relationship with Anya and Kasia and Piotr was. She forgot about Fenston and Ben and Alice. Out of her mouth, almost involuntarily came the single syllable, "Yes."

Piotr quickly took her in his arms and held her. "Yes," she said. "I feel it too. But I don't know what it means." As his gentle eyes studied her face, she remembered the half-truths. "Yes, I know what I feel, but I can't say I'm not afraid. Life is so complicated sometimes, it almost seems funny. Like it is deliberately playing some big jokes on us." Suddenly, they were kissing, an oasis of joy in the sorrow swirling around them.

Chapter sixty-five

A few days later, as she rushed down the steps to go to work, Piotr called to her from the kitchen where he had been steaming cabbage to make *hulupka.* "Do you have to leave right now?" he asked. "I wanted to talk to you about something without Kasia around. But I don't want to hold you up."

"Sure. I make my own schedule." She watched him carefully separate the wilted leaves and lay them out on the kitchen table. Slowly he measured out the seasoning for the meat filling.

"I've been thinking. I know you do research. I thought you could help," he paused and looked up at her as if she should know what he was talking about.

"Of course I'll help in any way I can. But what is it, Piotr?"

She waited, but he didn't look up at her. "Anya wants to try to find him. She thinks he's just away somewhere and that he doesn't know how sick she is. She begged me to look for him."

"Oh," Hattie's mouth fell open in shock. "And you're going to do it?"

"Can I not give her this wish? Even the convicts about to be executed, get their last wish."

"Are you certain?"

"Perhaps I want to find him, too."

"But why?"

"Anya thinks she still loves him. He should see what he's done. And I want her to see him as he is."

"Oh," Hattie's breath left her involuntarily.

"Will you or won't you help?"

"If it's really what you want. But let's think this through first."

"What's to think? He should be here. He should be made to suffer too. And not get off by just walking away."

"You really want that? What will it prove? Who will it help? Let it go. Wherever he is, he's suffering. Can't you let it go at that?"

"Why should I? He gets out of this without a scratch. And Anya dies."

Hattie's mind froze with all the terrible possibilities of what might happen if Piotr insisted on finding Ben. Piotr had already proved that the language barrier didn't exist for him. And he was smart enough to get on to Ben's trail in a few hours were he to set his mind to it. What would that mean for her? She spoke slowly, as if she were measuring the words. But she was really thinking of how she was shielding herself. "Think about what would happen if he did come back. He'd take Kasia. You'd have no claim on her. Then you'd have nothing. Please think about her, what's best for her. Leave Ben alone. For her sake, if not for yours and Anya's."

She looked down to see the neat pile of cabbage rolls that Piotr had made while they talked. She watched his practiced hands roll each bright green leaf around a small heap of spicy filling and secure it with a toothpick.

Still Piotr didn't look up. Nor did he speak. Hattie stood watching as if she could not do otherwise. There was something about the man, about the self-contained and orderly way he went about things, even the small things—the careful preparation of food, the lovingly recounted story—which made her want to be around him. Even now, with the awful truth of Ben's deceit and now her own between then, she did not want to move away. Held by his silence, Hattie waited.

Finally when he had filled and wrapped and secured the last cabbage leaf with its toothpick, he wiped his hands on the towel he had set over the bowl, and sighed heavily.

"Yes, of course you're right. But sometimes this rage comes to me. And I think the only way to rid myself of it is to find that man and make him suffer too. But of course this is not about me and my revenge. It is about what is best for Anya and Kasia. Thank you for helping me see that."

Halfway to the center, Hattie still felt the panic wash over her again when she realized just how vulnerable she'd made herself by her deceit.

Chapter sixty-six

Hattie was alone in the kitchen when Kasia came running in waving a letter.

"It's for you, Hattie. For you. But why do you suppose they wrote to Hattie Darling? Isn't that funny?"

Hattie felt the blood rushing to her face. Oh, God, how could this have happened? Did Athena give someone the address? She must have. But why? The terror grew in her as she looked up, hoping that Piotr was not around. Nonchalantly, she tried to take the letter from Kasia before he heard.

But he followed the child into the room and stood behind her looking quizzically at Hattie.

"What do you think it's about?" he asked. His voice was warm and calm as usual, but Hattie read something—suspicion or concern in his tone.

"What?" It was an uninspired answer, but all she could think of.

After what seemed like an eternity, Kasia handed the letter to Hattie.

Hattie Darling
c/o 321 Gordon Street
Hartford, CT

She drew in her breath and stared at it. They both stared at her.

"I don't know," she said. "I don't know what to say."

"Isn't it weird?" Kasia asked. Do they think your name is Hattie Darling?"

"There must be some mistake," Hattie said, regaining her thought process, which seemed to have stalled in shock. "It's from my daughter. It's her writing." Blessedly, Alice had only put her address and not her name on the upper left. "I told her to write to me c/o Darling at this address. She must have got confused and wrote it down the other way."

Piotr looked at her warily.

"Yes, that's it. That's the only thing I can think of. She must have worried that it wouldn't get to me and written it down wrong."

They both stood looking at her, Piotr with a measured expression. Kasia said, "Wouldn't it be funny if your name really was Hattie Darling? Then we'd have the same last name. Maybe we'd be related."

"We are related, aren't we, Little One? Aren't all people who care about each other related?"

"Yes, but you know what I mean."

"Yes, I do," Hattie sighed. "Thanks for bringing me my mail." And she took the letter from Kasia and left the room, hoping that she was not as shaken on the outside as she was on the inside.

In her room, she peeled open the letter from Alice, amazed at her own emotion and eagerness. She had not spoken to Alice on the phone since she had left Fenston after Ben's funeral. Obviously on some level, she had not allowed herself to feel the pain of their separation. Relief flooded her as she read her daughter's words.

> Dear Mom,
>
> I miss you so much. I can't believe we haven't been in touch for six months. I know much of what happened is my fault, and I hope you can forgive me. I'm coming back to Pennsylvania. They said I'd always be able to get my job back in Pittsburgh, but I thought I'd spend some time at the farm first. Athena gave me this address. She didn't say why you were there, except to get away. We have so much to talk about and figure out. I expect to be home for Christmas Eve. Will you?
>
> Love, Alice

Chapter sixty-seven

Though she knew Anya's health couldn't last, Hattie was taken by surprise at the wave of illness that overcame her the following week. Perhaps, as the doctor had suggested, she had been miraculously holding herself together until something was resolved, or until someone else had taken charge. That was clearly a role that Piotr welcomed. He met with the doctor again, made arrangements for home-care workers to start coming, and rented various stands and implements, as well as a special bed to make the sickroom more convenient.

Hattie stood back and watched in grateful amazement. Despite his soft, even demeanor, he was a person who knew how to deal with people and situations. For all his tenderness and softness, he was obviously used to being in charge and listened to. As much as possible, she tried to stay out of the way, ostensibly leaving each morning to go to her job and returning with groceries in the late afternoon in time to make dinner.

Hattie was afraid of the intensity of her feelings for Piotr. She avoided them by telling herself that it was an emotionally charged time and she was just reacting to her own displaced grief.

Often, though, she and Piotr met and the feelings would flare up. One evening he said, "Hattie, I feel like you are running away from me." He took her hand and kissed it. "There's so much pain in the world," he said, inclining his head toward the stairway and Anya's sickroom. "Can't we have the little bit of beauty and light we're allotted without having to worry about it or feel ashamed?" He took her into his arms and kissed her softly on the face, first her eyelids, then her cheeks, then her forehead, nose and finally very briefly and lightly on her lips. "Let's just be gentle with each other. We're both sad and wounded, but hiding it away from each other and ignoring what we feel, well, that won't make anything easier."

Wordlessly, she nodded yes into his chest.

Gradually, Hattie spent less time reading for the blind as she took over much of the running of the house. She cooked and cleaned and straightened like she had her whole life. Gradually, Piotr found his way into the kitchen too, bringing all manner of foods from Anya's childhood that he hoped would tempt her. He showed Kasia and Hattie how to make *pierogi*, the dumplings with potatoes and onions. The next night it was *bigos*, a tangy dish of *sauer-kraut* and special sausage he had to get across town in a specialty shop. Kasia's favorite was something her mother had always made as a special treat, *leniwe pieogi*, the soft dumplings made of cheese and eggs and flour and cooked quickly in boiling water and tossed with melted butter and cinnamon sugar. Hattie was glad to see Piotr and Kasia working side by side in the kitchen. She pretended to be busy in the other room while the chefs worked at Piotr's most special dish, *golabki*, rice and meat folded into cabbage leaf bundles, which resembled the little sleeping doves they were named for. Anya could only eat a few mouthfuls at a time, no matter now they coaxed and how she tried.

Chapter sixty-eight

By Thanksgiving Anya was nearly bedridden. The health care worker came every morning, and the rest of the time Hattie and Piotr were on call. Hattie gave up all pretense of working, explaining that it was a slow time; the company was in litigation and wouldn't be needing a lot of research just then. She didn't try to make the story any more convincing, as it seemed of little interest to anyone, beyond Anya and Piotr's grateful looks when she said she would stay on to help out.

She and Kasia were in charge of making the Thanksgiving dinner. The two shopped together and carried home all the fixings for a traditional dinner. It would be Kasia's first, since Ben had always been away working at Thanksgiving and Anya didn't celebrate the holiday. When Hattie saw Kasia's enthusiasm for the task, she drew it out over a few days, hoping to have a chance to talk. Kasia seemed strangely detached from her mother's illness, never speaking of it or asking a question. Yet it was clear that the child was suffering.

Chapter sixty-nine

Around the table laden with delicious food, a feast which Hattie and Kasia had delighted in preparing, was an aura of make believe. Or was it only in Hattie's mind? If only Anya were not dying. If only her love for Piotr were not so complicated. If only it were another time when celebration would be in order. She looked around and saw the acceptance in Anya's eyes, the sorrow in Piotr's and the fear in Kasia's. What did her own face reveal, so plain for everyone to read the emotions of her life?

Piotr had brought a bottle of champagne. Anya could only have a few sips. A small glass thimble was fetched from the sideboard so that Kasia could have a taste. She puckered up to the glass as if she expected medicine; small wonder, with all she'd seen of the potions and pills and regimen that were still not able to keep her mother alive. Piotr gave the traditional toast, "*Na Zdrowie*," he registered the irony of drinking to health with Anya pale and hopelessly thin beside him.

The turkey lay in its glazed skin and waited. Hattie removed her apron and sat, the mother at table, a role so familiar to her. Piotr toasted Hattie and Thanksgiving itself, saying how happy he was to be enjoying the American holiday. If Hattie was any example of how good Americans are, he could stay forever. Anya and Kasia clapped as Hattie blushed when Piotr lifted his glass to her. The two of them finished the rest of the champagne amid many giggles and Polish toasts.

Somewhere toward evening it was decided that Christmas would be early that year; they would celebrate in two weeks, an announcement that made Kasia jump to her feet. Later as she and Hattie did the dishes together, the child explained that they almost always had an early Christmas because her father had to be away from home for the actual holiday. "Special Christmases," Kasia said, because they belonged only to them. Everyone else was going around doing their usual things, school or work or shopping, and she and her parents were celebrating. She was allowed to take days off from school to make it more special.

"I got many presents. Last year a Chatty Cathy doll," she smiled up at Hattie who in turn was thinking of the holidays that she and Ben had shared, enjoying their home and friends and wonderful meals, while Anya and Kasia were here alone. A shudder went through her.

Kasia was sitting on the sofa with her mother, talking quietly about what toys she wanted this year. She had enumerated four or five things, when Anya held up her hand. "Remember that Papa is not here this year," Anya said evenly, though Hattie caught a glimpse of something behind her eyes. "You probably won't be getting as many gifts."

"Just because Papa is not here?"

"Because we already talked about this, you and I. Just because."

Hattie sensed Anya's frustration and embarrassment, as she tried to keep the conversation from escalating into an argument.

"I don't care. It's not fair. Why do I always have to have the worst things? First we have to have Christmas not on Christmas. Now Papa goes away and won't come back even for that Christmas." Hattie had retreated to the kitchen to avoid letting anyone see her tear-filled eyes. Piotr, so far, was keeping out of the discussion, though she could see by the set of his shoulders he was tensed to speak. As Kasia's voice rose, the back of her neck, the only part of her body Hattie could see, became bright red in rage. "It's not fair."

"Now dear, just calm down. You know you'll have a good Christmas. Just maybe not as many gifts as you're used to."

"It's all your fault anyway. Papa is gone. It's your fault. You're always sick and he doesn't want to be with us anymore." The child flung herself into the recesses of one of the chairs and threw her face into her hands. "It's your fault," she whimpered.

Anya struggled to her feet and went over to her daughter and pried her hands from her face with surprising ease. The child dove into her mother's chest, her back heaving with tears.

"Oh, Mama, why has Papa gone away? I didn't think he would stay away for Christmas."

Anya smoothed her daughter's hair and hushed her, rocking back and forth, "You know, Little One, how much your father loves you. Never forget that. We don't know what happened, why Papa has not come back. But we do know that if he can, he will. He loves you and would never leave you."

Hattie stood at the door strangling on her own emotions. She could see Piotr's face darkened with frustration. The impossibility of the growing love she felt for him tore at her. "Oh, what a tangled web . . ." ran through Hattie's thoughts as a refrain. She felt its threads tighten around her heart and heard Athena's admonition. Now she had enmeshed herself so deeply that she could not wrench herself loose.

Piotr stood and walked over to where Anya and Kasia were huddled comforting each other. "So let's talk about presents. But first we have to talk about jobs. Christmas is a lot of work and we're going to need everyone's help to make this a wonderful party." Despite the hollow ring his words had, like tin cans rolling down a wet street, they were all grateful that he had given them a way back to where they had been. Shaken by Kasia's anger and afraid of how the fragile air could at any moment become toxic, they were eager to stagger through the small space he had opened.

"I'll do the cooking," he said. "Since we've had the wonderful American Thanksgiving, I will make us a Polish Christmas. But like all great chefs, I'll need a helper." Kasia's hand went up immediately.

Chapter seventy

After Athena's surprise visit and Alice's letter, Hattie was more conscientious about her phone calls. She didn't want another shock. Though she missed Athena very much, she didn't think she could withstand another collision of her lives. In an odd way, she knew how Ben must have felt as he shuttled between the two women he loved.

In order to live fully inside what she was experiencing in Hartford, she had forced herself to stop thinking about Fenston. Like keeping Alice out of her thoughts, she had been pretty successful at excluding Fenston except when she heard Athena's voice. Then the lump of longing in Hattie's throat would become so large she could hardly squeak out, "Hi, Athena, it's me."

Through the fall, she had been given weekly reports about her neighbors, all of whom, according to Athena, could not exist another day without Hattie. Nonetheless, they had managed. Tom was home from the hospital without his appendix; the elections were over and Crystalle had elected John Whiten town supervisor, six weeks after he died. "So much for local politics," Athena quipped, "He'll probably do a better job than the rest of them." But the big news was that the Rodiri household had become interested in faith healing when Eddie's leg problems had been cleared up at a revival meeting. They had joined a Pentecostal Catholic group in Scranton and had taken to the highways to proselytize. This newfound fervor brought the family together; all their other problems subsumed in the search for new souls to convert. But there was bigger news yet.

"Paul's coming back. Got a card from him yesterday, Arizona, Tombstone. I think. Said he's about seen enough. Ready to come home," Athena all but crowed.

"Did he say when?"

"Nope. Just that he'd be back soon and missed everyone." Hattie wanted to ask if Paul had asked specifically about her but couldn't find the words.

"What's the latest from Hartford?"

"Thank God I asked Anya about her brother. Five days after you left, he was ringing the doorbell."

"Good. I'm glad for Anya and Kasia that he's there. Now let's talk about you being here. You've done everything humanly possible for them, even for you and that crazy sense of duty you have. Now, you have to let them be to work it out for themselves. You need to come home."

"I'm almost ready. But . . ."

"Almost? But? But what? Just get in the car and come home."

"I will very soon, I promise. I just want to stay a while to see Piotr get started, to help him. After all, he and Anya haven't really spoken to each other in twelve years. And he'd never even seen Kasia."

"What's he like?" An innocuous enough question, but Hattie knew at once that her voice had betrayed her, alerting Athena that there was something else, some kind of connection to this man.

"Oh, he's very nice."

"Yes . . . ?"

"Attractive," Hattie gave up the information hoping that Athena would be satisfied as she herself didn't want to examine her own tumultuous feelings about Piotr, afraid of what she might find.

"How old?"

"Didn't I tell you? He's fifteen years older than Anya. Fiftyish, I guess."

"Okay, attractive, single, fiftyish. Is there anything else you want to tell me about him?"

So much, Hattie thought. The way he holds his head when he speaks, as if speaking were a pact between two people. How his arms look when he rolls back his cuffs to wash the dinner dishes. His easy humor, the teasing by which he won Kasia over.

"A nice man," she said. "A nice man with a life of great sadness. And there's more of it to come."

"Well, don't take it on yourself. You've done enough there. Just come on home."

"Have you had snow yet?" Hattie asked, partially attempting to change the subject, partially because she suddenly had a clear view of how beautiful Fenston was in winter. She could see herself in twilight standing at her kitchen window. Those lines, "Watch the woods fill up with snow," came to mind. The beauty and peace of her farm, the land she owned both by birthright and by love rose in front of her, provoking terrible longing and loneliness. Suddenly, she knew how important it was for her to have the connection to the land, to that specific place.

"Six or seven inches last night. On top of the five from Wednesday. We're off to a good start this year. Windy, too. The kids are having a hard time keeping the lake clear for skating. Will just said last night he was going to get the cross-country skis ready. Maybe tonight we'll ski the lake path instead of walking." Hattie thought of her two friends, their nightly ritual of walking from their store and home the mile through thick woods to the shore of Chaplin Lake.

"Gibbous moon tonight. And with all this snow, it will be bright enough to read a book outdoors," Athena said, obviously relishing the prospect of her evening.

In the background, Hattie could hear store noises. She tried to call mid-afternoon when she knew Athena wouldn't be busy. After lunch there was always a lull in the trade. Athena had remarked she could leave the store empty from one to three thirty and nobody'd know the difference. "I hear you have a customer," Hattie said. "I'll let you go."

"It's just Clem. He's back talking to Will. Just one more thing. You'll never guess what Eddie and Eleanor are up to. Got it in their heads they are going to celebrate Christmas special this year, being as they got this new religion."

Hattie smiled as she imagined Athena's tongue in cheek expression. "Yes?"

"Eddie's over at their place, all his drills and tools and wires spread out all over the house. "I'm making a star of welcome and guidance for all who need it, Athena," she imitated Eddie's gruffness. "It's the star of peace."

"So I said, 'That's nice, Eddie. It will be a real nice addition to the rest of your Christmas display.'" Athena and Hattie both laughed. "Maybe you could put it over near Rudolph or the carolers, or up behind Santa and the sleigh."

Drawn into Athena's humor, Hattie suggested they move the life-sized plaster-of-Paris crèche to the right nearer to Frosty and put the star up behind the skaters and the giant candy canes, gingerbread men and Hershey kisses. "Or if they've let Halloween linger like they usually do, they might fix the star to a tower of pumpkins." Even her amusement at recalling the seasonal clutter of the Rodiri's front yard carried a tinge of longing.

"I mentioned something like that myself. 'Well,' says Eleanor, sweeping over to stand next to Eddie. 'Well, you can make fun if you want. But all the other stuff is going.

Now that we see the truth, we're getting rid of all the things that detract from the real spirit of Christmas. This year it will only be the crèche and the star.'"

Hattie could see the righteous quiver of Eleanor's face as she told Athena off. "'And as for the placement of the star. That has already been decided by the Good Book. Any fool knows that it has to be on the north side, so we're attaching it to the barn. That way, too, it will be seen for miles around. Eddie is making a huge pole and we'll put the star up there. It'll look down on us all, believers and non believers alike.' And you just know how she looked at me all smug and righteous, 'and maybe some of these others will get some sense in their heads and see the light of salvation beaming down on them from atop our barn.'" Athena's voice was the perfect blend of icy and huffy as she imitated Eleanor.

"I needed that." Hattie was still laughing when she said goodbye.

Chapter seventy-one

Kasia and Piotr struggled into the house carrying an enormous Norway spruce.

"Look, Hattie. Isn't it wonderful? Where's Mom?"

Anya was lying on the sofa, and Kasia rushed over to her. "Isn't it beautiful." Both their faces were lit by the child's enthusiasm.

"We had the best pick. I'm sure it was the first tree they'd sold, but it wasn't the first one we looked at," Piotr said, clapping his hands together for warmth. "We walked up and down at least three different tree places before *Malutka* found the right one." He looked at the child with great warmth and pleasure.

"Yes. The man selling the trees couldn't believe we were actually going to buy it. He said it was the best tree in the city. He agreed with us," Kasia added delightedly. "And I found it."

"She was a regular hawkeye, isn't that what you call it?" Piotr added and they all laughed. Piotr righted the tree in the stand, and Hattie rummaged the back cupboard where Anya had said the ornaments were and found three boxes of colored bulbs and lights, not nearly enough for the size tree Kasia had chosen. Hattie and Kasia made a quick trip to the mall to buy three dozen new bulbs and some lights and tinsel. As they left, Piotr asked them to stop and see if they could get a little package of straw, perhaps from the greengrocer.

The house was fragrant with new smells when they returned. Piotr and Anya had been in the kitchen and a feast was in the making. First they would have traditional *borscht* with *uszka*, the small swirled dumplings called little ears, which they resembled. Piotr had evidently called all over town until he found a butcher shop that had tongue, the traditional holiday delicacy, which would be served with dilled mashed potatoes. Piotr had carried Anya down the stairs so she could supervise the food preparation and tree decorating. She sat at the table and cut small jewels of dried fruit, which Piotr cooked and stirred until the bits of prune and apricot and raisins and lemon rind were plump and glistening, a holiday compote.

The table was set with the best things in the house, some linen napkins and a lovely old cloth with tatting along the edges that Anya said had belonged to Mrs. Morris. "It's nice to have her at our table for the holiday, isn't it? After all, she belongs here too." From her seat, Anya carefully selected plates and glasses. Then Piotr gave them each a small sheaf of straw. Hattie followed his lead as he lifted the cloth and placed a few stalks of straw here and there under it in places around the table, explaining to Hattie the Polish custom that reminds the revelers of the first humble Christmas scene, the imperative to offer hospitality to others. Kasia's eyes were large and questioning and luminous like Alice's had been at Christmas time, as she relished the unfamiliar customs of her heritage.

"I'd forgotten that too, Piotr. How many memories you've given me—thoughts of the old times with Mama."

Piotr's eyes misted over too, "Now, I wish I could say that I made the *babka*, then I could be sure it would be like the one Mama was famous for all over Warszawa. I bought it from the woman at the Polish deli, who promised me it would be delicious. So we shall see."

They ate in silence, intent on the food and the evening before them. Kasia's emergence from her shell was increasing daily. She looked at her uncle with adoration and he at her. Amid her joy and relief that Piotr and Kasia had bonded so easily, Hattie felt a small pang of sorrow.

Chapter seventy-two

After dinner, they took seats in the living room, Anya on the couch and Kasia next to her, Piotr and Hattie in the armchairs. The Old World sense of the room that Hattie had felt the first time she walked in the door was even more present with the tree lit and its soft light caught by tinsel glinting on all the surfaces.

Suddenly overwhelmed with happiness, Hattie thought: just let time stop. Let Anya not die, let Kasia not grow up, let Piotr not return to Poland, let no one find out what Ben and I have done. Since the evening when she and Piotr admitted their attraction to each other, Hattie had tormented herself with all the possible scenarios that might play out between them. How she could be so tortured and still feel the incredible peace of this special evening,

Hattie could not imagine. Yet she did. She wished only to hold the moment inside herself, knowing that it could nourish her through some bad times ahead.

"Time for bed, Kasia," Anya said. "Tomorrow will come only if you sleep tonight."

"But we forgot," the little girl said, dragging out the emphasis as if it should be obvious to everyone just what they had forgotten.

"What?" her mother answered.

"You know."

"I don't know. What is it, dear?"

"What we always do last thing at night when we put up the tree."

"Oh, yes, I'd forgotten. Hattie, could you turn off all the rest of the lights in the house?"

When the house was in total darkness except the small white lights on the branches of the tree and the dim wash of street lights and traffic against the living-room blinds, Kasia began in Polish a song her mother had taught her. Anya's breathy voice tried to follow along. Then Piotr's voice, thick with emotion, steadied itself and supported both voices and lifted and carried them through the verse to its sure conclusion. Hattie heard the Polish, not knowing what any of the words meant, but knowing it was a Christmas song, a song about the dream of peace and plenty, the joy a child brings to the sad confusing world.

Chapter seventy-three

After she put her nightclothes on, Hattie looked down into the living room and realized the tree was still alight. Thinking that she was the last one awake she hurried to unplug it and found Piotr sitting alone looking at the tree. After Anya and Kasia had gone to bed, she and Piotr had put the gifts they had bought under the tree. When they both judged their handiwork perfect, Piotr had gone up to his room. Hattie thought it odd that he had not said good night, but the evening had been so bittersweet she assumed he needed to be private with his emotions, an impulse she understood.

During the time that Piotr had been in the house, the emotional pitch between them had grown. Hattie felt it in her body, how it moved by itself in a new way, the way she sensed him next to her with small prickles inside her wrists and elbows. Had it occurred in a context devoid of risk and obfuscation, Hattie would have called it a delicious tension. When they were gathered around the tree earlier that evening, it had lessened to a merely warm familiarity. But when she entered the darkened living room and saw Piotr, she felt it leap within her.

He stood as if in answer. They both understood. They both accepted what the merest contact between them now would mean, and the inevitability of their touch. And yet he walked toward her and she toward him. Both of them knowing. So that when they kissed it was a determined hunger satisfying itself. But that was not enough. Gently he put his hands under her arms and lifted her to him. They were breathing into each other, pulling the air from each other's lungs, passing their life force back and forth between them. His mouth covered hers; his warm tongue traced her lips and moved as if he wanted to know each small crevice of her being. Hattie felt her legs grow weak with passion as Piotr and she slipped to the couch, she half sitting with him kneeling before her.

Even through her nightgown, she felt the warmth of his hands. Suddenly, he was kissing her neck and face and pushing his face into the coppery mass of her hair. "I can't . . . I can't do without you. I can't. Oh, Hattie, please let me love you." She pulled herself toward him, feeling herself moisten in greeting. Her own need was a frenzy inside her as he slipped out of his clothes and spread her legs with his hand, touching her there and there and there and making her want to shriek out for sheer wanting.

When he entered her, she caught her breath. With each movement, she felt the steady weight of his large body on hers pushing her, pushing them both toward climax, the giddy oblivion they were to give each other. As they struggled together, Hattie felt her body opening and opening to him, and always there was the next layer waiting for still more pleasure.

When she came, she was oddly aware of her surroundings, the lighted tree, the old couch, the obsolete wallpaper, somehow swirled together in the pleasure of the moment to make a place she'd never been before but knew perfectly. At the last moment, she tensed toward him as if she needed something else, something she could not name before she could tip into the healing chasm, and Piotr reached between them and touched the place where his body was connected to hers, and in that moment she fell. And he followed.

Later, as they sat demurely side by side on the couch, dressed as they had been when she entered the room, Hattie was surprised at herself. "They were right upstairs. Kasia might have come down and found us."

Piotr laughed. "She might have. But she didn't."

"Still, she might have."

"Should we always live as if every possible thing that might happen will? Do you think we should never take chances? Imagine if we hadn't taken tonight's chance. I think it was one of the Polish poets, I don't recall who,

who said, 'The train stops, the door opens and everything's different.' Isn't that so? About tonight?"

"Yes. It's so. If you're asking me if I'm happy? Yes, it's so."

"Then it was right?"

"Yes," she whispered. "It was right. For tonight."

"Then maybe this is right too. I was going to wait until tomorrow." When she saw the small box, she realized why he had gone upstairs. He handed it to her.

"It was my mother's, the only piece of jewelry she had. I think that my father had given it to her from his mother." The ring was old-fashioned filigree, a high setting with a small blue stone. "I want you to have it."

"Oh, Piotr. It's very special."

"I thought I'd never find someone I wanted to give it to. I've had it for thirty years and have waited. Now I want you to have it."

Hattie stood holding the ring for a long time, not saying anything, though her thoughts were a torrent. Finally, Piotr took the ring from the box and slipped it onto her finger. "A little big," he pronounced. "We can get it made smaller." He smiled.

"I really don't know what to say. My thoughts are so jumbled."

"I've thought and thought, too. Each night in my bed, I wonder what kind of person I am to be falling in love when my sister is dying in the next room. I go around and around the same idea. But it's futile; I can't stop one any more than I can stop the other. Sometimes we just don't get to choose the things that come to us. Either the good or the bad."

"I'm sure you know I've thought the same. Anya has come to mean so much to me." Hattie felt the tears in her voice and on her cheeks. "And Kasia, Oh, my God, what sadness she's had already in her short life. I don't think I'll ever get rid of the expression on her face when she understood what we were telling her about her mother's illness."

"Ah, *Malutka*," Piotr said, his voice also strangling with emotion. "No matter what presents she gets under the tree tomorrow, we can't give her what she needs, what children all need."

"No. All we can give her is a sense of being loved."

"You and I can give her that. Together. Maybe you haven't thought about what will happen when . . ." he paused, unable to put words to his sister's death. "But I think all night, what will I do? How will I stand it, just finding Anya . . . All these weeks remembering her voice, how she laughs and seeing her and then thinking of all the years I didn't see her. And now she'll be taken away again. But maybe something, maybe God," Piotr used the word God reverently and shyly, "maybe God made it so that if Anya had to die, that at least Kasia would have us, you and me, and we could take care of her and love her and love each other."

"Maybe God should have thought twice before he decided to make her an orphan in the first place." Piotr looked at her strangely and she realized she had implied that Ben was dead. Quickly she added, "Without a mother or a father in sight, she must really feel like an orphan."

"But we can be her family, you and me." Hattie didn't break the spell with the shadow of truth.

Chapter seventy-four

Each day Hattie and Piotr hovered while the health care worker was in the room with Anya. When she emerged, they read her for information about Anya's condition, and maybe a little hope. The first day she arrived she had met with them for a long time. Kasia was at school and they could air all their concerns, which added up to only one question, "How long does she have?"

Arlene Nichols sat at the kitchen table facing them, her hands idly picking at the tea bag label. She was a no-nonsense middle-aged woman with a frizzy perm and glasses on a string around her neck. She looked from Hattie to Piotr with great compassion, but her words were, it seemed to Hattie, straight out of a textbook: "It's a hard one. A case like this. A young woman. So inexplicable.

When it's a cancer, as it often is with the young, there's often so much pain that the family is grateful for the end when it comes. But here, she's not in terrible pain; she's very thin, but otherwise, you couldn't tell how sick she is. It's hard to accept that one day, and no one can tell you exactly when, her heart will just give up its struggle."

Hattie and Piotr both wept. And Arlene was a quiet presence around which their grief could display itself.

"Does she know how close it is?" Hattie asked.

"She's known for a long time. And I think she's ready."

"How can she be ready?" Piotr asked, his accent like his features clotted with emotion.

Arlene and Hattie were both silent. Who could answer his question?

Then Arlene said, "I think you should do whatever you need to make yourselves ready too. Often it's better for people, easier for them to accept the death of a loved one, if they feel they've prepared themselves."

"That sounds so easy. How do you get ready to lose someone you love? How do we help Kasia accept that her mother is dying when we can't accept it ourselves?"

"Of course, I don't really know you or know what Anya's life has been like, so I'm speaking generally. Maybe there are things you need to tell Anya. Things you need to settle between yourselves. Maybe you just need to spend a long time in her presence, in the same room with her silently. Maybe you can pray. There's no right way to do it. Like most important things in this life, we have to work hard at figuring them out for ourselves."

Maybe Arlene had taken courses to know how to help people through bad times, but if that's how she got so wise, Hattie was appreciative of her work. Though it was Anya dying, and each of them shared a little in that death, each was experiencing it in a singular way. Piotr took to sitting with Anya in the mornings while Hattie did a few chores around the house. Hours on end, he recounted every single thing he could recall about her childhood, flooding the room with the warmth of his memory and bringing to Anya the voice of their mother, the smell of the countryside outside of Warszawa and singing to her all their childhood songs. Often he sang long involved ballads in Polish and repeated a litany of the names of their neighbors and her childhood friends.

At noon, Arlene came. And then Anya slept. In the late afternoon, Kasia would bring her schoolwork for her mother to examine. Anya sat propped on the pillow, listening as Kasia read the new story in her book, the childish finger moving over the words as she pronounced each one carefully, a story about a circus day, a lost dog, a new neighbor. There were, of course, no stories about dying mothers or missing fathers.

Although Hattie and Piotr had told Kasia the truth about her mother's condition, the child seemed unable to process it. Every day she would predicate the future on her mother's recovery: "When mother is better, can we go to Disney World, get a new bike, make a picnic, have a puppy?"

"She knows the truth," Arlene said, almost echoing

the words of the school social worker that both Piotr and Hattie had visited. "She's just not able to admit it. Don't force the issue. When she's ready to talk, she will. In the meantime, she needs the comfort of thinking that her mother will get well." Glad, once again, for Arlene's advice, they allowed Kasia the imaginings that kept her world intact. Listening to Piotr's voice, dense and particular as matter itself, Hattie felt him willing Anya to live, his words holding her firmly to the earth.

Chapter seventy-five

After the night they made love by the muted light of the Christmas tree, Hattie and Piotr could not quiet their hunger for each other. All day, as they went about their sad chores, they were keenly aware of each other's presence. At night, after everything had been done to make Anya as comfortable as possible and Kasia was tucked in and asleep, Hattie would slip into Piotr's bed, her old bed in the back room. This was the room which had seen so many of her sleepless nights as she counted the blue cabbage roses, up one wall and down the other, multiplying and subtracting, losing her place, distracted by thoughts about how life seemed to have tricked her.

Those same roses presided over her joy, as she and Piotr made love and then held each other, whispering into the darkness. Often they cried, soothing each other until the first tender light alerted Hattie that it was time to return to the spare bed in Kasia's room. Piotr thought they should be more open about their feelings for each other to Anya and Kasia, but Hattie convinced him that the little girl didn't need to deal with any more change just then.

Piotr's love filled Hattie with awe that she should have found such joy where she least expected it. In the dark, she would trace his lovely mouth with her fingers as he spoke, feeling the accent that lent his words a peculiar stress and charm. Like Piotr, she knew the feeling of falling in love. Like Piotr, she had felt it only once before, a long time ago, that summer when Ben had first come to Fenston. After Piotr's initial declaration of love and his hope that together they could care for Kasia, neither of them spoke beyond the present, perhaps fearing that to do so would be to hasten Anya's death. So they lay in bed talking about their lives.

Hattie, warmed by this new love, spoke truthfully and with great tenderness of her unnamed late husband. Each night in Piotr's arms, she revisited her life with Ben. How together they had planted the apple orchard and repaired the roofs of all the outbuildings of her great-grandparents' farm. She spoke of the pleasure he took in buttoning on a fresh shirt after a shower, how he taught Alice to fish and drive. How his face stayed with her still, though the sorrow of his death had lessened. With no questions as rudder and no sense that they should be doing anything other than lying there talking through their lives, Hattie spoke until she had spent her soul's quota of words.

As she played over the epic of her own life, Hattie had a sense of a light coming on here or there in the forest of her history, drawing her into an episode she needed to recount. And each night when she had finished, she felt a kind of singular grace, a moment when she understood the meaning of her own life story, the value of remembrances totally without rancor or sadness. She saw her years as blessings, dependent neither on Ben's fidelity or her own estimation, but as something other. She had been inside of that life, guided by either wisdom or folly. And who was to say which?

She had done the best she could. And maybe Ben had too. After everything that had happened to her, she was no longer able to say that it was not possible to love more than one person at a time. She had loved Ben, and now she was coming to realize she could love Piotr and there were probably other men she could love as well.

When she fell quiet, instead of questions, Piotr stroked her hair as he would a child's; repeating gently, ever so gently: "Shush, shush . . ." So full were they of their own joy, that even though they were surrounded by the sorrowful penumbra of the house, they would lie with each other in total silence, breathing in and out the same darkness. Often after talk and laughter, they made love again.

Hattie had never experienced such intense erotic pleasure as Piotr was capable of giving her, as by touch and taste they quietly explored each other's bodies. He was a confident lover, solicitous of Hattie's pleasure. Often he lifted her above him, filling her with his passion as he watched the delirium seeping into her eyes.

Chapter seventy-six

Recounting pleasant memories led to deeper reveries, finding the lost spaces in Hattie's past. Suddenly, the period she had searched for, the pivotal days she had longed to recall, surfaced without warning. Piotr slept next to her. She felt the radiant warmth of his body and glanced over at his face, the handsome, kind features, the faint stubble along his chin, his hair askew from lovemaking. After he fell asleep, Hattie slipped into the dark well of her own history.

Ben had been right. He was home for two months straight right before they were informed of Gordie's death. Summer always went by so fast in Fenston. The early part, after their neighbors' spring planting, was given over to house cleaning and the cultivation of flowers. People literally lived outdoors all summer, eating all their meals on the porch or terrace and passing the early evening visiting back and forth and enjoying the light, balmy air.

The 4th of July celebration was central to the small town. A mile-long parade of floats and bands and strutting teams followed the fire engines through Fenston Corners and into the local fire company practice field. After the dusty parade, all the volunteer firemen, almost all the town's able-bodied men, would gather in the beer tent set off against one corner of the field.

Hattie remembered how she and Ben had walked through the lane of booths that sold food and raffle tickets. Alice had abandoned them immediately upon arrival to join her teenage friends. Inside the beer tent, a Country and Western band tuned up and began to play.

"Hey, neighbors," Will Wescott waved to them from a table inside, "I've been saving a spot."

Athena, who was talking to the people at the next table, looked up and smiled and shook the bandana she had worn around her neck, "Hot parading around all day! Now here's the reward."

Within ten minutes, they were surrounded by friends and the chorus of their voices nearly drowned out the band. Toward the end of the evening, Ben took her hand and led her out to the dance floor, "I think you might remember this." The band was playing "The Great Pretender," a golden oldie by the Platters, the group they had so loved in the early years of their life together. Circling Hattie's waist with his arm, Ben pushed his face into the drift of her long hair, "I love you, Hattie Darling," he said.

Smiling, she looked up at him, "What brought that on?"

"Oh, I guess it shouldn't come as any surprise that I love you."

"I didn't mean that."

"Then what?"

"You just looked so serious all of a sudden. What's that about?"

"I just wanted you to know I really do love you. Whatever else happens in my life or our life together, I do love you very much. And sometimes I don't tell you enough."

"Ben, you're scaring me. Is anything wrong?" In that moment, Hattie realized that Ben had been uncommonly quiet during the time he had been home.

"It's nothing."

"But it's not nothing if it's bothering you." Feeling her tension increase, she tried to search his face in the dark.

"Nothing specific, Hattie. I just got to thinking how much I love you. When I'm on the road, everything seems so far away."

"Is everything all right at work?" she asked, hoping that whatever was bothering Ben was that simple.

"Work's the same. Just that there's more of it. No, it's nothing. Nothing you need to worry about . . ."

"If it's a worry to you, I want to know about it."

"You're making something big out of a little comment. I'm not worried about anything. Guess I just have that odd feeling I get right before I go on the road. Like somehow something might change while I'm gone."

"Don't worry about that," Hattie laughed, relieved that Ben seemed to be shaking off his mood. "Nothing ever changes around here, you know that." And she pressed herself against her husband in the dark of the beer tent and he sang to her from the familiar storehouse of refrains they both loved.

The next afternoon, as he packed the car and Hattie helped him gather up things he needed to take with him, she recalled their conversation from the night before. A chill came over her when she thought that Ben might be suffering something he wouldn't share with her.

Kissing him goodbye she held on a little longer than usual, as if she knew that when she saw him next they both might have changed.

As that time nine years ago surfaced in Hattie's memory, tears sprang from her eyes as she realized she had finally located the place where her life and Ben's had diverged forever. There was a moment when it all came to her so clearly that she could hardly breathe. It was then, the summer she could not understand her own fear and confusion, that she had buried away in memories too painful to revisit. About that same time Hattie had begun to experience the crippling fear that had dominated her life for years. She lay in the dark feeling herself deeply in that old terror, connecting it finally with what she couldn't let herself know about Ben.

The next day, though she should have been exhausted with the emotional upheaval and lack of sleep, there was a new sensation of lightness throughout her body, which left Hattie feeling hopeful and at peace.

Chapter seventy-seven

That night, as she held Piotr's hand in hers and she kissed him softly, she told him that it was time for her to leave. In the tricky light of bedside candles, she watched his face darken with sadness at her words. In the silence, they heard the first broom tips of snow against the window. Piotr looked at her with unfathomable tenderness and said, "I know. Even though I dreamed and hoped it would be otherwise, when we were lying here each night, with all the things you told me about your life, I heard that too. That you would have to leave."

"You knew?"

"I heard it in the way you talked about your life. Your family's old house. The child you are missing, your own child. Seeing you with Kasia, well, I can only imagine how you were with your daughter." Still hand-in-hand, they were silent for a moment. "Days ago it came to me that you had been lent to me for this hard time. Lent but not given. I knew you would have to go."

"What will you do?" Hattie asked. "When . . ."

"I've thought about that too. I can't stay here indefinitely. Kasia and I will go back to Poland. I'll have to apply for papers for her, to become her guardian. Then she can get a passport. It might take a while, but eventually it will work out."

Hattie felt tears leaking from her eyes, slipping down her cheeks and landing on her bare chest. Knowing she'd never again have Piotr beside her or inside her, she felt another loss, another layer of sorrow slip over her.

In answer to her silence, he whispered, "You'll always know where we will be, where you can find us, when you want to. If that's the right thing for you."

"Yes," she said. "But in case I can't, I want you to take this and give it to Kasia when she grows up. Please remind her of me," and she slipped the ring Piotr had given her into his hand.

Chapter seventy-eight

At times Anya was so weak she could not walk unaided; then Hattie helped her to the bathroom and waited outside while she bathed. The day after Hattie told Piotr that she would be leaving, she heard a small thump in the bathroom. When Anya didn't respond to her call, Hattie opened the door and went in to find her naked, and on her knees, beside the tub.

"I wanted to use those bath salts, but I couldn't reach them," Anya said, pointing to a small linen sack, which had slipped from the shelf to the floor behind the tub. At first, she shifted her position, as if to conceal her body from Hattie's view. Quickly averting her eyes, Hattie retrieved the bag and sprinkled a handful of grains into the running water.

Suddenly, the room was suffused with lavender-scented steam, and Ben was there with the two women as clearly as if they had conspired to conjure him. A bond between them, his presence, filled Hattie with a sense of rightness. Anya reached to Hattie touching her arm lightly. "Hattie, I don't think I can . . . can you help me?" Hattie regarded Anya's body; the shoulders and breasts lightly freckled, the hipbones jutting against the skin, the nest of sandy hair at the parting of her legs. She could imagine Ben and Anya making love and felt no anger.

Hattie recognized that this moment, this encounter with Anya's physical self, was what she had most feared, most needed in order to let go of the final shred of pain and anger she had felt toward Ben and this other life. How beautiful every single body is, she thought; and how impossible it was to wish another person pain. Sorrow and forgiveness and regret that Ben's life could not have had some closure, asserted themselves in Hattie's heart. She reached out her arms to Anya and then bent and gently lifted her, the woman her husband had also loved, clear of the tub's edge. Both of them sighed with effort as Hattie lowered Anya into the fragrant and forgiving waters.

Chapter seventy-nine

Exhausted after bathing and dressing, Anya lay back in the bed against the pillow, struggling to catch her breath. The house was quiet around the two women. Piotr had gone to pick up Kasia from school. They would probably stop for hot chocolate, a ritual they both enjoyed. Hattie opened the shades, which had been drawn for Anya's rest, and started to leave the room when Anya said, "Wait. Before you do that. Hattie, there's something . . . something I've wanted to ask you."

Perhaps it was Anya's voice, maybe a thought drifting from Anya to Hattie, but immediately Hattie was alert. "Yes," she answered, trying to keep her voice steady.

"About when you came here. About the day you came. I've wanted to tell you something that's bothered me for a long time."

Hattie waited quietly.

Anya paused to regain her breath. "I don't know why, but for a moment I thought you had come to harm us."

"To harm you?"

"Yes, can you imagine? I needed to tell you that. I don't know why."

"You don't know why you thought it, or you don't know why you had to tell me."

Anya paused for a moment, as if trying to figure that out for herself. "Both, I guess."

Hattie thought back to that day, recalling the inquiring, suspicious, but oddly hopeful look on Anya's face. She held her breath afraid that after all this time she might still blurt out what had brought her to Anya's door. How accurate Anya's feelings had been, Hattie realized. She had come to harm them. She still had to keep herself from doing it.

"It was an odd thing, my showing up on your doorstep that way. You were right to be suspicious in a situation like that. But if you didn't trust me, why did you ask me to stay?"

"I've wondered that so often. I just don't know. Maybe for once I knew what was good for me." Anya's expression was tender as she looked up at Hattie. "I don't know what I would have done, what Kasia would have done without you here. I need to ask you to forgive me for having mistrusted you."

Hattie felt relief, as if they had steered themselves out of some difficult territory.

Anya gathered some breath and spoke again, "But I still keep wondering about how you got here. Who did you get the address from?" Anya said, pulling Hattie back to the crumpled piece of paper on which she had written 321 Gordon Street.

"The address?"

"Yes. You must know by now that there is no 123 or 213 or 312 Gordon Street. Or any other combination. There is only this block."

"I don't know," Hattie said her voice soft and clearly surprised by Anya's words. "I just don't recall how I came by it."

Anya's eyes were piercing when she looked at Hattie again. "So much has happened. You'll forgive me if I believe almost anything. Trying to make sense out of it. But sometimes . . . sometimes I almost think that Ben sent you. And if he did, I'm grateful that you came."

"Anya," Hattie began. "I . . ."

"Don't say anything. I didn't ask, I told you what I sometimes think. Please let me think it. It helps me to believe that he was watching out for us, even if he could not come himself."

"About Ben . . ." Hattie began, scarcely knowing what she was going to say next.

"Yes. I know. I don't think he'll ever come back now. I don't know what happened or why. But he'll never see Kasia again either." The incredible sadness in her voice touched Hattie.

"But you have only to think over your life together

to know that he loved you and Kasia. Whatever happened to him, whatever it was, could not diminish that."

"I try so hard to remember. I really do. But sometimes . . . Hattie, I don't know what I would have done without you."

Hattie started again, "I want you to know that however I came, I stayed because of you and Kasia, because I love you both very much."

"And you love Piotr too, don't you?"

Again Hattie was surprised. Anya had observed much more than they had thought.

"Yes, I do. Or at least I think I could. Love doesn't happen in a minute. There may be that initial feeling that can become love. But to love someone, to really love someone takes time." Then Hattie laughed. "Now that you've found out our secret, I think you need to rest. You'll be exhausted."

"Okay. But just one more thing, Hattie. Please, in the cupboard, there's a blue box. Bring it."

The cardboard box was much heavier than it looked as Hattie placed it on the bed before Anya. When she lifted the lid, the faint, musty melancholy of many lives rose about them. Inside, the pieces of fabric were a brilliant collage of texture and hue. Anya fingered a few of the remnants.

"Much of this came from Poland. I saved everything I brought with me and cut it into pieces. But here's some lace from the dress I tried not to make for Stan, the rest I used for my wedding dress, and here's Clara's piece, and here, fabric from Mrs. Morris. This is Kasia's baby blanket.

I've kept them all this time, thinking I would make something of them. But I never did. I want you to have it."

Hattie drew in her breath sharply, as if inspired by the scent rising from the old cloth. Suddenly, she knew it was time. Before she could think of how she wanted to say it, she blurted out, "You know, Anya, that I have to leave. I have a life somewhere else. Piotr is here now to care for you and Kasia."

"But I thought that you and Piotr," Anya said, her eyes widening with alarm.

"I love him, or I could love him—that's true. And it might have been possible. Sometimes the choices we make can't be explained except for our knowing what we sense is the only right thing for us. We just go in the direction that seems right and hope for the best. I was here when I needed to be, when you and Kasia needed me. But now I have to go."

Instead of speaking, Anya reached out to Hattie. And the two wives of Ben Darling lay in each other's arms as the room darkened and evening settled in around them.

Chapter eighty

Finally, it was that simple; that complicated. Hattie could easily imagine her life with Piotr and Kasia spread out in front of her, a kind of echo of her life with Ben and Alice. For a while, she almost convinced herself that she had been given a second chance. Not to say that there wouldn't be bad parts, maybe even worse than she had been through the first time round. But maybe she herself would be different, having learned some things along the way.

But there'd be the inevitable time when Kasia would have a certain look, a way of talking to her and she'd know that on some level the child had figured it out—Hattie having come to her and Anya deliberately, and not as the innocent bit of grace they both had imagined.

Ultimately, Hattie acknowledged that to understand

what had happened to Ben she had had to become Ben, forced to choose between two lives that must never know about each other. She could not make Piotr and Kasia part of her life in Fenston, nor could she go to Poland with them yet still retain her own life, the friends and family she loved. Right or wrong by anyone else's standards, she had made up her mind that Ben's secret would stay with her and Athena. She thought of Alice and a wave of tenderness rose in her. Surely the love they had for each other would overcome all the small wounds they had inflicted.

Opting for a quick goodbye, she told Kasia at breakfast that she was leaving, that she was needed somewhere else. Piotr stood next to Hattie while she told the child and focused on how much fun it was now that Piotr had come to stay with them.

Of all the wrenching emotional moments during the five months Hattie'd been in Hartford, this was the most cruel, the most difficult. Kasia cried and held onto her desperately. Piotr, helpless, stood watching. Feeling the little girl's small warm body in her arms, Hattie wavered. Perhaps she should stay—at least until Anya passed away. But then what? Her leaving might be even more hurtful at that point. If she left now, Kasia would have time to bond more completely with Piotr before Anya's inevitable death. They would see it through together and then find some way to go on with their lives. Silently, Hattie held Kasia, murmuring and stroking her silky blond hair, until the child's tears were replaced by small hiccups and sniffles.

Chapter eighty-one

Hattie left at noon and drove across the landscape that had divided Ben's lives for twelve years and now divided her own. She thought of Piotr setting out food for Kasia and himself and carrying a tray up the stairs to Anya's room. She saw the jumble of tablets and books and smelled the damp wool of Kasia's mittens thrown down on the hall table as she dashed in from her school day. It was a Thursday, and the Brownie uniform would be crumpled, the tan tights dusty at the knees from a day of school. The lovely everydayness of life, Hattie thought.

When she left the highway and headed down into the valley, the language and landscape she had chosen, she could see it all spread out in front of her. She opened the window and let the chill air rush in. Her eyes filled with tears as she turned onto the road toward home.

In the early winter dusk, lights were coming on as Hattie passed Fenston Corners, Wescott's Store, the post office, the fire hall, Wilson's Service Station and Shoe Repair. She smiled to see a small tree in the window and a new wreath at the door. Obviously, Paul had returned. Anxious to get home, she didn't stop to visit with anyone. There would be time for that tomorrow. Now she needed to be home. As she turned into the long drive to her old house, a flicker on the horizon steadied itself and beckoned, welcoming her home: Eddie Rodiri's bright, foolish and promising star.

Acknowledgements Page

356

Though writing is essentially an act of loneliness, it is seldom done alone. As I wrote this book, many people offered help, grace and wisdom, especially Marilyn Stewart, Jan Kulp, Ellen Alexander Conley, Judith Present, Margaret Karmazin, Susan Wyler, Janet Weinberg, J.C. Todd, Kayla McHale, Cass Dalglish, Roma Bross, Richard Moninski, Andrew and Marcia Felkay, Bill Shoff, Paul Kelly and my husband, Michael Downend.

Kielty Turner, daughter, friend and reader.

And my agent, Lisa Bankoff, whose belief in this book sustained me through its long gestation.

About the author

Karen Blomain

Karen Blomain, a native of Pennsylvania, has received two PEN USA Syndicated Fiction Prizes, numerous fellowships and residencies. She has published four volumes of poetry and has edited an anthology of regional poetry. She received an MFA in Creative Writing from Columbia University and has conducted writing workshops in France, Austria, Russia and throughout the United States.

Blomain and her husband, the writer and photographer Michael Downend, live in Maine and Pennsylvania.

The fonts used in this book are from the Garamond and Lydian families.